Praise for *Paradise Red*

'It's a story about compromise and chan[...]
up, in other words — but also a[...]
love. A high watermark in his[...]

'One of the best character-led, a[...]
teen fictions I know of.' *BookBag*

'K. M. Grant's spectacular novel w[...] gether the friendship, love and bitter rivalry of her wonderfully evoked characters in a finale to a superb trilogy of romance and adventure.' *Scottish Book Trust*

Praise for *White Heat*

'*Blue Flame* was one of the best teen books of 2008 so far. Its
sequel proves easily a match. K. M. Grant doesn't allow her
heroes a moment's rest: the pace is breakneck . . . Volume
three, *Paradise Red*, cannot appear too soon.' *Financial Times*

Praise for *Blue Flame*

'Grant handles the suspense well, and her main characters are
believable — even the dog. I particularly like the way in which
Yolanda never cares about her appearance or how muddy and
dishevelled she gets when having her adventures. And she has
woven such a gripping plot that I shall certainly be lining up
to read book two. I hope she doesn't keep us waiting too
long.' *Guardian*

'With this gorgeously and intricately braided novel . . . K. M.
Grant provides a top-notch tale of star-crossed lovers, court

intrigue, twisted religious hatreds and the mystical power of landscape.' *Financial Times*

'I found myself engrossed . . . Indeed, by the end my heart was in my mouth.' *Bookbag*

'This fanciful tale, set in the thirteenth century, takes the reader into a world of extreme religion, magical protectors and adventure . . . plenty to keep readers aged eight to twelve guessing.' *Aberdeen Evening Express*

'Grant's nuanced, thought-provoking look at the religious conflicts they face will resonate today. Though the themes are weighty, there is no lack of action, suspense, or romance here as Raimon and Yolanda struggle to save each other. A truly harrowing escape from a burning death and a heartbreaking separation will lead readers eagerly into the next book.' *Booklist*, starred review

PARADISE RED

K. M. Grant is an author, journalist and broadcaster. She currently writes for the *Scottish Daily Mail*. Her first book, *Blood Red Horse*, was a *Booklist* Top Ten Historical Fiction for Youth and a USBBY-CBC Outstanding International Book for 2006. The sequel, *Green Jasper*, was shortlisted for the *Royal Mail* Scottish Children's Book Award and *How the Hangman Lost His Heart* was an Ottakar's Book of the Month and a *Sunday Times* Children's Book of the Week.

PARADISE RED

K. M. GRANT

Quercus

First published in Great Britain in 2009
This paperback published in 2010 by

Quercus
21 Bloomsbury Square
London
WC1A 2NS

A CIP catalogue reference for this book is available
from the British Library.

ISBN 978 1 84916 065 0

This book is a work of fiction. Names, characters, businesses,
organizations, places and events are either the product of
the author's imagination or are used fictitiously. Any
resemblance to actual persons, living or dead, events or locales
is entirely coincidental.

10 9 8 7 6 5 4 3 2 1

Designed and typeset by Rook Books, London
Printed and bound in England by Clays Ltd, St Ives Plc.

for Liffy

A THIRD GREETING

Did I nod off? If so, I'm sorry. It's just that storytellers occasionally have to pause for breath and when you are as old as
I am, sleep is always lurking in the corner of the eye. I'm
awake again now, though, quite awake.

If this is our first meeting, you will not know that I, your
narrator, am the Amouroix-in-Occitan. That is, I am a small
snatch of land on the northern side of the Pyrenean mountains, one of the counties that make up the broader territory
once commonly called Occitania, which you may know as
southern France. I don't intrude much into these pages. In
fact, I pride myself on intruding so little that when I do,
you'll have to pinch yourself to remember who I am. I don't
apologise for that. I may be old and called a different name
but I have lost neither my spirit nor my looks. I am worth
remembering.

We may, of course, have met before, for what you are
reading now continues a story I have been recounting for a
little time. If we have not met, however, I need to tell you

about Raimon, Yolanda and the Blue Flame. Now — a story-teller's conundrum: how to enlighten new friends whilst not making old friends yawn?

The best way, in my opinion, is just to start, so I shall begin by telling you that I have been woken from sleep by the echo of Raimon laughing and that this surprises me. After all, Raimon's laugh at any time is rare enough but how can he laugh now? The ring on his finger — well, scarcely a ring, really just a strip of leather welded in the heat of the Blue Flame and given to him by Yolanda, the girl he loves — has etched both a black imprint on his skin and an aching groove in his heart. He and Yolanda certainly belong together, yet she is married to another, and, worse, though she wears the pair to his ring on a thong round her neck, has chosen to stick by that other in his hour of need.

It is not even as if that 'other' is a friend. Far from it. Yolanda is married to Sir Hugh des Arcis, the French Seneschal of Carcassonne, the guardian of the French king's standard, a red-tailed banner also known as the oriflamme. It is Sir Hugh who is set to crush the Occitan of which, as I told you, I, the Amouroix, form a part. If I tell you also that Raimon holds the Occitan dearer than his own life, you will understand why, as Sir Hugh's wife, Yolanda seems to have drifted far away in every sense. And Raimon parted from her in anger. It was not well done.

Then his home, together with the whole of my town of Castelneuf, is in ruins despite all the machinations of Raimon's other foe, Yolanda's brother Count Aimery. The count, whilst professing to be a true Occitanian, contrived to make his own deal with the French king. The Occitan might be overrun and my lovely lands forced to bow before the oriflamme but Aimery would be safe. Actually, more than safe, for he planned to trade his Occitanian title for a French title of grander proportions. However, Aimery miscalculated. Castelneuf, château and town, were burned on the French king's orders. Both Raimon and Aimery have been left to sift through ashes together.

Then there is the loss of the Blue Flame itself. This small living icon in which the soul of the Occitan is distilled has both saved Raimon's life and, some might say, ruined it. You see, if Sir Parsifal, the old knight who returned the Blue Flame to the Occitan in its hour of need, had not wandered aimlessly into the Castelneuf valley, Raimon would never have danced to its fiery tune, and had he not danced, there would have been no pyre and without the pyre, he would not have become the Flame's champion after Sir Parsifal's death. Without the Flame, he might have got to Paris in time to save Yolanda from her marriage.

If you are new to my tale, do not be confused. You can catch up with the beginning in your own time. For the present you need only know that the Blue Flame is now in the most dangerous hands of all, those of the White Wolf, a man who professes to be a loyal Occitanian but is, in truth, simply a religious fanatic, being the self-appointed leader of the Cathars, a sect who believe the earth and all its beauties to be the work of the devil. The Catholic French call him and those who follow him 'heretics'. Cathar heretics. Raimon just calls them wicked.

So, all in all, you will understand why I say it is a strange time for Raimon to laugh and I should say at once that his laugh is not the carefree laugh that occasionally rang out before Castelneuf was drawn into this bitter fray. Only a mad person could really laugh like that now. No. Raimon's laugh is squeezed through bad memories and stinging regrets. The life he and Yolanda might have led will never be because whatever the future holds, the past cannot be expunged. If it were possible to paint Raimon's laugh, it would be edged with black like an old-fashioned mourning card.

Having said all that, however, laughter is laughter, and Raimon is not brooding, at least not at this moment. I can tell this quite easily, since he has one of those cleanly etched, dark-framed faces across which all his moods flit openly, much like the shadows that chase across my jagged expanses. Indeed, not just his face but his whole body is seldom completely still, and even when peace does descend, it is less the stillness of repose and more the stillness of the diver about to leap. I love him for this.

Anyway, what would be the point of brooding? He cannot bring back Sir Parsifal, but although the old knight's absence, together with the loss of Yolanda and the Blue Flame, aches like a throbbing scar, none are entirely gone from him. He still feels Sir Parsifal by his side, usually urging a caution that Raimon is inclined to ignore, and the sky is full of Yolanda since it is of the sky that she smells. As for the Flame, it pulses as a cone of brilliant, prickling blue somewhere deeper than his heart, tugging at him as an impatient child tugs at its father's hand. On waking, he smells its sulphurous smoke. On sleeping, he feels as though the small silver salver in which it flutters has somehow jostled beneath his bedroll. And there is something else, something quite recent. Both waking and sleeping, he feels the Flame carries a message that remains just beyond his reach.

What is not beyond his reach, though, is the certainty that he will retrieve the Flame from the White Wolf. Like a rod of steel, this belief stiffens his spine, and if his spine ever softens, all he has to do is touch Unbent, the sword Sir Parsifal bequeathed to him on his deathbed. 'Fight for the Flame, for the Amouroix, for the Occitan and for love,' he hears the dead knight exhort him. And Raimon knows he will fight, fight to his last breath. He looks forward to it.

For the moment, however, Unbent is unsheathed not for battle but for polishing, almost over-polishing, by Cador, Raimon's self-appointed and eager young squire, and Raimon himself is not fighting but building. He is not building alone. Count Aimery builds beside him.

Are Raimon and Aimery friends or enemies? Certainly, they were enemies so long as it was Aimery's intention to betray the Occitan. Certainly, forgiveness and trust, those two staples of friendship, do not flourish between them. But now that Aimery's intrigues have so hideously unravelled, it is difficult to describe what they are to each other. It is practical expediency, not friendship, that keeps them working together. Both know that a château ruins is easy prey. At any moment, more French soldiers may come to complete the destruction they started, or a troop of random bandit knights could attack and finish the job for them. Also, though they have not yet quite reached my borders, Catholic Inquisitors, hungry for souls and brimming with highly imaginative ways of extracting confessions of heresy, are also moving slowly in Castelneuf's direction. French and Occitanian, Catholic and Cathar: the wars between them ebb and flow, with alliances forged in cunning and broken at will. At the time of my tale, not only Raimon, but the whole country simmers.

For the moment, however, Raimon and Aimery are straining bare-chested, hewing and hammering and heaving, working up a sweat though the air is freezing. And I, who can see everything, can tell you that though King Louis has betrayed Aimery and ruined the lands he inherited, Aimery's vision of himself as a great man at the French court still tempts him as a plump carcass tempts a wounded jackal. If he, Count Aimery of Amouroix, can only wrest the Blue Flame of the Occitan from the White Wolf and deliver it into the royal hand as he once promised he would, his fortunes may yet be restored.

This is what Aimery is pondering as he pulls his shirt back on, his flesh shining white and a little soft. Despite the activity, he is out of condition. He scratches the blond beard that broadens an already broad face just beginning to coarsen. Raimon's laugher irritates him. 'What's so funny?' he asks, his pale eyes darting.

Raimon gestures at a multi-coloured girl who is slithering towards them carrying a box the size of a cat's coffin, a skinny creature resembling a misshapen fawn – on closer inspection, a dog – under one arm. 'Laila's hissing at the ice as if it's insulted her personally,' he says, and calls out as he picks up his own shirt and slings it over his shoulder. 'If you hiss like a snake, Laila, you'll turn into one.' The cold makes his veins tingle as they used to when he and Yolanda took their first bathe of the spring. He touches his leather ring noting that he must oil it or it will crack, then tosses his icicled hair out of his eyes.

Laila opens her mouth to offer some sharp retort, slips over and crashes on to her front. The box, whose contents are a fiercely guarded secret, skitters away in front of her and her patchwork skirt flaps to reveal numerous jaunty underskirts. The dog, who rejoices in the name of Ugly, lands heavily and spins like a flailing skater. Still, the moment she can scramble to her feet, she whines concern for her beloved mistress, concern that is quite misplaced, for although giddy and panting slightly, Laila has enough breath left to let loose a torrent of curses. Guiltily, Ugly nervously extends a sympathetic and servile paw, a trick that Laila taught her when they met in the Parisian gutter. The girl, still cursing, takes the paw and then topples the dog over so that Ugly is upended again. Only now do the curses give way to a percussive chortle.

'A poisonous snake,' Aimery remarks drily to Raimon although it is his eyes that are snakelike, lingering as Laila dextrously rebalances her box on her head, makes a show of smoothing her dress over her hips and flips a dainty heel to reveal spiked shoes painted pink. A ripple runs through Aimery's grainy cheek.

A man shouts from above. Aimery drags his attention from Laila and tucks his shirt into thick woollen leggings. 'Ready?' he asks.

'Ready,' Raimon replies and drops his shirt on to the ground.

Above them, twenty feet of thick oak, honed and planed into a beam by dozens of woodcutters, has been raised on a specially constructed hoist attached to an enormous wheel turned by half a dozen sturdy oxen. Aimery and Raimon ease their way up the scaffolding poles towards it. This is a crucial moment, for the giant beam is one of six main joists for the great hall's new roof. When the five others are in place, the rest of the keep can grow and Castelneuf will rise again like a man rising from the dead. Raimon's father, Sicart, already perched high on the opposite wall, has taken hold of one side of the robust webbing sling in which the beam is cradled and is bracing himself. Instructions fly around. 'Take care!' 'A little to the right!' 'Don't let it swing too far over.' Nothing must go wrong.

When Aimery reaches the top of the scaffolding, he takes hold of the sling, while Raimon, more sure-footed, clambers over the rough cast stone to the squared niche in which the beam must settle. Another man does the same on Sicart's side. He and Raimon nod to each other. On the ground, the oxen are brought to a halt and men bind ropes into iron rings to prevent the sling from slipping. More shouted instructions. 'Keep the knots tight!' 'Just slip the loose end through once more.' 'Watch your back!'

Despite the care everybody is taking, the beam begins to swing as the wind strengthens. Raimon can feel sharp gusts icing his bare skin. He should have put his shirt on. 'It's straight now!' he shouts down, his teeth beginning to chatter. Then, 'Have you got it?' across the chasm to his father.

'Yes. Got it.'

'Keep it still.'

Sicart grunts, his arms aching. Damn the wind. Still, it is good to be doing something with his son. It stops him from thinking of his daughter, too devout a Cathar heretic for his liking, sitting below in silent mourning for the White Wolf, who, during the Castelneuf conflagration, snatched the Blue Flame but left her behind. She has said not a word since then.

Raimon is momentarily straddled over the niche. Once properly wedged, the beam will be a king amongst beams, set to last for a thousand years. At this moment, however, it hovers, ungainly as a heavy emperor being hoisted onto his throne. Everybody must keep hold. Just a touch from such a weight could send a man tumbling to his death.

'Are we all ready?'

'Push it over a bit.'

'Keep good grip.'

'More to the right –'

'Too much, too much –'

It doesn't matter to whom the voices belong. They are the voices of a shared endeavour. Except that just before the order goes to loosen the ropes and ease the oxen forward, Raimon has to bend almost double to sweep away a small piece of rubble. The beam must sit absolutely square and tight. As he stretches his fingers, there is a random gust. The beam shifts.

Aimery is immediately aware. His grip tightens then loosens, as if his hold has inadvertently slipped. The beam swings. The warning is swallowed. An accident can be so useful.

It is Sicart who suddenly shouts, 'For God's sake, Aimery. Duck, son!' The beam misses Raimon by less than a hair's breadth. Only then does Aimery find his tongue, adding his voice to the general relief. He apologises and re-catches the webbing. However, his apology is too effusive, his expression too innocent and when his eyes meet Raimon's, it is like granite meeting steel.

'Are you all right?' Sicart is leaning out, regardless of the danger to himself.

Raimon dusts himself down and raises an arm. 'I'm fine,' he calls back.

'Ready to try again?' Aimery almost trills. He seizes the beam and turns those granite eyes again to Raimon. 'I'll take better care next time.'

Raimon's lips tighten. Aimery is a fool to have given his secret ponderings away. Though he could so easily have died, Raimon is not sorry to have learned that his enemy is still his enemy.

They all re-arrange themselves. There is more shouting, more swinging, some grinding and grunting, a chorus of creaking ropes and a great rasping as the beam scrapes its way down amid gritty puffs of powdered stone. When at last it is still there is cheering. This is a good omen! Even the normally morose Sicart is grinning, helping more men to swarm up the scaffolding ribs to tap the beam for luck. The master forester carves his initials underneath those of the master mason. Aimery holds out his hand to Raimon. 'Beam in safe and sound,' he says. 'Sorry about the slip.'

Raimon cannot ignore the hand without causing

comment. The contact is momentary.

Two hours later, all five beams are in place. Tomorrow it will be the turn of the smaller joists. By the end of the week, if the weather holds, the rafters will be laid and the great hall will be closed against the elements. Everybody looks forward to that.

Yet they are unlucky. Before all the workers have reached the ground a few flakes of snow drift through the dust. There is disappointed muttering. It is late March, and spring should be on its way but this winter is being very persistent.

Raimon pulls on his shirt and Cador buckles Unbent to his back. The feel of the sword is very good. In Aimery's full vision, Raimon draws it out and tosses it from hand to hand, enjoying the filthy look Aimery cannot disguise. Aimery does not think Raimon should have a sword. Born a weaver, stay a weaver, that's Aimery's motto. Raimon presses the little flame that decorates Unbent's pommel hard into his palm and suddenly holds the sword above his head with both hands. Cador squeaks and leaps away. 'Catch,' shouts Raimon. He whirls the sword then tosses it. With more good luck than skill, Cador catches it by the hilt. 'Victory!' the boy yells, staggering a little under the weight, his whole face creasing with pleasure. Now he swaps Unbent for the rough sword Raimon carries all the time. Even after this tiny outing, he'll polish Unbent again.

Aimery, who has never seen his own squire's face crease like that, scowls as he wraps himself in a knee-length fox-fur, one of the few things saved from the French fire-raisers' looting. Laila is staring at him and at once he is again aware of pink heels and smooth hips. He coughs. 'I don't know why you're still here. I mean, why aren't you with Yolanda at Carcassonne? You're supposed to be her servant. How is she managing without you? And by the way –' he gestures at her hair – 'that's a terrible shade of carrot.'

Laila, whose corkscrew curls change colour almost every day, takes her time, tossing her head to dislodge the snowflakes and then blinks to draw attention to her eyebrows, each painted a different shade of turquoise and plucked into a perfect arc. 'If I'm still here, it's your fault.'

'Absolute nonsense. You're not a prisoner in shackles.'

'There's more to prison than shackles. I've no horse.'

'Take Bors or Galahad.'

'They're Raimon's.'

'So what?'

She sniffs.

Aimery exhales a long wintry blast. 'What you really mean is that you don't want just any horse. Bors and Galahad are too old and scarred for a *lady* –' he makes a derisive gesture – 'like you.'

Laila glares at him in the especially vicious way she has when somebody hits on a truth, and the glare has Aimery's blood flowing hot. This girl! He does not know whether to slap her or kiss her.

The sky chooses this moment to open and suddenly the snow is not floating but tumbling in huge wet flowers. Men are running for shelter and Aimery, hitching his jerkin over his head, sees in the corner of his eye a homing pigeon struggling to reach the loft he has had newly restored. He forgets Laila, just for a second.

'Sir Aimery!'

His squire, Alain, is making his way gingerly, trying not to slip. 'We've visitors. Around sixty, I'd say, coming up through the town.'

'Inquisitors?'

'No. They carry no cross before them.'

'Are they armed?' Aimery and Raimon both feel their swords.

'Yes, but their weapons are all sheathed. As far as I can tell, they're just seeking shelter. I think this is the start of a blizzard and it looks set to be a big one.'

'Close the gates,' Aimery commands. 'We've no room for them.'

'The barns are ready,' Raimon contradicts, 'the stables too and the temporary roof on the small hall makes it perfectly usable.'

Aimery taps his sword against his knee. 'And what will they eat?'

Raimon stands his ground. 'The huntsman's brought in meat and although we're short of grain, we've eggs and cheese. For God's sake, Aimery.'

Aimery clutches at his temper. He cannot afford to belittle and ignore Raimon, since his bravery during the fire and tireless work on the rebuilding means that those remaining at Castelneuf, from knights to beggars, have developed what, to Aimery, is a misguided sense of respect for him. He considers. Perhaps these people will have a use, and anyway, turning them away now will cause adverse comment. The French king sets a great deal of store by hospitality. If he were to hear that Aimery had closed his doors to travellers in need, it would be a black mark. Aimery bats the snow with the flat of his blade. 'Oh, let them in, then,' he says, making an effort not to sound grumpy, 'and be sure to tell them that even at this time of trial, the Count of Amouroix has not forgotten how to welcome strangers.'

Alain bows and vanishes amid the flurries before he has taken five steps.

Aimery turns his back on Raimon and heads for the loft. At least the birds know who is master. These speedy messengers will, he is sure, be vital for his future, for what he sends with them nobody knows except himself. The ladder steps are greasy and he can feel the wind on the back of his legs. Inside the loft is no warmer. The birds feel the chill too and are plumping up their feathers. Aimery's appearance has their necks jerking but few of them express any alarm. They are used to him. He peers round, then catches the latest arrival, blowing on his fingers before trying to unbind the little leather capsule in which the message is rolled. He swears as the pigeon flaps and pecks. Finding the binding too tough, eventually he just tugs the capsule off, pulls out a tiny scroll and reads it. It bears the royal crest. His ill temper subsides at once. Good, good. Nothing is over. Indeed, there is still everything to gain. He stuffs the slip of parchment in beside his dagger.

The bird hops away towards a nesting box, her head bobbing back and forth. In his rough hurry, Aimery has injured her leg. He catches her again. 'Well, my friend,' he says, holding her up in front of his face, and in her round eye, black as Raimon's, suddenly sees his reflection distorted into something squashed and bloated. He grunts and with a vicious twist born of his irritation with Raimon and uncomfortable desire for Laila, wrings the bird's neck. Her wings spread and beat just once before her head lolls and her eyes cloud. There is no reflection now. Aimery cradles her for a moment, glancing uneasily about. He should not have done that. She was a royal bird, after all. But when the other birds show no interest he relaxes, catches another and pets it. He reads his parchment again and then, before he descends, quite casually pitches the small corpse into the unforgiving arms of the gathering storm.

THE VISITORS

Some people speak of the dead of winter. I know nothing of that. I know only winter's sparkle, the crisp lace of frosted fern and the thick curves of drips frozen into polished beaks. In winter I am a fairytale country, soft and crackling underfoot, pearly ice adding a brittle, glistering lustre to the more workaday silver of my mountains. Today, a weak spring sun spits hazy diamonds and the late-falling snow transforms Castelneuf from a blackened heap into a shimmering stage set.

The visitors, naturally, are blind to the glamour as they struggle through the gate to the courtyard. Winter to the traveller means only hardship and potentially deadly delay. As the snow balls under their horses' hoofs, some of the women are weeping with exhaustion whilst the men stare balefully at the sky and occasionally raise a fist.

Alain has exaggerated. In all, there are nearer two dozen than sixty visitors. Nevertheless, they come with a deal of paraphernalia, mostly household rather than war. The majority are men, although there are at least half a dozen wives and daughters and four of the wives have very small babies tightly bound against the cold. They crowd into the small hall, shaking the snow from cloaks and boots and banging their feet to restore circulation.

One of the women, just a girl really, sits down and gratefully accepts the bowl of soup set on the table before her. As she bows her head to give thanks to God, she makes a neat circular movement with her right hand. At once, her father, a large man whose red nose and melon skin cheeks hump out of a speckled and bristling beard, stretches across as if to shield her. It is too late. Adela, who has been sitting motionless by the wall furthest from the fire, shovels herself up. 'You are of our faith?' she asks, her dulled eyes kindling.

The girl picks up her spoon and her smile splits a face almost unnaturally unlined and untroubled. With her white throat and hair the colour of corn, she looks like a doll that Adela once had made out of wool and wax and polished ram's horn. Adela doesn't remember the doll, but I do.

Adela does not wait for an answer. 'I, too, am a Cathar,' she says. 'My name is Adela Belot and I've taken the consolation from the Perfectus known as the White Wolf. Many people here did the same. Not that you'd know it.' She casts her eyes contemptuously about the room. 'They abandoned our religion when it got too hard.'

The girl swiftly spoons up her soup. 'The Cathar religion hard?' she says, and her voice is musical, a sweet voice for a sweet face. 'It doesn't seem so very hard to believe in justice and truth.' She licks her lips with relish. 'Perhaps your White

Wolf was a little over zealous. Some Perfecti are, even though they mean well. Oh! Thank you!' She gratefully accepts more soup. 'Our Perfectus at home is a nice man, quite gentle. I sometimes think of him as Christ's brother although I'd never tell him that because he'd be very embarrassed.' She twinkles and reaches for bread.

Adela is leaning forward. 'Did your Perfectus also tell you that only true Cathars can be true Occitanians? And did he tell you too that the Cathars now have the Blue Flame?'

The girl scrapes her bowl again then leans back with a contented sigh. 'That's better. I hadn't realised quite how hungry I was. It's hard to think about anything when your stomach's rumbling.'

Adela is annoyed. How can this girl be interested only in her stomach? 'Don't you care more about the Blue Flame than your stomach?'

'Of course.' The girl wipes her mouth. 'We're on our way to Montségur precisely because that's where the Flame is. Our Perfectus is there already, and all the other Occitanian knights that we know. I haven't taken the consolation, as you have, but I think I am as dedicated to the cause.'

'Be quiet, Metta,' her father admonishes and looks around fearfully. The girl taps his chest with affectionate reassurance before she turns back to Adela and notices the untouched food on her plate. 'You should eat. Look at you! You're flat in all the places you should be round!'

Adela blenches. 'I've told you. I'm one of the consoled, so why should I eat? To me, food is just the barrier that prevents us leaving this life and attaining life everlasting.'

'Is that what your White Wolf says?'

'It is.'

'Our Perfectus wouldn't agree, would he, Father?'

'Please be quiet, Metta.'

She is silent, but only for a second or two. Then she takes Adela's hand. 'I don't want to presume, but I really think your Perfectus must be mistaken. Food is not evil if you say the Lord's Prayer first. Could your Perfectus have misunderstood?'

Adela snatches her hand away. 'The White Wolf is not mistaken. He knows everything. He's a great man, perhaps the greatest of all men. He is the Keeper of the Blue Flame.'

The girl's smile lights up her whole face. 'Of course he is! But even the best and greatest men can sometimes be wrong!'

Bile rises in Adela's throat as she recalls the day when her mother, silent and trusting, starved to death because the White Wolf told her it was the will of God. He must be right, he must. She cannot afford not to think so. She turns on Metta. 'Of course good men can be wrong,' she says sharply, 'but not the White Wolf.'

'Then,' says Metta, with another smile, 'he must be right, only he's certainly a very strict Perfectus, the strictest I've ever heard of.'

'It's what the Lord demands,' Adela insists.

'Oh no,' says Metta. Disconcertingly for Adela, her smile is the same whether she agrees or disagrees. 'I don't believe the Lord demands anything except that we love him and allow him to love us.' She licks her spoon again. 'That was the nicest soup I've ever had. Does your White Wolf —'

'That's enough, Metta, I mean it,' interrupts her father, adding in a low voice to Adela, 'you shouldn't listen to her prattle. She fell from a mule basket when she was a baby and hasn't been quite the same since.'

'You mean she talks nonsense?

The knight hesitates. 'I mean she talks a little too freely.' He glances at her with concerned affection.

Aimery and Raimon have come in from helping to cover the tools against the weather and catch the last of the exchange. Aimery touches Metta's arm. 'So,' he says, and his tone gives nothing away, 'you follow the Cathar creed?

'Metta —' her father warns yet again.

'Let her answer,' Aimery says pleasantly enough.

The girl is unafraid. 'We did when this lady first asked,' she nods gently at Adela, 'and we still do now!'

Aimery ignores the joke. 'It's brave to say so.' He scrutinises her carefully. 'The Counts of Amouroix, and I am the current holder of the title, have always been Catholics.' He glances over at the fat priest supping hugely in the corner. 'That's our priest, Simon Crampcross, and my uncle was an Inquisitor.'

The girl's father gasps but the girl is quite unmoved. 'Indeed,' she says, her eyes twinkling. 'We forgive you.'

At this, Raimon laughs out loud and Metta, noticing him, is startled to find herself blushing.

Aimery bristles and forces her attention back to him. 'You think our differences are a joke?' He shouts over to the fat priest. 'Simon Crampcross, come here! We've heretics in our midst.'

Metta's father looms large. 'I've already explained, Sir

Aimery,' he says quickly, 'that my daughter's a bit simple. You should take no notice. Now, if you don't mind, we must see about our things.' He cloaks Metta as a bear might cloak its cub and hurries her away.

'I should stick them all in the cellars,' Aimery says deliberately loudly as Simon Crampcross shuffles over, his long tongue all over his fingers, his shirt spotted with meat pudding.

'It's not the Cathars who burned down your château,' Raimon points out.

'That's true,' says Aimery. He pokes the priest's stomach with the hilt of his dagger as he calculates how to turn this situation to his advantage. He stops prodding as something occurs to him. 'Go back to your dinner, you fat fool. Fill those bulges and reflect on how you seem to have ended up on the wrong side.' He strokes his beard as Simon Crampcross lumbers off.

Raimon narrows his eyes. The wrong side? What's this new nonsense of Aimery's? He wonders if the priest knows something.

He does not. Bemused, for he has served the Catholic counts for nearly a decade, Simon Crampcross's balding pate shines with the effort of eating and shuffling as he too tries to gauge what is in Aimery's mind. Is the count about to turn Cathar? Is he just joking? Has he gone mad? Since the fire, after all, Aimery has been unpredictable and temperamental as a stabled bull. It would be far from unthinkable, so the priest realises with horror, even with Aimery's history of taunting the Cathars, that he might suddenly decide to throw over his

Catholic faith and join them. It was, after all, the Catholic king who burned his château. Only one clear thing. He, Simon Crampcross, must stay firmly in the chapel until he sees which way Aimery's wind really does blow. Surely even Aimery would not hurt a man in the house of God, although – and Simon Crampcross almost chokes on the remains of a pickled pig's trotter – he has heard of an archbishop in England who was murdered in his own cathedral. Fear bubbles up through his mountainous layers and he belches uncontrollably.

Raimon's gorge rises. The smell of Simon Crampcross must make even God sick – not that Raimon cares about God, at least not Aimery's God, or the White Wolf's, or the Inquisitors'. He had begun to care for Sir Parsifal's God, but Parsifal is no longer here. He goes back into the snow to breathe cleaner air and finds Cador at his heels.

The boy is munching on an old bit of bread and opens a mouth full of crumbs to catch the snowflakes. 'When will we get the Flame back from the White Wolf?' He stamps legs achy with growing pains. He wants action.

Raimon can feel the cold seeping through his boots. 'I don't know. It won't be easy.'

'All the more reason to get started.' Cador shakes the snowflakes from his ears like a puppy.

'What makes you so sure I can actually do it?'

'Well, we have to, don't we?' Cador carefully includes himself. 'The Flame belongs to the Occitan. You're the champion of the Occitan and I'm your squire.'

Raimon shivers. He does not feel much like a champion at this moment. 'Champions can fail, you know.'

'But you won't, Sir Raimon.'

'Just Raimon, please.'

It is a well-chosen response, making them both laugh, albeit a little painfully. Parsifal, if you remember, was always disclaiming his knighthood on the grounds that he didn't deserve it and Raimon always ignored him. A history of shared expressions is a warm history. Cador chews cheerfully. 'You'll succeed because you've got Unbent and me. What else do you need?'

Raimon considers. He does not need to love the Occitan more. That would be impossible. To Raimon, it is the place of which his bones are made, the place from which Yolanda has sprung, the place in which he first saw the Flame, the place in which he wants, eventually, to grow old. If he fails the Flame and the Occitan dies, he will be left in limbo, a man without a country, a lover without a beloved, a boat without an anchor. He cannot explain this to Cador. Instead, he condenses it. 'I need to feel like a knight,' he says.

'You'll feel like a knight when you get the Flame back and Mistress Yolanda comes home and everything is perfect again.'

'You sound like a troubadour.' The words are jesting but Raimon's tone is curt. 'Only they believe in happy endings.' Nevertheless, the little boy's unflinching optimism is infectious. Raimon curls his finger again to feel Yolanda's ring and allows himself to remember the evening she floated like a starfish in the river, her skin glowing like a dusky pearl. Snowflakes fall on his hair and remind his scalp of her fingers kneading away the tangles in his head. For an instant, intruding, he sees Metta's blushing face. He pushes out his lower lip.

When the wind finally drops, the snow falls straight down and soon both Raimon's and Cador's arms are ridged white. Cador throws his head back and closes his eyes. On impulse, Raimon bends down, makes a snowball and pops it into the boy's mouth. Cador's eyes fly open as his tongue flies out. Then he bends himself, deftly rolls another ball, skips away, throws it and hits Raimon smartly above the ear. He gets two back for his pains, one on each cheek. 'Now it's war!' the boy cries joyfully. Raimon hesitates. A knight must watch his dignity and this is hardly a time for larks. But a snowball explodes on his chin and in seconds he and Cador are at it full pelt, two sparkling warriors in a spangled mist.

Their game is stopped when a tightly packed snowball pitched by Cador slams into the chest of somebody who unwisely chooses this moment to emerge into the courtyard. He protests.

'Apologies, Sir Knight,' says Raimon quickly, and recognises Metta's father.

In his mottled bearskin, Sir Roger de Salas is even larger outside than in and, close to, Raimon can see two deep chasms cut into that humped face, chasms that circle his nostrils before disappearing into the mountain of bristle. He spreads huge, knotted hands that Cador reckons, with awe, must take almost a whole sheet of steel to gauntlet and he moves with an air of concentration, as though always having to remember where every bit of his largeness is. Disparate though they are in size,

Raimon can see a distinct resemblance between Sir Roger and his daughter, for her guileless sincerity is simply a prettier version of Sir Roger's apologetic courtesy. It is Cador who notices that Sir Roger's stockings are full of holes, that the leather thongs on his boots have rotted away and the hilt of his sword is rusted. 'You have a neglectful squire,' he says with the unabashed candour of the young.

'I have no squire at all,' comes the regretful response. 'I let him go some months ago. He was a good lad, though.'

'If he was good, why did you let him go?'

The knight's breath turns cloudy. 'Oh,' he says vaguely, 'my wife thought it best. He wasn't really one of us.' He stops.

'You mean he wasn't a heretic?' Raimon is quick to accuse.

Sir Roger doesn't want to answer but the silence forces him.

'No, he wasn't,' he says. 'He was a Catholic so we didn't think it safe to keep him, either for himself or for us. You know how it is.'

'I do not,' says Raimon haughtily. 'I'm neither Catholic nor Cathar. I am an Occitanian.'

The knight regards Raimon with more attention. 'I wish more of us had the courage to say that,' he says, somewhat to Raimon's surprise. 'Indeed, I wish I'd had the courage to say it to my wife, God rest her soul, and to my son before he left home. My wife was a Catholic, you see, and my son still is. We're a divided family, I'm sorry to say. Perhaps if more of us were like you, King Louis would be thinking twice before sending Inquisitors and his army to finish us all off.' There is silence. The knight leans back, his melon skin wrinkling. The bearskin sags.

'So, you're going to Montségur,' Raimon says quickly. A big man deflating is a pitiful sight.

Sir Roger sighs. 'Montségur will be our last stand, both as Cathars and Occitanians. This is what it's come to.'

Raimon kicks at the snow. 'You'll meet the White Wolf there.'

'So I'm told.' Somewhat absentmindedly, Sir Roger begins to make a snowball of his own, rolling it between soup-plate palms. It is the size of Cador's head.

'I'm surprised Metta had never heard of him. Is he not a Cathar hero?' Raimon watches the knight carefully.

Sir Roger packs his snowball tightly. 'A hero to some, perhaps, but I've kept his name away from Metta. She believes our faith to be a gentle thing, as do many others. But he's our leader now and since he's called us to fight, what can we do but answer his call? He has the Flame. He calls us in its name.' He pitches his snowball against the remains of a far gatepost.

'Well aimed!' shouts Cador. 'Oh, well aimed, sir!'

Sir Roger gives a rueful smile and begins to gather up more snow.

'Why follow where he leads?' Raimon asks, his voice low and urgent.

Sir Roger pitches his new snowball gently and then holds up his hands in mock surrender at the volley of Cador's returns. 'Where else is there to go now? Who else is there to follow? We've made too many mistakes to recover. Everybody's going to Montségur.'

Raimon shifts. 'Don't you wish to spare your family?'

A spasm crosses Sir Roger's face. 'Metta's life is in God's hands.'

The old knight's gently patronising tone has Raimon exploding like the snowball. 'Don't treat me as you treat your daughter! What's the matter with you?' He raises his fists and Cador raises his also.

Watery eyes peer out beneath the knight's badgery eyebrows. 'I love my daughter,' he says simply. 'I treat her as she must be treated.'

Raimon drops his fists, conscious that it is the height of boorishness to raise them against a visitor. 'I've been rude, Sir Roger,' he says, his contrition cold but genuine.

The knight holds up both palms to indicate acceptance and dismissal. 'No need,' he says.

They all gaze over the snow.

'You know,' says Sir Roger, seeking something – perhaps justification for what he has chosen to do, perhaps some reassurance – 'it could be worse. At the final reckoning at Montségur, I'm sure the French king will spare our women and children and those of us who die will die for God under the Occitan Flame.' He stamps a foot. 'And you can never rule out a miracle, you know.'

'The Flame won't save the Cathars.'

'You think not? What will it do, then?'

'I don't know.' This admission emerges sullenly.

Sir Roger pauses. 'Do you never wonder if it's you who's wrong and the White Wolf right?' He contemplates his ragged boots. 'But it's true, what you say about Metta.' He gives a deep and troubled sigh. 'I shouldn't have brought her.

She should be at the beginning of something, not the end. She deserves life and love and children, not to be stuck in some fortress whilst the world dissolves around her.' He shakes and a whole mountain of snow falls from him. He begins to roll another ball. 'Now then, Sir Squire.'

'My name's Cador, squire to Sir Raimon of the Blue Flame.'

'Well then, Cador, squire to Sir Raimon of the Blue Flame. I'll bet you think I can't hit the top of that post. Do you see the one? On the right near the pigeon loft?'

Cador squints. 'I bet you can't. It's too far away.'

'Too far, eh? We'll see. Off you go and shout when you're ready.'

Cador has to take giant footsteps, for the snow is deep.

The knight watches, flipping his snowball from vast hand to vast hand. When he throws it, the ball hits the gatepost with an enormous wallop. 'See,' Sir Roger says to Raimon with childish delight. 'Miracles do happen.'

Raimon says nothing.

The evening settles and a kind of cosiness prevails in the hall. Outside, a night wind gets up but in here, everybody, including the dogs, basks in the glow of the hearth. Gratitude for shelter, squashed though the shelter is, soothes everybody's jangles and as the world outside crackles and freezes, the talk is not of war or Inquisitors or Perfecti but of past winters that have come late and stayed long, of the qualities of oak or ash for keeping hearthstones hot, and of the sighting of an unexpected early bud on the alders by the river. Even Adela's habitual glower softens into something more

dreamy as the voices drift about, rising and falling, occasionally speared with flashes of laughter. Bowing to repeated
requests, Gui and Guerau, the Castelneuf troubadours, gather
themselves together and begin to chant a winter tale so
familiar that people only half listen. Eventually, their voices
fall away. Then, Laila rises. Without a word, she breaks the
sleepy spell, leaving Aimery shaking his head in disbelief and
the visitors gasping.

The girl's hair is stark white this evening, in honour of the
snow, and her skin ice-blue. She has painted Ugly silver and
the dog shimmers along beside her mistress looking faintly
shy. Laila, not shy at all, stands on a trestle and stretches her
spiky arms, one up and one down, palms flat like a Hindu
goddess. Ugly sits below and begins to lick herself clean, so
that soon her tongue and teeth are as silver as her coat. She
glances unhappily at her mistress. She'll surely be punished
for this, but Laila has forgotten all about her.

By the very force of her own silence, the girl forces silence
on the hall and then begins to mime the story of a winter star
who falls to earth and is trapped under a stone by a
ponderous mountain god. The star pleads for her freedom
and the god says he will grant it if she will dance for him. But
as she dances he is careful to keep one of her dainty feet
shackled so that she cannot spin away. Bending and writhing,
her body hypnotically sinuous and supple, Laila becomes the
story and, mesmerised, the children of both resident and
visitor creep closer, longing to help the 'star' in her agony.
Laila waits until they are almost on her then suddenly, her
foot snapping free, she is transformed from fairy into hornet,

buzzing and stinging. The children scream and rush back to their mothers, plucking at their arms, quite certain that they have been bitten.

Laila growls contemptuously and then, like Ugly, the children are forgotten. Now she turns comical tease and has the men in the hall rocking with nervous laughter at her overblown coquetry whilst their wives lower their eyes. Finally, she commands wild applause by descending from the trestle in a fountain of holly berries conjured up apparently from nowhere.

She accepts the adulation, her white hair fizzing, bowing more like a queen graciously accepting the homage of her subjects than like an entertainer grateful for the applause. To his surprise and pleasure, she reserves a tiny, special bow for Aimery. He doesn't return it but his eyes follow her until she vanishes through the hall door.

As soon as she has disappeared, Raimon, who stood throughout with his arms folded, moves forward. Now it is his turn, and Cador, who has been watching Laila open-mouthed, finds Unbent taken from him. Cathar or Catholic, this may be the last gathering of Occitanian knights in an Occitanian hall. Gripping Unbent's hilt, Raimon holds the sword high and begins to sing:

> In Occitan there hovers still
> The grace of Arthur's table round.
> Bright southern heroes yet fulfil
> The quest to which they all are bound.
> No foreign pennant taints our skies,
> No cold French king snuffs out our name.

Though we may fall, again we'll rise
No Grail for us, we burn the Flame!
The Flame, the Flame, the Flame of Blue,
Sweet Occitan, it burns for you.

His voice is not the rich voice of a troubadour. He has no skills, as they do, to inject subtle tints of melancholy or rejoicing to play the audience like a lute. He simply sings the words and means every one. Sicart, slouched slackly with sagging jaw and closed eyes, sits up. Sir Roger, mountainously slumped, straightens his back, and the whole hall listens rapt.

As he finishes, Raimon wonders if now the knights will feel the same urgency as he does and rise, drawing their own swords. But they do not. Instead, they seem content to shake their heads and wallow in the easy shallows of nostalgia. A feeling of utter loneliness engulfs him. He is the only one, it seems, who wants the Flame to burn in an Occitan free from the twin curses of authoritarian religion and the French. He and Cador. A weaver-knight and a self-appointed squire. Two amongst all these. As he gives Unbent back to Cador he is aware of Aimery raising an ironic tankard. The count no longer seems the least bit impatient with his guests. Indeed, he now oozes such charm that Raimon wonders the visitors do not find it as unnerving as he does. But then Aimery vanishes, no doubt sniffing after Laila, and Raimon's attention is called elsewhere. More logs are piled into the hearth. Another cask of wine is opened. Metta tries to draw Adela nearer the fire. The stories go on.

It is in many ways a pity that such an evening ever has to

end, but end it does. As everybody nods off, most not moving from their seats, Raimon settles himself on a pile of wolf-skins and tucks Cador in beside him. The boy is soon asleep but Raimon tosses and turns.

The arrival of the visitors has made everything more urgent. If Raimon is not to allow the Flame to perish with the White Wolf at Montségur, he cannot delay much longer. Yet from all he hears in the general gossip of the height and impregnability of the fortress, climbing in and stealing the Flame will be impossible. No – he corrects himself – not impossible. Nothing is impossible. There must be a way. There is always a way. He makes plans and discards them. Then something occurs to him that he does not immediately discard. He frowns and glances over at the snoring Sir Roger and then, further back, to where Metta is sleeping rather more quietly behind a hastily strung-up curtain. He shakes his head but hours later he is still fretting. It would be bold, so bold that it could work. Perhaps God is on his side after all.

He gets up and slips outside. After the mugginess of the hall, the cold hits him like a hammer. The snowclouds have been blown away and there is just black and white and indigo. Even the braziers the huntsman lights in the kennels for the hounds and dogboys are burning too low to shine through the window slits. Raimon breathes in, and then out. 'I'm coming for you, just wait for me,' he whispers to the Flame. Then he holds out his arms as though Yolanda were about to fall into them. He knows it is foolish. Yolanda can hardly materialise from the stars. But still, standing like that, he can hope.

AT CARCASSONNE

Fifty miles away, Yolanda is sitting in a pool of lamplight biting her nails — a new habit she cannot remember starting — her dog, Brees, pressed close against her side, his large hairy bulk a protective bulwark between his mistress and the draughts from the shuttered window. Yolanda may call out Raimon's name and long for Castelneuf but Brees is perfectly at home because his home is simply where she is. He yawns and scratches the blanket. It is too clean for perfection but it will have to do. Yolanda stops biting her nails and buries her hands in his thick bristly neck. 'I know you want me to lie down,' she says, 'but I just can't.'

Yolanda is not her husband's prisoner. She is not locked in a dungeon, but neither is she free to go. Since she learned of the destruction of Castelneuf, Sir Hugh des Arcis has had to post guards outside his wife's room because, as she reminds him unceasingly, she only married him so that I and all my lands would be safe, and though Hugh protests that he had nothing to do with the burning of the château and villages, she will not listen. To her, his promise is broken so her wedding vows are dust.

She has often thought of escape but it is not easy. Many-towered, proud Carcassonne, over which King Louis's oriflamme now flies, may be an Occitanian city but it is filled with Sir Hugh's men. What is more, they have spilled beyond the long, castellated defences and are camped in neat rows around the leafless vines spread for miles like skeletal dwarves. With Frenchman and Occitanian forced to rub shoulders, the atmosphere both inside and out prickles with suspicion.

Not that the French find it uncongenial in Carcassonne. Not at all. They have come as conquerors, which is always pleasant. If they are edgy it is because, though strong and mighty, they are permanently disconcerted. For a start, beyond its sturdy double walls and the two, purposely discon-nected, portcullises, the city is full of traps for the unwary: staircases leading nowhere, false floors and gates opening not into the city proper but into slaughter yards from which the blood never entirely dries. Though the French knights set clerks to draw maps and force local people to act as guides, they never feel they quite know where they are or where they might end up. Furthermore, the stone that in the sun glows so blindingly golden can, in a moment, turn dead grey. A visitor spying Carcassonne from afar would not know whether to rush through the gates in hope of welcome or creep past for fear of ghouls. Though they know they are secure, somehow the French intruders feel permanently threatened.

This is not good for Yolanda whose guards, in their anxiety, are sharp-eyed and so rigidly dutiful that she cannot even go to the watercloset without detection.

Tonight, in the next door chamber to hers, Hugh is also wakeful, pacing about under a domed stone roof that he sometimes fancies is descending slowly to trap him, as he once trapped a spider in a vase. When they arrived here just before the winter set in, Hugh was wounded and sick, so the place has become heavily overfurnished with tables and chairs and chests of medicines. The large bed in which, though brought from his house in Paris, he finds it so hard to sleep, sits opposite a hearth that could heat a room double the size. A writing desk has been placed wherever space can be found and on a large round table, squashed between bed and door, are several empty pitchers, a quantity of discarded goblets and twists of paper bearing the blotchy hand of an apothecary. Occasionally Hugh finds the soles of his boots glued to the rugs by the remains of unidentifiable meals. He hates this room.

He is not thinking about the room now, however. Nor, though it should be, is his mind full of King Louis' plans for the Occitan, or even of the Blue Flame that he must capture. As he paces, he fingers the long scar on his forehead, the remains of the wound that nearly killed him, and thinks of his wife.

He repeats 'my wife', the phrase which she utterly repudiate, as he pushes irritably past the two knights who have kept watch over him since he was carried in here. After eleven years in his service, lean and ambitious Amalric and swarthy, loyal Henri recognise his moods yet they do not know what is troubling him now. He glances at his reflection in a silver dish that has found its way on to the writing desk. Below the scar, a grave face stares back through fading blue eyes just emerging from bruised pouches. He turns one way and then the other. His chin is smooth. The barber has shaved him well, carefully tracing round the burn on his right cheek that will also fade in time. He opens his mouth. He still has all his teeth. He bends and as his hair falls notices a white streak amid the blond. He peers more closely, hoping it is a trick of his imagination and his heart sinks when, on closer inspection, he sees that the streak is broad and the white well-established. When did this happen? He moves his hand from scar to scalp, as if a touch might bring back his natural colour but then drops his hand and braces himself.

Oh God, here comes another. When will they stop, these awful rushes of panic which, since he was wounded, have begun to creep from behind, like burglars. The wave that is about to hit him is so dense he is surprised that Amalric and Henri don't see it and leap to his defence. He sways away from the desk and steadies himself against a wooden chest, his legs buckling slightly. He knows he is being stared at and tries to beat the weakness off and stand square. If he can just hold on, the feeling will pass. It must. But it does not and he begins to sink.

Amalric seizes a lamp and Henri grabs Hugh's shoulders to heave him on to the bed. On the way, he grabs one of the dirty goblets. 'Quick, Amalric, stick a posset in here.' Amalric untwists a paper and swirls the powdered contents round but when he tries to force the drink on Hugh, Hugh bangs his hand upward and sends the goblet flying. The knights exclaim loudly. Hugh begins to rage. The knights drop him. They have no idea what to do. Amalric runs next door and only when Hugh hears a voice that is neither Amalric's nor Henri's does the panic begin to recede.

'What do you want? What's going on?'

He wipes the sweat trickling on to his collar. Yolanda is in the doorway, one hand resting as always on Brees's head, her face masked by a long mess of uncombed brown hair. He coughs to test that his voice will not squeak. He can take nothing for granted. 'I don't want anything and nothing's going on,' he says when he can trust himself.

Henri harrumphs. Hugh glares at him. 'It's too hot in here, that's all.' He walks to the shutters, forcing purpose into his shaking legs, and throws them open. Then he goes straight to the fireplace and smashes down the logs. They crack and roar and spark, making the room even hotter. Hugh keeps hold of the poker until his hands stop trembling. 'I shall ride tomorrow,' he says abruptly.

'The apothecary says –' Amalric begins.

'I said I shall ride tomorrow.'

Amalric catches Henri's eye. Perhaps a ride will restore their lord to his normal self better than any quack's preparation. 'We can see what the hunting's like round here,' Amalric suggests. 'The hawks'll be glad of an outing.'

Letting go of the poker, Hugh pushes his hands together behind his back until the very last of the tremors have ceased. He sits on a bench, out of the light, barely hearing a word that has been spoken. *What's the matter with me?* His heart quails. What happens if he begins to shiver and shake as he leads the knights in the assault on Montségur? Sweat prickles again, only this time it is cold.

Yolanda is still standing in the doorway.

'Leave us,' Hugh says to the two men. Yolanda turns, trailing her sage-green night-robe. 'Not you.'

Yolanda stops quite still, always holding tightly on to Brees. Hugh gestures for her to come nearer to the fire, for though she is warmly wrapped, her face is pinched and drawn. The gauntness adds a certain distinction. She looks older than her fifteen years and she carries her left hand as though the wedding ring Hugh obliges her to wear is too heavy for her finger.

'Yolanda.' This is not the moment for what he has to say. It really is not. Indeed, in many ways there could not be a worse moment but he cannot wait. He stiffens his back. He is Sir Hugh des Arcis and he is her husband. He touches the signet ring on the fourth finger of his right hand. He will speak and he will get his way. 'Yolanda,' he blurts out more briskly than he means to, 'I want a son.'

He can tell that she heard him because her stillness alters in a heartbeat from mutinous to stunned. Even her dress no longer twitches in the draught. Brees whines and nudges her leg. Her only movement is a tiny pulse in the hollow of her neck. Hugh waits, and she keeps him waiting a long time.

Lots of men might say the same words to their wives, yet Yolanda had never, ever thought to hear them from Hugh. Indeed, in the five months since their wedding, bowing to her wishes, he has made no attempt to force himself on her. More than that. He has been kind to her. Until her home was destroyed and he would not let her go, she had learned to think of him as a friend. Though she had married more than unwillingly, she wore his ring without fear, which is why this declaration hits her like a stone and she is surprised to find herself still standing.

Hugh is not looking at her. 'If I die,' he says, 'my family dies out with me and I have lands, Yolanda, lands that need an overlord. Without a son, the king will give everything that's mine to whomsoever he chooses and the des Arcis name will be forgotten. Why should that be when I have a wife?'

Silence.

'Can you understand, Yolanda?' He takes a candle and kneels before her. Brees sticks out his tongue. Hugh ignores him. 'Look,' he says, and he holds the light near the white streak in his hair. 'I'm growing old.'

She ignores what he's trying to show her, glances at the great unmade bed and then at the door. Should she run now? Should she scream? If he so much as touches her hem, she'll set Brees on him. They make a curious tableau.

He gets up slowly, making no move towards her, and puts the candle down. She begins to breathe again. A cool voice inside her head tells her to think before she does anything. After all, despite the shock he has just given her, she does know this man. They have travelled together. They have even shared a chamber and remained quite separate and it is not his way to use violence against a girl. But then, and the cool voice becomes less cool, this man wants a son and that is a powerful want, more powerful, perhaps, than any other. That kind of want might well override ordinary scruples. To get a son a man might feel justified in doing almost anything.

She swiftly pulls an oak chair between Hugh and herself and clutches the back of it, unconsciously folding her skirts about her legs like armour. 'I'm not your wife any longer. The bargain is broken.'

'We've been through that, Yolanda. You *are* my wife.'

She manages to keep her head. He has always been susceptible to reason. 'Perhaps I couldn't give you a son.' She tries not to sound pleading. 'Perhaps I would just have a daughter. Perhaps I couldn't have a baby at all. Perhaps even if I did, they would all die, like they did with your first wife.'

A faint shadow darkens Hugh's face. 'Perhaps,' he says quietly, 'but that doesn't alter the fact that I want a son and that you, as my lawful wedded wife, should be my son's mother. If a daughter comes –' he shrugs – 'I will care for her, of course. But I need a son.'

She crosses her arms in front of her. Brees, sensing real fear, rolls a grumbling purr round his throat. 'How could you even imagine I would agree?' She can feel the vibration in the top of Brees's head.

'A man can always hope.'

She crunches her fingers through her hair and a lock snags on his ring. She tugs at it and then bursts out, 'Please don't do this, Hugh. You're the king's chosen knight, the Seneschal of Carcassonne, the keeper of the oriflamme and the hero –' her voice is bitter – 'of the destruction of the Occitan. You don't need me. You can have anybody you want.'

'I want you.'

'That's ridiculous.'

He is stung not by her anger but by her contempt. All her sweetness, the sweetness that first drew him to her, is turning sour. And suddenly, he wants to hold her, to tell her that he loves her even though he knows that she will never love him. He wants to declare that though many women would be happy to give him a son, he wants *her* son and he wants that with every fibre of his being. He wants to ask why she cannot see how perfect their union would be, not just for himself but for the Occitan and for France. Together they could join north and south in love rather than bloodshed. They have been given the chance, as few others have, of creating something great because a child of theirs would be a beautiful and rare creature, a matter for rejoicing. Can't she just forget Raimon and be happy?

But he says none of these things because he has never spoken such words to anybody. How, then, could he find the courage to say them to somebody who does not want to hear them? Instead, he picks up a goblet from the table and is grateful when the wine makes him cough.

Yolanda is trying not to shiver. Eventually, she speaks again. 'I didn't think you were like other men,' she says, her voice surprisingly calm. 'I didn't think you would stoop to their standards. I didn't think you'd treat me as part of your war of conquest.'

Ah! She knows just how to hurt him. He takes another slug of wine. 'As you observe, I am the keeper of the king's oriflamme,' he says mechanically. 'I have under my command two hundred knights and five thousand soldiers.' He stops. It occurs to him that if he is to do what he intends to do, he must actually do exactly as she says: he must think of her as part of his war of conquest. Indeed, he must suppress all thoughts of her as the girl he loves and wishes to protect from hurt and dream only of his future son, a honey-gold child to warm his cold castle of Champagne. Once he has a son, he will let Yolanda go. Perhaps, in time, that will be enough to gain her forgiveness. He tips the last of the wine down his throat. 'Do you know what Henri and Amalric and, I dare say, most of the other knights believe?' he asks.

She does not move.

'They believe you make me less of a knight than I should be. They believe you've turned my head. They believe you sap my resolve and cloud my judgement.' He pauses. 'They believe I should have had Raimon executed when I had the chance and that I should have taken you by force on our wedding night, as a proper husband would have done.' She reverses fast and flattens herself against the wall. He does not move. 'Of course, had I done that,' he carries on relentlessly, 'by now you might well be having a son and we would not be having this conversation.'

A log falls and he starts, feeling the panic rising again. The goblet falls from his hand as he sinks down and grips the arms of his chair. The wave engulfs him, smothers him, then passes over. 'Christ in heaven,' he says furiously. He glares at Yolanda.

She is not glaring back. She has seen his weakness and is making one last attempt. 'Nobody despises you. Your knights and servants admire you.'

'Oh, don't humour me.' He leans forward and wipes his brow on his sleeve. 'You think that because their words are respectful I don't see their expressions? I've led men for many years, Yolanda. I can tell what they think by the way they pull on their gloves.'

Yolanda waits, then with sharp, determined movements, eases off her wedding ring and drops it. She has nothing more to say. She stands poised for a moment then, when Hugh does not move to stop her, runs back to her own room. As she slams her door, the ring is still rolling.

Hugh sits for an hour staring at it, and only after he hears the bells calling the monks to early prayers does he pick it up, touch the band where it touched her and lock it into a chest containing other precious things. Then he goes to the desk. Carefully, he moves lamps into position on a large map, already spread, on which is drawn a fortress amid the detailed contours of a loaf-shaped hill. Above the hill, his clerk of war has painted the Blue Flame. Hugh finds a page in the passage and sends him for fresh ink. No matter what his own preoccupations, the king has issued his orders and Hugh must calculate how best to carry them out. He traces the hill with his finger then stops. In the guttering candle, the Flame has taken the shape of Yolanda's face. Her expression is harsh and unyielding. If she is to bear his son, he knows he had better get used to it.

THE CONVERT

At dawn two days later, Raimon pulls on his boots. Stepping over Sir Roger, he tiptoes past Adela, asleep outside the warmth of the tender circle of women, and notes with sadness that though she is not yet twenty-five, suffering and self-righteousness have shrivelled her features. Her lips, which always owned a disapproving curve, are a little crusted, like those of an old woman. He looks carefully at Metta. She sleeps neatly, her arms clasped lightly together and her pretty lips slightly parted as if hoping for a kiss. Raimon wonders at the endless variety of women. Yolanda sleeps like neither of these two. She sleeps either curled like an animal, her head rounded into her chest, or with her limbs at odd angles and her hair an explosion. Is she sleeping now? His legs cramp. He steps outside. If he is to put into action the idea that now nags, he must begin the preparations today.

The sky is grey and promises a bitter day. He rounds his lips and blows out, pulling his blanket closer and wishing he had a better pair of boots. He sees the huntsman coming out of the kennels amid a swirl of hounds.

'They're so beautiful.'

He turns to find Metta beside him, her hair unbrushed and without a cloak. At once, he unwraps his blanket and throws it round her. 'Here. You'll die of cold. You looked completely asleep a minute ago!'

She smiles her thanks. 'I woke when you passed. We should share,' she says, taking the blanket gratefully, 'or it will be you who dies.' She opens the blanket without any coquetry. Raimon hesitates for a moment and then they are huddled together.

The hounds are sniffing about, finding places to do their business. The dogboys who are, as their name implies, almost dogs themselves, and to whom the huntsman is both mother and father, follow with little shovels. Metta laughs. 'Our kennels were not so close to our château,' she says, 'and we never had boys like these.'

'They're mostly orphans,' Raimon tells her, 'or boys people reckon are a bit soft in the head.' They watch two collide as they both dive for the same piece of dirt. He whistles down and the dogboys stop and wriggle at him.

'Some of the hounds are bigger than the dogboys,' Metta observes.

'Yes,' replies Raimon. 'The bloodhounds could eat one quite easily for breakfast. The huntsman sometimes threatens.' A look of such horror greets this that Raimon laughs. 'Don't worry! He loves them!' He finds it easy to speak to her. This, and her unexpected presence beside him, makes up his mind. His plan is not mad. It is rich with possibility. Perhaps Sir Parsifal himself is behind it.

Metta blushes. 'Tell me the hounds' names,' she says.

And so it begins. Metta will be Raimon's ticket of entry into Montségur. He will attach himself to her and her to him so that when the visitors leave, he will leave with them and when they get to Montségur, he can stride boldly through the gate at Metta's side. To everybody at the château, Yolanda has abandoned him for Hugh. Why, then, should he not fall in love with this peaceful creature, tender as a peach, whose gentle voice would be perfect balm for any bruised heart?

He runs through all the hounds' names, adding little stories as Yolanda used sometimes to do. Metta is quickly entranced. He is just pointing out Farvel, the huntsman's favourite, when Sir Roger appears. 'Metta!' he says reproachfully. 'It's too cold for you out here.'

'Yes,' she says, 'too cold for all of us. But Raimon had a blanket and we shared it.'

'Nevertheless, go in now,' her father admonishes her.

She smiles and kisses Sir Roger's horny cheek before slipping out of the blanket and back inside.

'She was just asking about the hounds,' Raimon says with casual innocence, although he knows his face is red.

Sir Roger grunts. Below, the hounds sing when the huntsman brings out a horse and swings on. A falconer, already mounted, falls in behind and two more men armed with nets and bows bring up the rear. They are heavily muffled and the falconer is swearing as his horse tries to keep its feet.

'Oh dear!' Sir Roger exclaims as the horse slips and bangs

its knees. 'I suppose they're going out for extra food. We're causing a good deal of trouble.' He gazes anxiously at the sky. 'I hope they get back before the weather closes in again.'

Raimon, glad that Sir Roger has ignored his blushes, tries to reassure him. 'They've an hour or two yet. I'm afraid you'll not be going anywhere for a while.'

'No,' says Sir Roger, a worry line parting his eyebrows. 'I suppose that would be madness.'

'Mad and dangerous,' says Raimon and wonders when Sir Roger will guess that, for Metta, the danger is in remaining here. His conscience twists, but he must get to the Flame, he must.

Typically, it is hawk-eyed Laila who first notices how much time Raimon and Metta spend together. 'What do you see in that simpleton?' she asks him on the third evening. Snow has been falling since before dusk and now lies in a second or even third lumpy blanket over the ice packed below. Everybody totters gingerly as if temporarily disabled.

'She's not a simpleton,' Raimon says. 'She's good and kind.'

Laila snorts.

For many days following, the sky, low and thick, wraps Castelneuf in a luminous cocoon of half-light that gradually blunts the visitors' impatience at the delay to their journey. There is food, there is comfort, there is Laila and her tricks and, of course, there are always stories. Most beguilingly, in the fog of this half-ruined eyrie, they feel beyond the reach of the ordinary world.

'She's not a simpleton,' Raimon repeats the following week when Laila again badmouths Metta. 'She may not toss balls in the air and wear pointed heels but that doesn't mean she's not just as clever as you.'

Laila humphs. 'Yolanda would find her very dull.' Their eyes clash. Laila's lashes are splashed yellow, like a tiger's.

'Yolanda isn't here,' Raimon says shortly.

The girl grimaces. 'When she returns she's going to find things a bit different.'

'You mean she'll find you as Aimery's countess?'

Laila does not even blush. 'Why not?'

'You don't even like him.'

'You don't know what I like.'

'You like making trouble.'

'*You like making trouble!*' She pouts and imitates his voice. It is all he can do not to shove her out of the way. 'And you're so perfect?' She throws back her head and her curls dance. 'Why not admit it, Raimon. You're just as bad as the rest of us, calculating your own advantage. I can only think that the ninny-girl's father has offered you money to forget Yolanda and take the half-wit off his hands.'

Raimon lunges but she easily evades him and skips off to find Aimery in the courtyard. Raimon does not follow. Instead he kicks at the snow because, as is her gift, Laila has struck hard where she knows it will hurt most.

Yet he must continue his courtship. The Flame needs him and he cannot think of another way to save it. So he avoids Laila and allows himself some satisfaction as the pieces of his plan fall easily into place. Already, Metta seeks him out. Already, she trusts him. Already, their names are spoken in the same breath. Yet this, Raimon begins to realise, whilst it may ensure him entry to the fortress of Montségur, may not get him to the Flame itself. If he is to pass as the White Wolf's friend rather than his enemy he will have to go further. Under Metta's guidance and the canopy of love, Raimon will have to pretend to convert.

The very thought makes his skin crawl and he wonders whether, after so many public and forceful denigrations of Catharism, any conversion is plausible. And even if it is, how will he cope with the snide remarks about having eventually 'seen the Cathar light' he has spent so much time and energy denouncing? Will he be able to bear the look in Cador's eyes, or the gossip and sideways glances? Yet a conversion, which the White Wolf would be obliged to welcome, is a more certain key to the Flame than even Metta.

He persuades himself. Metta's Catharism, after all, is a gentle thing, quite unlike the evangelical implacability of the White Wolf's. She never speaks of starving people to death or of leaping voluntarily on to funeral pyres. Though she might believe the world to have been created through evil, Metta's God is not an arrogant seeker of revenge and punishment. Rather, he is the God of Love. If anybody, therefore, was to lead him to a new understanding of the Cathar faith it would be her.

He begins to ask her questions. She answers with open pleasure. The only thing that disconcerts is that Laila now never leaves him alone, creeping up when he least expects her. She cares nothing about his beliefs. What makes her hiss and spit with increasing venom is his betrayal of Yolanda. And she does not confine herself to whispers. Sometimes, at supper in the hall, with her eyes darting from Metta to himself and back, she demands loudly 'How can you?' He toys with the idea of telling her the truth but discards it. To Laila, information is ammunition and he could not trust her not to use it for some purpose quite of her own. Nor does he tell Cador, but this is for the boy's own protection. What he does not know he can never be made to reveal.

But what of Metta herself? Ah, what indeed. She hears Yolanda's name occasionally, but Adela reassures her and anyway, when Laila shoots her barbs, they are deflected by the innocent shine of Metta's good nature. She will not believe ill of Raimon, not now, although Raimon knows that in the end, when she discovers he has used her, she will hate him. This, curiously, he finds he can bear. Much more unbearable, almost intolerable in fact, is the knowledge that he will have corroded her simple trust as rust corrodes iron. That is what really haunts him.

Yet the call of the Flame is always stronger than even his worst moments of guilt. He cannot abandon it to the White Wolf. Nor can he stand by as it is captured and carried aloft through the streets of Paris as a final sign of Occitanian subjection. He hardens his heart. Iron can be cured of rust. Perhaps Metta will understand. And it is not, he tells himself, as if his seduction is entirely false. He likes her, likes her very much, and she quite naturally seems to gravitate towards him. Yet he could never love her. That is pure pretence. You see, running or swimming, riding or harvesting, even just lying in a hollow plaiting grass, he and Yolanda have always been equals, whereas with Metta he is always the protector. If

Yolanda is a wild thing, Metta is a domestic pet and, apart from Brees, he has never loved one of those.

The mountain fog thickens and the atmosphere thickens with it. Though more snow seems impossible, more falls. The visitors settle in and Raimon works hard. When food runs a little short, he makes sure that Metta and her father have more than they need. When Sir Roger complains of stiff limbs, he searches out the apothecary and digs through the snow for a struggling medicinal herb. At Metta's behest, when starving deer are seen scraping the ground on the opposite hillside, he takes Cador and half a dozen men with pitchforks of precious hay to spread about. Over the last, he teases Metta gently. 'I thought you Cathars believed that starving to death is not the worst way to go.'

Metta will not take this as a joke. 'I told you on the first night we were here that our Perfectus teaches that the fast to the death is wicked, and anyway, you have to volunteer for it. The deer certainly haven't done that.'

Raimon pats her arm. Metta puts her hand on his. 'Christ fed the five thousand in the Gospel,' she says earnestly. 'I'm sure some of them must have brought animals. He will have fed them too.'

'Is that another piece of wisdom from your Perfectus?'

'Actually, I've never heard the Perfectus speak of it.' Her round eyes twinkle.

'How do you know it, then?'

'I've read it myself, in the Bible.'

'You read the Bible yourself?' Raimon is genuinely surprised.

'Why not? As I keep telling Count Aimery, Christ doesn't need priests to interpret his good news,' she says. 'We can understand it perfectly well ourselves.'

Raimon takes a deep breath. 'You make the Cathar faith sound so different. When you speak, it sounds less like heresy and more like common sense.'

'It *is* common sense, Raimon,' she says, quite radiant. 'That's why I believe it.'

Later, at supper, and bringing Adela into the discussion, Raimon asks Metta more questions, some of them highly sceptical so that Metta has to persuade him of the answer. When he and Adela speak, both are aware that this is their first real conversation since their mother died.

After supper, Laila disappears and when she reappears she has painted her face green. 'It's the colour of treachery,' she says to Metta, who smiles and turns away. Raimon wonders again if he should take Laila into his confidence and again decides against it.

The first really clear dawn seems like a miracle and in a splurge of boyish excitement Aimery orders the farrier to nail planks on to runners. 'Sledging!' he cries. 'Why ever not!' Everybody rushes out, thrilled to see the sun, and a long sweep is made, the longest Castelneuf has ever attempted. Stretching from the château gates down through the town to the river, with enough bends and curves to satisfy the most ardent adrenalin-seeker, eager hands roughly bank up the snow on each side in an attempt to keep the sledges on course. A carnival atmosphere prevails.

Only Adela resists and Metta sits with her, trying again

and again, with no success, to get her to see that joy and faith are not incompatible. Adela's responses are stubborn and surly but Metta has boundless patience. Sicart hovers until at last he bids Metta go outside. 'This is a grand day,' he says. 'Don't miss it.' Metta is torn. 'Go on,' Sicart urges. Metta succumbs, pats Adela's bony shoulder and then hurries into her boots.

Ignoring Laila who, using Ugly as a prop and to the amusement of some, is exaggeratedly shadowing his every move, Raimon tucks Metta into a sledge, pushes off and leaps on behind her. 'Take care! Oh, do take care!' shouts Sir Roger. 'Don't go too fast!'

Raimon holds Metta by the waist as they lift their feet and the runners find their path. Leaving Laila behind, they gather speed and Metta's hair whips out from under her fur hat, wrapping itself round Raimon's face. The thick hanks exude a scent of rosemary and mint, a lovely smell, but Raimon can hardly stand it. He doesn't want fair hair, he wants brown. He doesn't want rosemary and mint, he wants the musty smell of Brees. Metta holds herself stiffly and jolts against him with every bump. Yolanda would mould herself to him. He and Metta are two. He and Yolanda are one. The joy of the run vanishes. Raimon cannot bear what he is doing.

Impacted from the many sledges that have gone before, the snow is unforgiving and the sun, glancing harshly off the solid mass of crystal, blinds. If Metta feels Raimon's stiff resistance as they glide and swerve and scrape, she says nothing. When they spin dangerously close to the road's edge, where the banking has already given way, she cannot help screaming, but there's no stopping now. As the pace increases, the cold slices through their furs and leathers and skin, stinging like a nettled knife.

At the horse-troughs, the feeder stream suspended mid-flow, they slow. The road is flatter here. Metta shivers. 'Shall we go back?' Raimon says at once.

She turns her head. Droplets have peppered her white skin. Another man might have compared her to a fairy queen. 'I've never felt so terrified in my whole life,' she says. 'If I didn't have you behind me, I'd have died fifty times. But isn't it wonderful! Please, let's go on.' She raises her feet, Raimon pushes off and the runners are hissing once more. His face aches and his lips are as raw as his heart.

They slide to an ignominious halt at the bank of the river and Raimon has to grab Metta to stop her rolling in. 'It wouldn't matter, it's quite solid,' she cries.

'It's very deceptive, river-ice,' Raimon tells her but she is not listening. She is laughing, high on love and thrills. 'I've never, ever done anything like that before. Nobody on earth can have gone so fast.'

They watch others coursing down and listen to the screams of those who don't stop in time. Metta claps her hands together, blows on them and stamps her feet. 'Shall we walk?' she asks. 'It's too cold to stand.' She motions to the bridge, a new one rebuilt after the fires and complete enough to use. 'Can we cross?'

Raimon watches a streak of vermilion. It is Laila, perched on the front of a sledge with Cador and another knight behind. Her hair is plaited, with beads woven cleverly into the ends making them stick straight out behind her like two herons' beaks. Even as her sledge bangs and crashes, almost flinging her off, she is throwing out her arms to Aimery, whose sledge is running beside hers, not plain like the others, but all strung about with fancy bells and silken ribbons. Indeed, it might have been decorated with Laila in mind. His only companion is Ugly, whose ears have flipped inside out as she folds her skinny frame to avoid the worst of the pebbled spray. She is terrified. Laila calls her, and in a daring swoop, scoops her away from Aimery. Whooping with delight, Laila ostentatiously covers the quaking animal in kisses.

They all hit the bottom together and Cador somersaults smartly off whilst Laila, abandoning Ugly, whirls like a merry-go-round.

'I don't believe Laila's afraid of anything,' Metta sighs.

'More fool her,' Raimon says more curtly than he should, then shouts for Cador. 'Will you pull our sledge back to the château? We're going to walk.'

Cador leaps up, nods and shakes himself like a pony. Laila is running to the river, slithering down and jumping about. Raimon opens his mouth to shout a warning. Then he shrugs. Let Laila do as she likes.

Spears of blood begin to flow once more through Raimon's ears and lips making them itch. He takes Metta's arm to ensure she does not slip and then uses the excuse of a narrow track to let go. As they walk in single file, he strides just too fast so that she must scurry to keep up. Her lack of complaint irritates Raimon more. He knows how unfair he is being but for fully a quarter of an hour he cannot help himself.

The path soon vanishes in the pristine hush and Raimon hardly realises that they have walked straight over the boundary wall and are in the Catholic graveyard. 'Take care,' he warns Metta. 'Don't fall over a tombstone.' He takes her arm again, and as suddenly as it arrived, his ill temper vanishes. How dare he snap? None of this is Metta's fault. He guides her round gently, their footfalls making deep indents until, though there is nothing to see in the white flatness except some animal tracks, he is sure they must be in the separate place set aside for the Cathar dead. He halts. 'My mother's buried in here,' he says.

'Oh,' Metta responds, at once full of sympathy. 'You must miss her.'

'Every day,' Raimon replies and draws his dark brows together. Another lie and he surely need not lie all the time. 'Actually, Metta, that's not true. There are days when I don't think of her at all. It's only when I hear the snatch of a song or smell bread baking, then I wish I could just – could just –' He cannot go on. What he is saying now is not a lie, yet is tainted by its use as another hook to draw Metta to him.

'I'd like to have met your mother,' she says after a while. 'Do you think you're like her?'

'No,' says Raimon quickly. 'She was nothing like me.'

Metta stands, waiting for him to take the lead as is her habit and Raimon feels again that rush of resentment. Now he welcomes it because it helps to harden his heart. 'I wanted to be a good son to her,' he says, 'but I failed her in the end.'

'Why do you say that?'

Raimon finds he has to walk on, picking up his feet and placing them carefully so as to make clean imprints. As he walks, he bows his head, swinging his hair over his face. 'She wanted me to believe as she did. And I did try, Metta. I even took part in her consolation. It was just that the White Wolf — I told you, remember? He told her she couldn't eat. It seemed like murder.'

'It wasn't murder but it was wrong,' Metta says, following in his footsteps.

'Perhaps I was too quick to believe the worst of the Cathar faith and believe me, when my mother died, I wanted to believe the worst.' He stops when he thinks they are directly beside his mother's grave and turns. Metta moves until she is standing over his mother, a cosy angel in wool and fur. 'But now?' she prompts.

Raimon takes a deep breath and does not draw back. 'I don't know. But these last days, talking to you —' He shrugs. 'It's too late, though, isn't it?' He finally lifts his face to her.

Metta smiles her innocent smile. 'It's not too late,' she says. 'Many people come to our faith who have spent their lives denying it.'

'I suppose they do,' he says, and thinks *careful, careful* as he presses on. 'Sometimes, when I'm with you, it does seem the only way to make sense of everything.' He feels two bright lying spots under his eyes. Yolanda would have recognised them at once. Metta puts them down to the cold. She clamps her hood tightly under her chin. She is a perfect model for a Madonna, Raimon thinks rather bleakly, because she is a girl without angles, a girl in whom a man might bury himself and find all the comfort in the world. His quicksilver resentment turns again to remorse. She does not deserve this.

'Come,' she says, conscious of a certain hollowness in his cheeks, 'let's get back into the warmth.'

As they retrace their steps, snow from the branches above drops on to her head. 'I've been talking to Cador.' Her voice is light. 'He tells me you're the bravest knight he's ever served and from the stories he tells, I think it may be true.'

'I'm the only knight he's ever served and I'm not even a knight.' Raimon moves in front of her so that she cannot see the workings of his face. 'Walk in my footprints again. That way your feet won't get so wet.'

With happy companionship, Metta slots in. 'It's an honour to be walking in the steps of the Knight of the Blue Flame,' she says.

He stops short and spins round. Has she guessed, or is she making fun of him? But she is incapable of either guessing or jesting. She is simply complimenting him in a way she knows will please him. Why this should be the last straw, he does not know, but it is. He cannot deceive her any longer. He will get the Blue Flame another way. 'Metta,' he begins, but it is hard. He is only used to revealing things to Yolanda.

She stands expectantly. 'I'm listening,' she says.

Where to start? 'I love this place,' he says.

'Yes,' she answers. 'I know that.'

'No, you don't know, not really, not in the way I want you to know. I'd do anything to save it from harm, anything. Do you understand that? Anything.'

'Yes,' she says again. 'That's why Cador calls you the Knight of the Blue Flame.'

'It's more complicated than that. You see —' But he gets no further for a shriek has Metta clinging to him, and very quickly another shriek follows, high as a banshee, so that the hairs on both their necks rise and they begin to run as fast as the snow will allow, Raimon kicking great clods aside and virtually swinging Metta off her feet. They slither back across the bridge, still clinging together.

Downriver, a crowd has gathered. Dropping Metta, Raimon pushes through to the front where he finds Laila, soaking and crying, belabouring Aimery. The pink dye from her hair has run into the chalk with which she has whitened her face, giving her a skinned look. Aimery's hands and clothes are also pink-blotted as he fends her off. 'Jesus Christ, Laila!' he is shouting. 'You're the very devil.'

Two men are carrying something between them. Dread sucks all Raimon's breath into an echoing howl. 'Cador! Oh my God, Cador!'

But it is not Cador the men are carrying: it is a skinny, hairless dog. 'Ugly!' Raimon exclaims. 'Oh, for goodness' sake.' His relief fires his anger. 'That poor brute. What did they do to her?'

'You knew it wasn't safe,' Laila is screaming at Aimery, 'yet you still threw the bone into the river. Why were you even carrying one?'

Aimery finally grips her hands behind her back. Her petticoats flap, garish and dripping. 'It was the end of my breakfast. I wasn't thinking about the dog when I threw it.'

'Why didn't you jump in to save her?' Laila is writhing, trying to face him, but he has her too tight.

'I knew I'd be too heavy. Christ in heaven, you idiot! The ice couldn't even hold you.'

'You could have tried!' She ties herself into terrible, murderous knots.

'Like you did? What good did that do?' Aimery is puce, for he almost cannot hold her, and the puce clashes with the pink as Laila's screams ricochet round the valley. 'Let go of me! Ugly! Ugly!'

Raimon has reached the dog and is kneeling. Ugly's eyes and mouth are open giving her a look of faint surprise. She is already stiffening.

'If I let go, do you promise not to hit me?' Aimery seems determined to turn this tiny tragedy into something of a joke. He lets go.

Laila kicks out at him then rushes to Ugly and takes the dog's face between her blotched hands. 'Wake up,' she orders. 'Wake up at once, Ugly. Don't you dare ignore me. Wake up now this minute.' There is a click as she shakes the dog and the jaw closes. She repeats her order, her voice rising and rising until Raimon puts his own hands over hers. 'She can't obey you, Laila,' he tells her flatly. 'She's dead.'

For a long moment Laila remains still. Only Raimon can see the struggle going on inside her and the tears she refuses to shed. Aimery will not have that satisfaction. Raimon grips her hands tighter as she shrinks into herself.

A large shadow is cast over the snow. 'Well, I'm really sorry about the dog,' Aimery blusters, 'but be honest, Laila, you never liked her much. You were always making fun of her. In fact, you treated her abominably.'

A tremor shakes Laila from top to toe. Raimon wonders if she is at last going to break down or whether she will conjure a dagger from nowhere and stab Aimery straight through the heart. Instead, however, she turns chilly as the river. Under the chalk, Raimon can almost see her skin stiffening like Ugly's. She leaves her hands for one more moment beneath his, as if gathering strength, then she whips them out and springs up. Aimery mockingly puts up defensive fists but she simply tosses her head. 'Well, there we are,' she says breezily, hands on hips. 'There were already too many ugly creatures in the world.' She seizes a sledge. 'Come on! What are you all waiting for? Let's go!'

Cador creeps to Raimon's side. He is weeping unashamedly. 'I was pulling the sledge up the hill. I was too far away,' he sobs, bending over the corpse. 'Poor dog!'

Raimon is taking off his cloak. He wraps Ugly in it and picks her up. 'We can't bury her until the ground thaws.' He looks around. Laila is slithering up the hill as fast as she can go, talking nonstop. Her voice is shrill. She does not look back.

Cador, Metta and Raimon set off back over the bridge, Raimon in front carrying Ugly, Metta in the middle and Cador behind. The sun's rays are still dancing. Why not? The sun does not care about a dead dog. But the burial party are all huddled, thinking of the cold and the river and the knocking of a small, desperate head against unyielding ice. They bypass the graveyards and find a small clearing in which a completely circular drift of snow has settled. Raimon lays the bundle down and he and Cador scrape out a hole. When it is as deep as they can get it, they lower the corpse whilst Metta offers a simple, heartfelt prayer that the dog's spirit may be at peace. When the prayer is over, Cador stares at the misshapen bundle, his grief giving way to incomprehension. 'How can she be dead, just like that? She was so happy this morning. It doesn't seem possible.'

Raimon casts a glance at Metta and is aware that his earlier desire to unburden himself has vanished. He will stick to his plan. 'Perhaps it's for the best,' he says, noting, and not to his credit, a new piety in his voice. 'At least Ugly now has eternal life that can't end in death.'

Cador frowns. 'Are dogs granted eternal life?'

Metta answers. 'We believe that a dog cannot take the consolation and become a Perfectus, but a dog is a living thing and every living thing is important to God. When animals I love die, I always tell myself that if Christ cares even for the sparrows in the air, he'll certainly care for something bigger, so I'm quite certain that he'll have a place for Ugly.'

Cador looks more cheerful as they pile the snow over the dead dog until, in the end, only a last leg sticks out in final supplication. Raimon covers it up as Cador sculpts a lumpy headstone. 'How do you write Ugly?' he asks.

'Letters are quite hard, aren't they?' Metta has the virtue of never sounding disapproving.

'Do you find them hard too?' Cador asks. 'I did know them, but I've forgotten.' Like Laila, he does not like Raimon's attachment to Metta, but unlike Laila he has made no comment, and he certainly could not complain that she is unkind. When she takes his finger, he is quite willing that they should scrape out Ugly's name together.

Once they are back over the bridge, they stop and look at the water. Already, a thin sheet has formed over the murderous hole. Metta shrinks deep into her cloak. 'Poor Laila.'

'Why do you say that?' Cador juts an angry chin. 'She just ran off. She didn't seem to care at all.'

'Oh, she cared,' Metta replies. Cador remains disbelieving.

Half an hour later they reach the château gates. Sir Roger is waiting. 'Thank goodness you're back,' he booms. 'Everybody tells me there's been some kind of accident with a dog.'

'There was, sir,' Raimon says, 'but Metta's safe.'

Sir Roger looks at Raimon, then at his daughter and then back to Raimon again. 'I hope so,' he says and Raimon's heart lurches as, without a smile, Sir Roger takes her inside.

In the Cold

Yolanda is crouched by her bed, her lips bared in a snarl that only gradually subsides. Hugh has left her although his presence still reverberates. He came to her, as he warned her he would, then left without laying a finger on her. She did not snarl when he was with her. This snarl came after, from the animal part of her, the part she does not want him to see because if he thinks of her as an animal, it will be easier to treat her like one. When he was here, hard-eyed and grim, she stood, forbidding Brees to move, matching him look for look. Not a word was spoken until finally he had blinked first and retreated. Only then did she crouch and now she must get up. He will be back and that tactic will not work again. If only Laila were here, she might poison him. She must get out.

She crawls over to the door and puts her ear to it. One of the guards is leaning against it. She can hear the creak of his leather jerkin. He is sighing with boredom as he tosses dice, but how can that help her? She tries to clear her mind. Hugh has still not locked her in – he would not stoop to that – but if she emerges, the guard will follow her like a shadow. She goes to the window and throws it wide. Here there is more possibility if she thinks herself agile enough to find footholds in the stone. If she slips, however, she'll be smashed to smithereens in the courtyard below. And she would have to leave Brees behind. She slams the window shut and Brees's paws scratch behind her as she paces back and forth.

Food is brought. More in hope than expectation, she ties it into a bundle and hides it under the bed. She reopens the window and this time leaves it swinging. She listens again at the door. The guard has changed his recreation now. He is kicking something. She pulls the door a fraction. At once he is blocking out the light. 'I heard a noise,' Yolanda says.

The man, thickset and with a complexion like custard, picks something up to show her. It is a goat's bladder, roundly stuffed with straw.

'Oh,' she says. 'You like to play kick ball?'

He nods.

'I'd like to play too.'

He squares his shoulders. 'It's a man's game.'

She ignores that and opens the door fully. Two chests, lids agape, are set, one at each end of the anteroom. She raises her eyebrows. 'I have to get the ball into the chest,' he explains.

'I can see that. But isn't it a game for two?'

'Two or more, but I can practise on my own.'

'Can I try?'

He is dismissive. 'I've told you, it's a man's game.'

Yolanda is already out and gathering her skirts. She is deliberately hopeless. Far from landing in the chests, the ball bangs randomly off the walls. Brees pursues it in his lumbering way and Yolanda shouts at him to leave it. The sentry stands, his arms folded, until Yolanda teases him, kicking the ball through his legs. He cannot resist. Soon they are both concentrating and when Yolanda makes a lucky score, the man grows purple with frustration and begins to play in earnest. When the score is even, he relaxes and shows her how to use the side of her foot to push the ball round. They chase each other, Yolanda's skirts riding higher and higher, until suddenly, with a wallop that makes her spine jolt, she pitches the ball hard at the edge of the door frame and watches it spin into her room and right out through the window. 'Oh no!' she cries, 'Oh no! Just as I'm beginning to enjoy myself. Quick. Go and get it.'

'I'll shout down,' the man pants, and leans out. 'Eh! You!' Nobody hears him.

'Get it quick,' Yolanda begs. 'I'm just beginning to think I can beat you. I'll close the window so it can't happen again.' She whisks about, to stop him from thinking. 'Look! Couldn't we expand the game? If perhaps if we move one of the chests into my room and play across the way instead of down we'll actually have more space. Getting it through the door itself can count as some kind of score and getting it through the door and into the chest can be a bigger score. That'll be a real test of skill.' She begins to move her feet, as though trying it out. 'Like this, or perhaps like this.'

The man sucks in his cheeks. His legs are twitching. He wants to play. He wants to win.

Yolanda now busies herself pulling the chests just an inch

this way or that as though this is her only preoccupation. She is amazed at the man's obvious passion for what seems to her a ridiculous pastime. Nevertheless, she stokes the passion up. 'Now. Do you think the chest's absolutely in line? And should I shut Brees away? He's not really an asset to the game, is he?' She finds an old belt and calls the dog to her.

That seems to convince the sentry. 'I'll be straight back.' He runs towards the nearest set of stairs, then, just as Yolanda is fishing her outside boots from under the bed, thinks the better of it and runs back. Yolanda feigns to be inspecting her footwear. 'I really think I'll kick better in these,' she says. 'You've got to agree that you've an advantage. Your boots are much tougher than my velvet slippers. Did somebody bring the ball upstairs?'

'No, but –' The man is so torn between pleasure and duty, it is almost laughable.

'Look,' Yolanda says, all reason and logic. 'There are more guards at the bottom of the steps – and do you really think I'm going to vanish when the score's two/one to you?'

The man grins and disappears.

Yolanda yanks the laces to secure the boots, seizes her thick cloak and the bag of food and flees the room in the opposite direction, with Brees pounding behind her. She does not know her way about but since rooms lead off rooms and passages off passages, it is easy to hide when members of the household approach. She pushes downwards all the time until finally, through an unguarded basement storeroom, she is rewarded with the street.

Here, the lights that illuminate the main thoroughfares

and gathering places are her enemy, so she pulls Brees close and squeezes down funnels between walls that smell of old bones. Sometimes she hears her name being shouted and Brees's hackles are permanently up for the air is alive with the ghosts of other fugitives. Soon Yolanda has no idea where she is, but she doesn't care.

In the end, it is Brees who forces her into the open. Smelling a cat, he jerks away in pursuit and Yolanda has to follow for she dare not call his name. When, finally, he halts, it is at a large iron grill loosely set into the road. 'Good dog!' whispers Yolanda, rather to Brees's surprise, for he knows he has been bad.

The hole is a squeeze but the tunnel is slanted, not vertical, so they both slither down to the bottom. It is an old sewage conduit and Yolanda can just stand up. Most people would gag but she breathes in the acrid stench as though it were the lavender her mother used to wear. Sewers may be vile but they lead to rivers. She pushes on, her legs soon soaked up to the knee and Brees's tail quickly thick with sludge. Who cares? They have only to keep walking.

That was the easy bit and had they known what awaited them, Yolanda might not have been so jaunty.

Once out of the sewer, over the river at the least busy of the fords and two miles or so from Carcassonne, they find the blizzard from Castelneuf has moved east. Snow is now falling here, snow that quickly thins to aggressive white hail that clatters against their heads like a relentless barrage of shatter-proof marbles. Even under the dense fur of her hood, Yolanda feels under attack and all the fierce joy at their escape soon dissolves in the bitter struggle to keep going.

The cold out here is of a completely different order to anything she has ever felt before. It has a solidity about it, like rock, and the warm flood of sewage has now turned her skirt into a stiff frozen board that clangs heavily against her legs. Worst of all, though her feet push on, she senses she is getting nowhere. Everything looks the same all the time. Now the wind gets up in sneaky, skinny draughts that deposit powdered ice into her nostrils so that she sometimes has to open her mouth to gasp, which, in turn, makes her chilled teeth ache and rattle. Her tongue tastes of steel. A stream of water would run from her eyes except that it freezes before it hits her cheek and even her hands are frozen because the snow has somehow needled its way inside her gloves. Yet though the gloves are quickly worse than useless, she cannot bring herself to peel them off. Bare skin is unthinkable.

She soon becomes frightened less for herself than for Brees. The dog's head may be large and his coat an oily matted rug but it is no match when the wind becomes a sheer, shrill, glacial howl, determined to flay him alive. His steps are slowing and under his stalagmite fringe, his eyes are closing. When he begins to lean heavily against her, Yolanda knows they must find shelter or perish.

Briefly, she toys with the idea of going back. That would be the sensible thing to do. But she cannot, will not, submit to Hugh. She tries to encourage Brees on but hardly dares turn her head to him for fear of giving the wind another opening into her ear. And anyway, what is the point? Though he is so close, he is nothing but a bluey-white mass, shuffling on pillars of grey.

He stumbles, but she beats him until he rises. It is either a beating or death. They must keep moving, however slowly. Then she too closes her eyes, only for a second but her eyelids weld together. She tries to prise them apart and then gives up. Even the dark seems white.

She begins to sink, then beats herself as she beat Brees and grits her teeth. *Think of other things.* She pictures words being branded like red fire on to her back. No, not red words, blue. *Think of the Flame, think of it as a bridge, one end in your heart, the other in Raimon's. Think of it deep inside Brees, burning hot and thick, like soup. Soup, soup.* She recalls herself and Raimon tossing the hay in the hazy afternoons of summer. Now she is reliving the day they tried to ride his mother's pig. And see, see! Here is her tenth birthday, or was it her eleventh, when he gave her a catapult armed with pebbles he had collected from the very bottom of the lake. Where is the catapult now? Why didn't she take more care of it?

She moves a little faster as though, if she is quick, she might step back into that other life. Too fast. She trips and spreadeagles with a cry, her eyelids torn cruelly apart and the bag in which she has stuffed food crushed against her side. A gust raises her dress and at once, her legs and back are peppered with diamond nails. *The wind is the greatest enemy*, she thinks as she lies helpless. *If we can just get out of the wind, we may yet survive.* She clumsily rolls and her dress cracks like a biscuit. Brees is a snow ghost. 'Brees! Brees!' She prods him, her gloved hands misshapen blocks on the ends of her arms. *Help us!* she cries silently. *Help us!* She begins to swing her arms wildly, banging against the dog, trying to break the shell that is smothering him. Then, in her last despair, she opens her mouth and laughs and cries and just has time to scream Raimon's name before she misses her footing completely and, snatching at Brees, they tumble together.

At the bottom of their fall, they do not find themselves in a miraculous home built by elves or fairies, the kind about which Gui and Guerau sing. They have simply fallen over a shallow overhang above a river Yolanda had not even realised was frothing and spouting less than three yards away. The water is confined within its winter banks so they do not get wet, and the earthy roof under which they crawl affords a tiny respite. When Yolanda is able, she sits up, and though the blizzard still rages, she can make out trees. For the first time for hours, the landscape seems to have some shape and this itself is like a miracle.

The overhang is not much use really, but before it tapers off to expose them again to the full force of the storm, there is a small indent, gouged into the river-rock by some natural means but deepened by animals. Yolanda pushes into it and finds that she has slammed a door in the wind's face. She can breathe again.

But though she tries to pull Brees in beside her, the hole is too small and narrow so he must sit sentinel in front, with only his tail sheltered. It does not wave and he makes no sound, not even when the birds who have ventured out drop as small, pearly corpses into snow, nature's gift to starving hawks.

Night falls and passes, although the light hardly dims as the snow reflects upwards. Yolanda's furs and woollen under-garments, her lined boots, her gloves and the hat melt and cling. She feels like a damp statue. Her eyes are dry, though, powdery dry and there is a permanent high hum in her ears. Her nose, the end of which feels hard as a stylus, still runs but she has given up wiping it.

It is Brees's tail, such a loyal, pathetic, bedraggled thing, that finally makes her move again although it takes her ages to decide which bit of herself to shift first. Her buttocks are flattened into plates. She tenses a muscle in her left leg. It obeys but scarcely seems to belong to her. She tenses it again and then drags her foot to the side. That really doesn't belong to her. She pulls the other one. Her whole body creaks. Pockets of warmth she did not know she was harbouring dampen and chill. She feels colder, much colder, than when she was still, but the sight of Brees's tail keeps up the tiny momentum.

Eventually she is on her knees and her breaths are like milky pendants in front of her. She purses her lips, then cries out as the top one cracks. No blood runs out to soothe the wound. It remains raw and biting for a moment or two before dulling to the flat ache of everywhere else.

Gingerly, she extends an arm and touches Brees's back. Nothing. Not a quiver. She pats him, her breath making bigger pendants that shimmer over him before dissolving. 'Brees.' He does not turn. Now she is blasted by hot terror. 'Brees! Brees! Brees!' She lifts her fists and pummels his back and sides, shattering the frosted carapace that has fully enclosed him and never ceasing to call his name, demanding that he drag himself back from wherever he is. 'Brees! Brees! Don't leave me!'

It is as she pummels that she realises the sky is now a

flawless blue. And there is sun. She blinks. The storm has passed. What is she doing under here? She must get Brees into that sun. 'Shine on him, oh, just shine on him,' she implores. Unable to get through to him with her fists, she resorts to kicking him, provoking exquisite but frightful pins and needles as the tiny veins in her feet expand. The agony makes her kick harder.

It is her screaming, however, that finally brings Brees back from the brink. An ear jerks. At once, Yolanda is hopping round, pulling and slapping, yanking and hollering and throwing herself on top of him. By the time she stops, her scalp is sweating and Brees is shuffling on four stilts down to the river to drink. She follows him into the warm and bursts into tears. Nothing, ever, has been as welcome as this heat. In moments, the steam rises from Brees and in minutes, opening his mouth in a gargantuan yawn, he lifts his leg and urinates.

Some time later, they eat and begin to walk again. After a while, Yolanda has to take off her hat and Brees, dripping, pants a little, his tongue striped pink and grey. From some-where to their right beats the metallic *chwit, chwit, chwit* of the nuthatch. There is movement amongst the creepers. On their left, the river has ceased to froth and now thrusts its way conversationally through the settled white glitter. Yolanda swings her gloves. Brees is alive. He is warm. She is alive. She is warm. Together they are going home to Raimon and she is never going to leave him again.

THE LIE

Since Ugly's burial, Cador is happier that Raimon likes Metta but is too observant not to see the attachment growing beyond the friendly. After the sledging day, Raimon spends more and more time in her company and less and less in Cador's. In the evenings, he sees Raimon not only staring at the girl as though there was nobody else in the room but also listening and nodding when she speaks of her faith with much more care than he used to listen and nod at Sir Parsifal. Not that the boy utters one word of criticism and every evening, after Raimon has bidden him a distracted goodnight and he is warmly burrowed under his furs and blankets, he tells himself that soon Metta will be gone and everything just as usual. But in the wakeful dawn, he wonders. Raimon hardly mentions Yolanda now and if Cador brings up her name, his lips purse and his voice becomes distant. The question hovers over the boy's head. Can Raimon really be going to give up on Yolanda so easily? He scoffs at himself. Of course not! Giving up Yolanda would be as impossible as giving up Unbent. Yet now that the idea has taken root, he cannot get rid of it. And then he panics. If Raimon can give up Yolanda, maybe he could give up Cador as well. After all, it would not be hard, amongst all the visitors, to find another boy, one better at his lessons with the sword, or one who can saddle Bors and Galahad without standing on a box. He throws off his bearskin and begins to polish Unbent yet again. Perhaps a brighter gleam will bind himself and Raimon irrevocably together.

Preoccupied, it takes Raimon a while to notice Cador's agitated dejection but he also knows that if Cador believes in his attachment to Metta and his conversion to Catharism, others will be more inclined to believe too. Nevertheless, it is dreadful to him to see the boy so miserable. 'Parsifal would be pleased with the way you keep the blade so sharp and clean,' he says one day as Cador wipes more invisible dirt from Unbent. 'Do you miss him?'

Cador nods.

'I miss him too,' Raimon says. He kneels, takes a cloth himself and spits on it. 'We can't live in the past, though, Cador. We must look to the future.'

Cador stops polishing. 'Does that mean forgetting every-thing – everybody – in the past?' he asks, with characteristic directness.

Raimon stares fixedly at Unbent's silver flame. 'Not forget, Cador, but we sometimes have to accept that things change.'

'You mean what you feel for people and what you believe? Those things change?'

Raimon tries not to wince. 'Well, yes,' he says, and he rubs at the flame as though his life depends on it. 'Sometimes, for instance when we learn more about things, we find that what we've been wrong, or at least mistaken. Wouldn't that be a good reason to change?'

Cador now raises his head. 'Is that what's happened to you about the Cathars?'

'I've listened to Metta and what she says makes sense. You've heard her too, Cador.'

'But what about the White Wolf? What about the Flame being the Flame not of the Cathars or the Catholics but of the Occitan? Was that all wrong?'

Raimon's cheeks tighten. He polishes and polishes. 'As I say, Cador, things change. Now that the Catholics have burned the Amouroix and even Castelneuf itself, we can't just go it alone. We've got to take sides and in a choice between the Cathar Occitanians and the Catholics, I choose the Cathars. Don't you see that I have to be on one side or the other?' He drops his cloth and picks Unbent up. 'The Flame would expect no less now that the last battle is in sight. Do you understand that?'

The boy takes a deep breath. 'No, because you've always said there should be no division, that we are all just Occitanians.'

Raimon's heart leaps with joy. Cador will always hold true. But it also beats with sorrow that the boy's faith in the knight he has chosen to serve is being so sorely tested.

'I don't think Sir Parsifal would understand either,' Cador continues miserably.

There is a long pause. 'I think Sir Parsifal would understand that I do what I think is right,' Raimon says shakily. He gets up. He can bear no more.

As he stumbles away, he feels the boy's arm tugging at his. 'I just want to know one thing.' Cador's eyes are huge.

Raimon wants to stop him. 'Cador –' he warns, for he does not know if he could lie outright to those eyes. But Cador's request is something quite else. 'I just want to know that you'll never abandon me,' he whispers.

Raimon lets out a deep breath and takes both Cador's hands in his. 'I'll never abandon you,' he says. 'Whatever happens, Cador, I would never, ever do that.' The boy scrutinises him hard and then his face clears, although not entirely. Nevertheless, it is the best that can be done.

Raimon goes straight back into the courtyard, where the place is beginning to look busy again. Stripping off his jerkin, he steadies himself by brushing snow from the timber. Work begins again today on the great hall roof and in three days, four at most, the roads will be passable with care, and real life will resume. When he has finished this job, he goes to the stables and speaks to the visitors' grooms about fodder for the journey. Leather is being oiled. Oats are being sifted. The smell is no longer of snow, it is of a household on the move.

Just when he is leaving, he finds Laila lurking in a corner next to Galahad's stall. 'Anybody would think you were Aimery,' she says, 'giving orders and treating the place as your home.'

'It is my home.'

'No, it's not.' She pulls herself up so that she can straddle the partition. Galahad's ears flick back and forth. Laila kicks the boards from both sides. 'You don't deserve to live here any more.'

Raimon knows this tone. Though Laila's skin is unpainted today and her hair its natural red, she is in a dangerous mood. He strokes Galahad's nose and braces himself.

'One smile from that smug yellow corncob and you just forget all about Yolanda! How could you?'

'I've told you before. Don't call Metta names, Laila.'

'Why not?'

'It makes you look ugly.' He chooses the word deliberately and Laila flinches, which gives Raimon a moment of guilty satisfaction. Well, she should never have called her dog such a thing. In seconds, she has recovered and is off on a tirade against which, eventually, he blocks his ears, unblocking them only for her final flourish. 'You set yourself up as a knight, Raimon, but you're just as faithless as a butcher's boy.'

'You may remember that it was Yolanda who chose to go with Sir Hugh,' he says coldly.

'What did you expect?' Laila sharpens a barb. 'She's the daughter of a count and you're only a weaver.' She drums her heels in triumph.

Raimon is ready for her. 'If I'm only a weaver, what does it matter what I do?'

Laila leaps off the partition. 'It doesn't matter to me, not one jot. But you see Yolanda's not like us. She's actually got a heart, the poor fool.' She jabs a finger in his face, and a multitude of bracelets jangle up her arm. 'You could at least have been careful of that.'

When she is gone, Raimon leans his head against Bors's neck. He must either make his final move now or give up this idea. This is his moment of truth. He hesitates for only a second before finding Sir Roger and asking to speak privately to him. He wastes neither time nor words. 'I think you know what this is about, sir,' he says. They are in the room in which Parsifal spent his last weeks, one of the few rooms to survive the fire intact. Aimery has this room now, but since he is busy, it is the room in which they are least likely to be disturbed. Raimon tries not to look at the bed in which Parsifal died, now shoved untidily against the wall, its covers scattered. The rest of the room is piled high with discarded clothes and weaponry. Raimon takes a deep breath. 'I want to come with you to Montségur.'

Sir Roger squints. 'Do you, my boy?'

'Is it such a surprise?'

Sir Roger folds arms thick as tree trunks. 'I suppose not.'

'Will you be happy to have me riding in your company?'

'In my daughter's company, you mean.' Sir Roger's lips disappear into a cave in his beard as he scrutinises Raimon more carefully than Raimon finds comfortable. 'My daughter loves you,' Sir Roger says. 'But you already know that.'

'We — we — we get on very well, sir.'

'Come now. You've made sure of more than that these past weeks.'

Raimon has to keep his voice very steady. He tries not to touch Yolanda's ring. 'Metta has taught me many things. She manages to make sense of so much that before seemed senseless.'

'In what way?'

Raimon swallows. 'Well –' he knows he is colouring, but he cannot stop now, 'she's made me understand the Cathar faith.'

Sir Roger looks Raimon up and down. 'And you like what you hear?'

'Very much, sir.'

Sir Roger pauses. 'Enough to become one of us?'

Now Raimon has a moment of blind panic. Yet he does not search for weasel words with which to comfort himself, nor does he cross his fingers as some would do. He just lies because that is the path he has chosen. 'Yes,' he says.

Sir Roger hums for a few moments. 'So – you would like to ride with us as a true Cathar, and take up your place at the last stand?'

'I would.'

'And this has all come about because you love my daughter?'

'I can't deny the two are connected.'

Sir Roger takes long moments to make up his mind, but at last a slow smile spreads. 'I'm not going to pretend that what you say doesn't please me,' he says. 'I like you and I think I'm a good judge of character. So, very well, Raimon. Ride with us. It will be our pleasure.' The old knight's handshake is almost the worst thing of all.

They are leaving the room when Sir Roger scuffs his boots. 'Do you think there's somebody here could mend these things before we leave? Your squire said they were a disgrace and they are.'

'I'm sure there is,' says Raimon.

Sir Roger does not really care about his boots. He has something more to say and eventually comes out with it. 'Look,' he says. 'I really do believe that you're a good man but let me also warn you. I'm not given to violence except in war, but if I find you're playing games with my daughter, do you see these hands?' He unfurls them slowly, for full effect. Raimon has seen smaller hams. 'You'll find them round your neck.'

For the rest of the day, Raimon feels those gristly fingers round his windpipe and at early evening retreats to the kennels.

The huntsman is feeding the brazier. He nods at Raimon and then goes to Farvel. The dog is poorly and the dogboys are sitting silently on their haunches in a circle around him. A few are gnawing at bones. Raimon hunkers down. 'How is he?'

'Not good,' the huntsman says. He sits and takes the hound's head on his lap. When he croons, Farvel's ears twitch.

The dogboys shuffle up and pat Raimon's legs, encouraging him to make himself more comfortable. One offers him an old knuckle of pig, which he politely declines. The huntsman croons on and gradually the fingers round Raimon's neck disappear although a large cold stone in his stomach remains.

Then, in a blast of cold air, Aimery appears. 'Ah, this is where you are, Raimon.' He pushes between two of the dogboys. They know better, with Aimery, than to object. 'I'm glad to find you,' he says, tossing aside the pig knuckle.' He contemplates Farvel and frowns. 'Will he recover?'

'He may. He may not,' says the huntsman without looking up.

'Are all the bitches ready to whelp?'

'Don't you worry, sir. Farvel will leave behind a fine crop of puppies.'

Aimery taps his fingers then turns to Raimon. 'We need to talk.'

'I don't believe we have anything to talk about.'

'Oh, come on, Raimon. You know we do. We must talk about the Flame.' Raimon stiffens. Aimery hauls him up and bundles him into a corner, out of the huntsman's hearing. 'Can I speak candidly? Raimon shrugs. 'You see, I know what you're doing,' Aimery says. Raimon's face closes. Aimery jabs him in the ribs. 'Let's put all our cards on the table here since we both want the same thing.'

'And what would that thing be?'

'To get the Flame for the Occitan, of course,' Aimery says, keeping his eyes fixed on Raimon's. 'The last thing we want is either for King Louis to have it or for the Cathars to claim it as their own.'

'You've changed your tune.'

'Of course I have!' Aimery is beautifully affronted. 'For goodness' sake, Raimon. The king has burned my home and how could I ever believe that the Flame belongs to those damnable heretics?' He clears his throat. 'Don't you see, we're just the same now, you and I. We are both Occitanians fighting for the Occitan, so –' he grins – 'I'm going to do just what you're doing.' Raimon feels a cold thread run down his back. 'Yes,' says Aimery blithely, 'I'm going to turn Cathar, go to Montségur and we can get the Flame together.'

The stone in Raimon's stomach turns to acid as Aimery waits, with some enjoyment, for him to respond.

'What do you mean, turn Cathar?' Raimon tries not to stammer. 'Your uncle was an Inquisitor, for God's sake.'

'Don't be so stupid, Raimon. I'm going to do just as you're doing and pretend, although I'll not stoop quite so low as to use some poor girl as a stooge. I'm going to brazen it out quite on my own.'

Out of all the things Raimon has expected, he has not expected this. He pulls at three long straws and begins to plait them. 'So that's why you've been so nice to the visitors.'

'Didn't you guess?'

Raimon throws the straw down. 'And what do you intend to do with the Flame if you get it?'

Aimery is smiling brightly, although there is a slight — very slight — hesitation. 'I shall bring it to Castelneuf and set it up as a beacon for all Occitanians,' he says in his most churchy voice.

'I don't believe you,' Raimon fires back.

'You don't?' Aimery fills his voice with mild affront.

'No.'

'For goodness' sake, Raimon. What else will I do with the Flame? You don't have a monopoly on loyalty and righteousness you know. You're not the only one who cares about the Occitan.'

His words are so plausible that had there been no incident with the beam and no hesitation, however slight, Raimon might believe him. After all, Aimery has grown up in the same landscape of silver, green and gold as he has. Just like

Raimon, Aimery too pledged his boyish allegiance to the Occitan and only the Occitan. As boys, both of them were fed the same myths and romances and both understand the region's obstinate otherness, its desire to hold itself apart from the more mundane world of everywhere else and particularly France. They have both sung the Song of the Flame. The Occitan can never mean nothing to them.

But the grainy face with its blond, concealing beard and palely inscrutable eyes is not the youthful Aimery. That Aimery has been disappearing, little by little, for years and has now vanished altogether. Raimon knows he is right about that. He considers. 'Let me go for it,' he says at last. 'Why risk the two of us?'

'I was just going to suggest the opposite. Why don't I go to Montségur and you stay here to supervise the building work,' Aimery replies gaily. 'After all, if this old place is to be the home of the Flame, it needs to be carefully prepared. Refortified, with the Flame burning on high and both of us defending it, would even King Louis dare launch an assault?' His tone is wholly satirical but Raimon cannot challenge him. Aimery would denounce Raimon without a qualm. Nevertheless, Raimon is determined about one thing. 'I'm going to Montségur,' he says.

'Well then, we'll go together. Funny that your new love will imagine you're going with her. I wonder when you'll tell her the truth?' Aimery grins nastily. 'But I have to say, I hope you really have given up on Yolanda because I hear from Sir Hugh that she's quite settled as Lady des Arcis now. She has outgrown you just as I was sure she would. But to put her mind completely at rest I shall send her a message telling her the good news about you and Metta.' Aimery is playing Raimon like a fish, dipping half in, half out of the truth as it suits him. He strides back into the main kennel and drums his fingers against Farvel before moving towards the door. 'Now, huntsman. I'll hold you to that promise of a good crop of puppies, and don't let that old hound die. We need him to flush out the enemy.' He twirls his sword at Raimon.

'I wish you and Sir Raimon godspeed,' the huntsman says.

Aimery flinches. 'Raimon's not quite a "sir" yet,' he says crisply.

Raimon follows Aimery to the door. 'And why will anybody at Montségur believe you're a real Cathar? Everybody knows that you're a Catholic. They'll need a bit more than your word.'

Aimery laughs and draws Raimon close. 'Come on, weaver. Use your brain. They'll believe me because my château and lands have been burned by Catholic King Louis. I'm a Catholic victim, don't you see, and victims often convert. Actually, I've already spoken to Sir Roger. He didn't even blink.'

After Aimery has gone, Raimon returns to the brazier and sits for a long time. The dogboys settle beside him and the huntsman does not chivvy them away.

At dinner that night, the hall rings with discussion about the journey. Metta is sitting by her father and looks up immediately when Raimon eventually enters. She has been waiting. 'Oh! You're white as a sheet. Come near to the fire!'

Laila is perched on a stool. 'Yes, nearer the fire, Raimon,' she smirks, saccharine sweet. 'Your poor little self might catch cold and that would never do.' She scowls at Metta, who blinks and smiles back without any rancour, which makes Laila hate her even more.

Raimon approaches, but only for a moment. He does not even hear Laila. As soon as Aimery is surrounded by others, he leaves again because if Aimery has sent Yolanda a note, he must send another. He fingers his ring as he hurries to the loft.

It takes him some time to capture a bird for he is entirely unpractised, and then spends more time trying to discover some distinguishing mark to indicate where the bird is from. There is none so he must take his chance. He has already written his note. It is very short. 'Whatever you hear, I'm keeping faith.' He does not sign it. There is no need. He binds on the capsule and pushes the bird out.

A quarter of a mile downriver, Aimery, warned by Alain that Raimon had gone to the loft, is standing in the lee of a coppice, a hooded falcon on one arm and a small lantern in the other. It's still just light enough to see although when the pigeon comes, its camouflage almost fools him. Only its speed gives it away. He grins broadly as he removes the falcon's hood and casts her off. She circles, apparently blind to her prey. 'Come on, you dimwitted fool,' Aimery mutters as the pigeon speeds on and the falcon disappears into the clouds. Then, from the clouds she reappears, only this time honed and plummeting. The pigeon stands no chance against a long hind killing toe fully extended. It lands with a small thump in a heap of dead leaves and by the time Aimery gets there, is a mass of bloody plumage. Aimery rummages in the feathers, finds the leather capsule and reads the contents before tossing both away. '"Keeping faith", indeed.' He wants to laugh but the laugh won't come so he grinds his heel so hard into the blood and bones at his feet that the startled falcon rises into a tree. When she will not come down, Aimery picks up a stone and shouts. Frightened, the falcon takes off and Aimery, after following her fruitlessly for fully quarter of an hour, is left to stalk back to Castelneuf quite alone.

THE RING

The following evening is the last the visitors will spend at Castelneuf. The journey will not be easy for though winter's grip has eased, the aftermath is treacherous. Spades must be wielded to make the road leading to the river safe enough for carts. The emerging mud depresses.

The daylight hours have passed in a tumult of packing and repacking, shoeing and reshoeing of horses, filling and emptying sacks and barrels. Nobody knows what to expect at Montségur. Should the travellers take more than the food they will consume on the week's journey, just in case? Or will there be an abundance at the fortress making it a waste of effort to provide more? They scurry about deciding one thing then another.

An hour after dusk the temperature has dropped again adding an edge to the travellers' appetites.

Raimon has already begun his round of goodbyes and his reception amongst the household servants has not been good, which is hardly surprising. Like Laila, many think him a faithless turncoat. *At least I've deceived them successfully*, he thinks grimly as the laundress refuses to take his hand. He rolls Yolanda's ring with his thumb. It affords a measure of comfort.

He goes last to the kennels and finds a dismal scene. Farvel has died and the huntsman's usually steady hands tremble as he sews his faithful servant's body in to a thick pall of straw. The dogboys are weeping. Entering, Raimon sees Farvel's empty set at once and drops to his knees. The huntsman watches how he kneels, how he holds his head, how his body leans, reading him as he reads his hounds. He starts sewing again.

At last, he finishes with his needle and gestures to the dogboys to lay Farvel's body gently on his set one last time. Their sniffling turns briefly to a howl that fades only when the huntsman reaches for his horn and blows 'gone away'. He blows it again and again. In this confined space, the peal is intense enough to wake the dead, which is perhaps his intention although Farvel never moves.

Raimon cannot delay. He swallows a huge lump in his throat and tries to be matter of fact. 'You've probably heard that I'm going to Montségur with the visitors.' He dreads disapproval but the huntsman does not look disapproving. Instead, he does something quite unexpected. He gestures to the dogboys to leave Farvel and gets them to stand in the most orderly manner of which they are capable, which is about as orderly as a tumble of twigs. Only then does he address Raimon in his gruff growl. 'I hear what they're saying about you.' Raimon stiffens. 'They say you've turned Cathar because of some girl.' Raimon bites his tongue. The huntsman's contempt will be bitter.

But the huntsman has something else in mind. 'I don't know about that,' he says. 'I only know that a hound on the scent is always to be trusted.' Then he walks with Raimon to the door and throws it open, gauging the tenor of the night with quick short sniffs. 'Are you on the scent, Sir Raimon?'

For a second, Raimon wonders if the huntsman is scoffing, but only for a second. The huntsman is like Metta. He does not scoff. It is such a relief to answer with absolute truth. 'Yes,' he says, 'I'm on the scent.'

The huntsman nods. 'Good hunting, then.'

At supper, the noise is too plentiful for the troubadours to sing and anyway, the time for entertainment is over. Gui and Guerau hang up their instruments. Aimery sits on the dais surrounded by his household knights, highly voluble and handing out detailed instructions as to what must happen at Castelneuf in his absence. Nobody knows what to make of his conversion or his decision to go without them to Montségur but they barely question him. Some will leave, most will stay, for his interests are their interests. Aimery seems unconcerned.

A quick, fussy Castelneuf knight with a reputation as a panicker is put in charge of the rebuilding and another knight, slow, methodical and an enemy of the first, in charge of defence. Their mutual dislike will keep their ambitions at bay. The garrison will be very small, which makes some knights concerned for the château's safety. Aimery reassures them. 'There's nothing here for King Louis now,' he says, 'and

Sir Hugh des Arcis will not return. He's my brother-in-law and, besides, the Amouroix is no longer of interest. They're done with us. And if Inquisitors come prying when they hear of my conversion, who cares? There's precious little left to burn.'

As a last bit of business he sends Alain to the chapel where Simon Crampcross has been lurking all this time hoping to be forgotten. He sweats as he is prodded like a fat cow into the hall and his eyes swivel between Aimery and the game pies.

Aimery stands. 'Ah, priest!' His voice rings out. 'Begone! This is a Cathar château now, and though you may call me a heretic, I'm proud to say that I've seen the true light.' He scours the room in search of scepticism but everybody is wisely inspecting their boots.

Simon Crampcross does not argue. With surprising speed for a man of his bulk, he lumbers out and Raimon is left wondering if this is all part of Aimery's act or whether Simon Crampcross believes his banishment to be genuine. He does not wonder long, however, because something else is brewing.

Laila, her box of tricks open beside her and her top lip curled in anticipation, is lounging against the hearthstones, dangling a plump saffron-coloured slipper embroidered with fishscales from one toe. Raimon guesses at once that the slippers were a present from Aimery – perhaps in recompense for Ugly – although how Laila could have accepted slippers as an apology for a dog, Raimon does not know. She is delicately picking at a chicken leg with small white teeth. Free from any painted artifice, she has a kind of shocking nakedness about her. When she sees Raimon looking at her, she closes her box, locks it with her toes and very slowly sticks out her tongue.

Aimery, aware of Laila's every breath, coughs and bangs his knife on his platter. 'It seems,' he says in a slow drawl, 'that for some at least the snow was heaven-sent. My lords, do you lack all powers of observation? Are you blind? Raimon frowns. 'Gentlemen, can't you sense it?' Aimery can hardly contain his enjoyment. 'Love has blossomed in our midst.'

There is a purr of approval. Everybody loves a lover.

'Now, Raimon,' Aimery searches him out. 'Don't be shy. It doesn't become you. We've all seen how you and Mistress Metta de Salas have grown close and we all know that tomorrow you will ride together.' He raises his goblet. 'I'm sure the whole company wants to wish you well.'

Raimon sees Metta colour. Any reluctance on his part will be a humiliation for her. He must sit beside her. Laila pushes her way in, too, and sits on the opposite side of the trestle, next to Adela, little quivers of excitement erupting beneath her skin. The awkwardness is palpable and to soften it, Metta makes a gentle joke about the dogboys. Laila laughs harshly and much too loudly making Raimon prickle all over, his knuckles white against the dark cloth of his jacket.

At what Raimon afterwards realises was a pre-arranged signal, Laila, fingers flashing, pounces on his leather ring. 'Isn't now the time to take that old thing off?' She tugs at it. Speechless, Raimon pulls back, upsetting a flask of wine. Its contents spill everywhere but though her bodice is splashed and ruined, Laila is not deterred. 'If you're going to

Montségur with Metta, you should wear only her ring!' She will not let go. 'That's what real lovers do, isn't it?'

Metta tries to push the conversation elsewhere. 'Do all orphan boys go to the kennels, Raimon? Do you have any dog-girls?

Laila bats her aside, then seizes her hand. 'Metta! My dear Metta! Don't *you* think Raimon should wear your ring? After all –' she stands now, to command everybody's attention – 'it's not quite right, really, if Raimon loves you, that he wears a ring in honour of another man's wife.'

The hall falls silent. Laila lets go of everything and sits, grinning.

'Really,' Metta says quietly, 'it doesn't matter.'

But Sir Roger is standing. 'Another man's wife? What's this, Raimon?'

'I thought he would have told you,' Laila spouts piously. 'He wears it for Aimery's sister, Yolanda, only she's married to Sir Hugh des Arcis.'

'I've noticed the ring but that can't be true!' Sir Roger's fists are like haunches of beef.

'You tell him,' Laila says to Raimon. 'Go on.'

Raimon swallows. 'Lady des Arcis – Yolanda – and I grew up together,' he says, trying to keep his eyes unclouded. 'You know that. And I – I – I freely admit that we were very fond of each other.'

Laila's voice grows harder and louder. 'Oh, a little more than "very fond", Sir Roger. Unless, of course, Yolanda is a liar. Let's ask Raimon. Was Yolanda lying when she told me she loved you and you loved her?'

'Yolanda doesn't lie.' He feels as a man feels on the prow of a rocking ship.

'It really doesn't matter,' Metta insists. 'He can wear her ring. After all, we're not betrothed or anything.'

But she is no match for Laila. 'Betrothed in all but name,' she flashes. 'You've been quite the clever miss. He's turned Cathar and is going with you to Montségur. Don't pretend you don't know that he's bound to you himself. If not for your sake, don't you think for Yolanda's that he should take off her ring? After all, even Frenchmen know you shouldn't wear rings given to you by one person if you're in love with another.'

Raimon rises. 'I mean no disrespect to Metta by wearing Yolanda's ring.'

But Sir Roger is dismayed. He looks from his daughter to Raimon and back to his daughter. 'There's an easy way to sort this out,' he says. 'Just take off the ring.'

'Father! I *really* don't mind,' protests Metta. 'Raimon has not said he loves me.'

Her father turns on her. 'But he has behaved as if he does and is that not what you hope and believe?'

Metta's lips tremble. 'I — we —'

'I repeat. Has he not led you to believe in his love?'

'I believe he — I believe —'

'Enough!' shouts Sir Roger. He will not have his daughter made a spectacle. 'Raimon, if you are a man of good faith, before our journey begins, take off that ring. The painted girl is right. You have courted my daughter, so what possible use is another girl's ring now?'

Raimon knows, without even looking, that Aimery has his legs outstretched, his arms folded and is crowing silently.

Cador, standing behind Raimon, refuses to be silent. Though he longs for Raimon to throw Metta over, he leaps to his knight's defence as a good squire should. 'He can just wear two rings,' he calls out. 'He's got two hands, after all.'

Everybody laughs except Sir Roger, whose bluff face has taken on a determined set. 'My daughter is no man's second choice. It may be true that there's been no formal betrothal but I insist that you remove that ring. In fact, you should take it off and –'he tugs at a jewelled ring on his own hand – 'wear this instead.' His huge frame towers over Raimon, holding out his offering. 'I repeat. Take that one off and take this as a sign of good faith.'

Raimon is motionless.

'Perhaps the leather one's too tight to remove,' Metta says, still trying to help.

This makes Raimon twist Yolanda's ring quickly for he senses Laila gathering herself up to grab him again. The ring shifts as the leather slides. He never knows quite how Laila's fingers dart, but in a second he is empty-handed. 'I'll have it now,' she crows, stashing the leather ring down the front of her dress. 'And I shan't betray it.' Her eyes flash victory.

Raimon's torture is not yet over. With Metta still watching, what can he do but take Sir Roger's ring? The jewelled band, flat and shining, covers the precious stain Yolanda's ring has left. Only when he sees it is firmly on does Sir Roger sits down amid some cheering, though nobody is quite sure what they are cheering about.

Raimon also sits and the dinner continues around him. Metta speaks to him. He answers mechanically. Her father's ring sits as heavily on his finger as Sir Hugh's sat on Yolanda's before she tossed it away. The worst thing is that he can see the slight bulge in Laila's bodice where Yolanda's ring is lodged. It is so near. Occasionally, Laila's hand brushes against it. Raimon knows she is aware that he is following her every blink, and knows, too, that she is enjoying it. Yet he can do nothing until, finally, the food is cleared and she vanishes. Without a word to Metta, he at once grabs a flare and goes after her. She cannot hide from him. He will have the leather ring back if he has to wring her neck to get it.

He does not have to go far. She is waiting. 'Looking for me?' His flare gutters as he manhandles her up the chipped stones of the spiral staircase and into a tiny archer's alcove that bulges into the wall. 'Give me back my ring,' he commands.

'No.'

'I'm not going to beg. Just give it to me.'

'You? Beg? It never crossed my mind.'

'For God's sake, Laila, just hand it over.'

'Why should I? You don't want it any more. You've a much grander ring now.'

The dark in this alcove has a peculiarly rank quality about it, partly because the arrowslit lets in only a sliver of half-light and partly because generations of archers, unwilling to abandon their watch, have used it to relieve themselves. Laila feels the stickiness through her slippers and scrunches up her toes. Raimon makes a move and her hand flies to her breast. Less than two feet separate Raimon from his treasure.

'Give it to me.' He is begging now and he knows it.

'You don't deserve it. You've betrayed Yolanda.'

'I'll not take any lessons in betrayal from you,' he sparks back. 'Your dog's eyes were barely shut before you were accepting presents from her murderer.'

There is a tiny silence. Then, 'If you want it, come and get it,' Laila hisses and though he can see so little, Raimon knows she is showing those white teeth again. His blood flows thick and dark as Laila curls away from him, her breathing short and sharp like a vixen in a trap. He could so easily smash her ribs. That is what he wants to do. But she is a girl. He half steps back, reining himself in, then hears a faint, contemptuous purr. It is too much. He leaps and the air parts and closes as they claw at each other, Laila's nails raking Raimon's face, Raimon's fingers ripping Laila's shift. Neither makes any noise, not when Laila draws blood, not when Raimon cracks and bruises her shoulders. There is so little room in the alcove that they find themselves thrust together, rocking and shoving in their shared boiling fury, Raimon's superior height and weight equally matched by Laila's wild abandon.

I do not know what would have happened had Aimery not come past. Perhaps Raimon would have killed Laila. Certainly, he feels for her neck, wanting to snap it as you might snap the stem of a poisonous weed. Or perhaps Laila, with the knife she has concealed at her belt, would have killed Raimon. But Aimery does come past and sends a soldier to drag them out. Hauled into the light, Raimon at once feels ashamed although Laila, her clothes in tatters, feels no such thing.

'Well, well,' Aimery leers, his face creasing with amusement. 'A cat fight, if ever there was one.' He chucks Laila under the chin. Raimon is surprised that Laila doesn't kick him. Instead, through her panting, she purrs again, this time the purr of a coquette. It is too much. Raimon breaks away and disappears down the stairs. Behind him he hears Aimery laughing.

Unable to face anybody, Raimon sleeps in the kennels that night. Before he lies down, he removes Sir Roger's ring. Yet in the morning, when his breath is calm and his bruises cold, he replaces it. He was a fool to fight with Laila. It has achieved nothing. He must just trust that whatever Laila does or says, Yolanda will get his message. For himself, there is nowhere to go but onwards towards the Flame. He washes his face in the hounds' water trough, stares hard but with no admiration at his reflection, and pulls straw from his hair. In the courtyard, he finds Cador with Galahad and Bors. Despite their lack of exercise, the horses' coats shine. 'They're ready for anything now,' Cador says as he hands over Unbent.

Raimon nods and straps the sword to his back. 'And we are too?'

'Certainly are!' Cador grins. A journey is always exciting and today, for the first time, he has managed to saddle Galahad without standing on anything. He must be at least two inches taller than he was when the snow first fell. He has saddled the pony from whom he will lead Bors but Raimon stops him from mounting. At first Cador thinks he is going to be forbidden to come. His mouth is already open in protest. But Raimon has made a decision. 'Leave the pony,' he says. 'It's time you rode a proper horse. Climb on to Bors.' The boy's look of delight is a timely gift and Raimon keeps it in his heart for a long time to come.

INTO THE FORTRESS

The sun is strong and the branches dripping by the time the procession begins to wind its way down from Castelneuf. Laila, her eyelids heavily shadowed with green and her brown shoulders almost bare, stares after them from an upper window. Aimery has tried to persuade her to come with them but to his surprise and disappointment, she has refused, so now he is riding with Sir Roger at the head of the party, talking loudly. He dissembles shamelessly and unnecessarily, telling Sir Roger that even before the firing of Castelneuf by King Louis, Catharism was stealing up on him. 'I've always been a seeker after the truth, haven't I, Alain,' he says, moulding his lips primly at his squire. 'So if we're to make a stand under the Flame, I want to be part of that.' Alain nods. It is best always to agree with his master. Sir Roger waits until Aimery has finished and then hangs back.

Cador, of whom Bors is taking good care, finds himself congratulated by Sir Roger on his elevation from the pony, and then sent on a silly errand so that Sir Roger can settle his own horse next to Galahad. He sees, with approval, that Raimon is still wearing his ring, and also notices that Raimon seems surprisingly ill at ease in the saddle. 'You usually ride bareback?' he asks. It seems a good way to crack through the awkwardness left by the previous evening.

'I prefer it.'

'I haven't ridden bareback since I was a boy.'

Raimon gives the faint smile he feels is expected.

'The girl Laila is not with us?'

'No,' Raimon answers.

'She's a strange one, and no mistake,' Sir Roger muses, 'and I can't say I'm sorry to leave her behind.'

'Laila does what she likes,' Raimon says shortly. 'She says she's going to go to Carcassonne but she goes nowhere unless it suits her.'

'And nobody minds? Nobody forces her?'

Raimon fiddles with his reins. He does not want to speak of Laila.

Sir Roger presses closer. Though deeply concerned for his daughter, he feels, somewhat unaccountably, that the business of the ring was not well done. But this is not his only concern. 'I am hesitant about bringing this up when the count has been so hospitable,' he says, his tone slightly over-confidential, 'and I've no reason really to believe otherwise, but do you think he's quite genuine in his conversion?' Raimon looks straight between Galahad's ears. 'I mean, perhaps it's just the way he speaks, but he hardly seems a natural Cathar and he doesn't listen to Metta as you do. I don't want to arrive at Montségur with a fraud in our midst.'

Raimon concentrates hard on the rhythm of Galahad's walk. 'Aimery wouldn't open his heart to me,' he says in the end.

'But you've known him a long time.'

'You must ask the count himself.'

Sir Roger rolls a little and his raw-boned, skewbald horse shortens its stride. 'I've a bad feeling,' he says.

Under the pretext of correcting how Cador holds his reins, Raimon moves away.

The journey settles into an uneven pattern, half noisy chattering as spirits lift, half nervous whispering at the prospect of what is to come. While at Castelneuf, when Sir Roger's household spoke and sang of the Flame and Montségur, their hearts were full of romance. Now, as reality looms, the romance fades. The Flame may be at Montségur but under the fortress's craggy prominence many of their bones will whiten. Though when the sun is out they speak with bravado, when the sun sets, they are fearful.

Sicart, who did not try to dissuade Adela when she declared her intention to go to Montségur too, listens as she exclaims as usual about God and the White Wolf, but now adds her open desire for martyrdom under the Flame. 'I'm going home!' she cries, glittering without warmth. He forces himself to sit with her though she scarcely feels like his child. Though she and Raimon are within an arm's reach, he realises with awful clarity that he matters to neither.

The first evening they are beyond my boundaries they set up camp on a plateau whose trees have been cleared for building. Beans and lovage grow in straggles, with a broken fence to keep out the pigs. Raimon leaves Unbent with Cador as he helps gather wood for fires. It is Metta who gets Adela momentarily to swap prayer for help in boiling up some pottage. They eat and huddle together for warmth. Nobody sings or sleeps much.

The dawn hides the distant peaks in fog. The wagons get stuck and all the men, whatever their rank, must put their shoulders to the wheels. When at last Raimon can swing back on to Galahad, he pushes forward, away from the main party. Today Sir Roger becomes a little over-keen on patriarchal confidences. The hours drag. Even with Unbent in his hand and the Flame burning in his heart, Raimon feels as lonely as his father. Much of the time he ignores Sir Roger and tries to pretend that Yolanda is riding alongside. Yet, without her ring on his finger even she seems ghostly. Galahad, feeling his master's inattention, picks his own way.

'Tired?' Aimery asks blithely.

Raimon jerks and picks up his reins. Sir Roger has gone and he did not hear Aimery approaching. 'No.'

Aimery caresses his arm conspiratorially. 'How we've fooled these poor cabbages, you and I,' he chortles. Raimon will not answer. Aimery coughs. 'Well, now is the time to make a plan. When we reach Montségur, we should probably –' Sir Roger rides up again to the place he has begun to think of as his own. 'Ah, Sir Roger!' Aimery exclaims. 'Raimon has been singing Metta's praises and berating me for daring to disagree that it was providence rather than just the weather that steered you to Castelneuf.'

He chatters on and on until Raimon gallops away. Balls of

snow from Galahad's hoofs smack Aimery's horse smartly on the nose. 'Really!' the count says, turning wide eyes on Sir Roger as Argos throws up his head, 'men in love behave very strangely.' And he goes on to tell Sir Roger, in a loud voice that carries clearly through the crisp air, how Raimon deserves to be a knight because he prides himself on never telling an untruth. He paints the saintly picture so thick that he risks Sir Roger rumbling the joke. But Sir Roger is a simpler soul than Aimery. He believes him partly because it seems true, but mainly because, for Metta's sake, he wants to.

INTO THE NIGHT

By the time Yolanda and Brees reach Castelneuf and run, as best they can, up to the gates of the château, they are skin and bone. Few acknowledge them for there is almost nobody left. Despite Aimery's plans the day after he rode away the château began to empty. First to go were the upper servants, the steward, clerks and craftsmen. Next, the two knights he left in charge quarrelled quickly, irrevocably, and perhaps purposely so that they could leave too. And who can blame them, for despite Aimery's assurances that Castelneuf is of no interest, it is rumoured that the Inquisitors who are on their way south still have Castelneuf on their list of places to visit. No knight intends to burn for Aimery. Better to find another lord to serve.

So by the time Yolanda and Brees stagger in, the only remaining inhabitants are Gui, Guerau, the huntsman, the dogboys and Laila, of course. It is she who pulls open the postern gate and drags the exhausted travellers through, hiding her happiness at seeing Yolanda again behind a nurse's scolding. It is she who half carries Yolanda into the small hall and stokes up the fire, sending the troubadours for furs, food and more logs. It is she who strips Yolanda of everything she is wearing and rolls her up in blankets. It is she who, as soon as a pot soon boils on the hearth, feeds Yolanda and Brees hot broth, a spoon for one and a bowl for the other. Though Laila would never say so, as she clucks and fusses she is so glad she could sing.

Brees recovers more quickly than Yolanda. Before an hour has passed, he shakes off his covers, wolfs down an entire loaf of bread and seizes a leg of mutton from the table. Yolanda's lips are too cracked to smile. Besides, the soup hurts her mouth and very quickly her stomach can take no more. When she turns from the spoon, Laila rummages in her box and pulls out a salve which she pastes on to Yolanda's whole face before beginning to tease out her hair. Even this is too exhausting. Yolanda's head lolls so Laila stops and files her own nails instead.

Yolanda dozes, then wakes and only then notices that there are no footsteps, no voices and no other people. She tries to free her arms from her woollen cocoon. Laila clicks her tongue. 'Stay still, for goodness' sake.'

The paste has eased some elasticity back into Yolanda's skin and though her lips sting, she forces out two words. 'Where's Raimon?'

At once, Laila swipes up more salve with her forefinger. 'Don't speak,' she orders. Yolanda blinks and turns and is faintly reassured to see Gui and Guerau hovering.

Laila wipes the salve on Yolanda's eyelids and resumes her work on her hair. Her fingers are slow and gentle, then faster and less gentle as her temper gets the better of her. 'Oh, why not tell you straight?' she explodes. 'He's fallen for a simpering idiot of a girl called Metta who set her cap at him after her father and his household sought shelter here from the snow. They've all gone to Montségur and Raimon's gone with them — well, gone with *her*. It's the last stand of the Cathars, don't you know.' Her voice mimics Sir Roger's gruff roll perfectly but with an added twist that loads it with ridicule. 'Last stand of the crackbrains, more like.' Her fingers tug, eliciting a yelp.

'Raimon's gone?' That is all Yolanda hears for the moment. 'That's what I said.'

Yolanda has to find some way of not drowning from disappointment. 'He's gone for the Blue Flame,' she says mechanically. 'That's why he's gone.'

'No, that's not why,' Laila contradicts, and her fingers snap. 'Weren't you listening? He's gone with a girl — and Aimery.'

'Aimery?' Yolanda says stupidly.

Laila grabs a comb. 'That's why the place is empty. Now listen more carefully to what I'm telling you.' She repeats what she said about Metta, with a few disobliging additions, until she is sure Yolanda understands.

During her recitation Gui and Guerau return and they all speak at once. 'Yes, Aimery's turned Cathar as well. Dismissed Simon Crampcross — everything.'

Laila interrupts. 'It's the girl. It all boils down to her. I'm not saying she's a witch but she certainly cast her spell. You should have seen her, swinging those yellow plaits. They weren't even painted.'

Yolanda tries to focus. 'I don't believe you. A girl trap Raimon? Never.'

'Oh no? Where is he then?'

Yolanda makes her voice quite firm. 'He wouldn't abandon me. He's gone for the Flame.'

Laila stands with her hands on her hips. If Yolanda's heart is not to be broken, she needs to despise Raimon as much as Laila does, so her upset on Yolanda's behalf makes her cruel. 'You're quite sure of that, are you?'

'Quite sure. He loves me and I've come back. I should never have left him.'

'He's left you.'

'I know him better than you do, Laila. He hasn't.' Yolanda will no longer remain in the cocoon. She emerges and sits with the blankets round her shoulders. The pair to Raimon's ring swings on its leather thong. Laila's eyes narrow. Slowly she reaches into her bodice and draws out the ring's pair. 'It's true that you did once know him better than I do, but I wonder if you know him at all any more.' She holds the ring up to the light.

Gui and Guerau retreat. They do not want to see this. They close the door behind them.

Yolanda stares at the ring, but even now she is disbelieving. 'How have you got that? Is this one of your tricks, because if so it's a wicked one.' She swallows.

'It's not a trick.'

'Then you must have stolen it. Admit it. You've taken it

from him. You must have done. Raimon would never give it up.'

Laila tosses the ring from hand to hand. 'I did steal it, in a way,' she says.

'There then.'

'I stole it after he swapped it for a jewelled ring given to him by Metta's father.'

Yolanda still clings on with desperate obstinacy. 'No. That's not true. You stole it from his finger because you're jealous. You've never liked him.'

'You're right,' says Laila, livid that Yolanda will not believe her, Laila Hajar Mais Bilqis Shehan, who has stood up for her all these months. 'I *have* never liked him. He's not good enough for you. You should marry a prince or a king and he's just a weaver.'

'How dare you!' Yolanda cannot leap up, but she struggles to her feet. 'Get out of here and take all your tricks with you. You can leave Ugly though because she deserves a kinder mistress than you will ever be.' She looks about, suddenly realising that Ugly is not here either. 'Where is she?'

'Ugly's dead,' Laila says quite casually although her whole face tightens until it is nothing but points and angles. 'Aimery threw a bone on to the river ice and she fell through and drowned.'

Yolanda stares. 'Drowned? Oh, God! Under the ice? The poor little thing.' She gives a long shiver and draws the blankets close, suddenly freezing again. Her eyes fix on the ring but all she sees is the dog.

Laila sits beside her and strokes her back. She will not speak again of Ugly. 'I'm not lying about Raimon,' she says. 'It's true that he didn't want to give up the ring, but when Metta's father offered him another, along with his daughter, well —' she pauses. Yolanda's shoulders are shaking. Some girls would have stopped now but Laila determines to drive her point home. 'He sledged with her, Yolanda. He ate food from her plate.' She pauses again. 'He took her to visit his mother's grave.'

An inarticulate sound bubbles up from somewhere.

Laila adopts a more practical tone. 'And men accuse women of being fickle!'

The fire crackles. As though some frozen core is melting, hot, slow tears carve neat stripes down Yolanda's dirty face. You might expect sobs but there are none, for these are not childish tears from some momentary upset or easy tears from a lovers' tiff. They are the kind of tears we rarely shed because they spring from a well that, once emptied, we feel nothing will ever fill again.

Even Laila's chin trembles as she passes Yolanda a rag for her nose. And suddenly she is crying, and her tears, too, are genuine. 'Ugly didn't deserve to die like that.' Then she dashes her weakness away with the back of her hand. 'Her death'll be paid for, never fear about that,' she whispers. 'I only hope the Inquisitors don't get to Aimery first.' She sneezes and her eyes are bright as washed diamonds.

'Oh, the Inquisitors too? Haven't we had enough misery here?' Yolanda cries.

'There's never enough misery, apparently,' says Laila, grimly gay. 'Only in stories is misery rationed and sadly we don't live in a story.'

Yolanda wipes her cheeks. In her disarray, she looks much more like Yolanda of Amouroix than Lady des Arcis. When her chest has stilled, she looks about. 'If everybody else has gone,' she asks, 'why are you still here?'

Laila's face closes. 'Because I am,' she says. Then she pokes Yolanda in the ribs. 'I was waiting for you, of course.'

'How did you know I'd come?'

'Did you ever think of not coming?'

Yolanda slowly shakes her head.

'Well then,' says Laila, pushing back her curls, and adding with foxy piety, 'since there was no appropriate horse on which I might come and seek you, it was my duty to stay and wait where you would first seek me.'

If times had been different, Yolanda would have laughed. A dutifully pompous Laila is highly comic. Instead, she wants to know something else. 'Why did Gui and Guerau and the huntsman stay?'

'So many questions! How should I know? Too comfortable? Nowhere else to go? Lack of imagination? Actually, if you really want to know, the huntsman stayed because some of the bitches are about to pup and the troubadours stayed because both are secretly in love with me.'

Yolanda still does not laugh for her eyes are fixed again on the ring. When she puts her hand out, Laila places it in her palm where it sits, cracked and misshapen, but still the closest to Raimon she can get. She folds it hard into her fist and tries to imagine Raimon with this other girl, talking to her, listening to her, looking at her. Does she smell of the sky, as Raimon once said Yolanda did? Is her skin milky-white rather than Yolanda's grubby tan? Does she wear pearls around a perfect neck? She tries to imagine the scene during which, in front of this new girl's adoring eyes, Raimon took off the leather ring that she and he forged together in the white heat of the Flame, and replaced it with another.

Her imagining is not a form of self-torture. What she really hopes is that all of these scenes will be quite impossible to imagine at all. Then she will surely know that Laila has distorted things. But it turns out that Yolanda can imagine the scenes only too well. After all, Raimon was so angry when they parted. No — worse than angry. He would not have discarded her out of anger. He was disappointed and hurt, a far more dangerous combination. How can she blame him, then, if he seeks solace with somebody more sympathetic?

The ring bites into her skin as she glares about the room in an effort not to cry again. She finds little comfort in what she sees. There is almost nothing of her past life left in here now. What the fire did not destroy has been pushed around so much that were it not for the hearth and the windows, their shutters untidily half open, Yolanda would hardly know she was in the small hall at Castelneuf at all. The rushes on the floor have all been swept out and, with the walls stripped bare, a chamber built for cosiness is now just a chamber. What is more, the whole place smells quite different. It has lost, finally, any smell of her mother.

She rocks back and forth. This is the last straw. Raimon has gone and her home is not even her home any more. Somehow both have left her behind, caught up in events in which she seems to have lost her part. She never saw the fire here. She never saw Raimon fighting it, or him and Aimery together discussing the rebuilding. She never saw the Cathar visitors. Instead, she is the visitor — worse, she is a visiting stranger.

After the heat of the tears, a dismal bleakness descends. She shuffles back to the hearth, where she sits with Brees on one side and Laila on the other, her mind quite blank.

Laila does not want to stare into the fire so she gets up, gathers together a heap of expensive-looking rags and expertly begins to patch a bright green shift. She seems to have been busy. Her special chest is half covered in clothes in various stages of transformation. 'In a perfect world there'd be no men,' she says, watchfully conversational now and trying to draw Yolanda in. 'I really don't care for them at all.' She finishes a seam, takes the poker and stirs the fire into an ashy mess.

'What shall I do?' Yolanda asks, more of herself than of Laila. 'Should I go to Montségur myself?' She finds her teeth chattering again.

'Here. Wrap yourself in this.' Laila heaves Brees off an old wolfskin and drapes it on top of everything else that already engulfs Yolanda. She kneels and begins to rub her feet. 'Look on the bright side,' she says. 'Your toes are quite pink so they're not likely to fall off from frostbite. Toeless feet are quite disgusting.' She rubs hard. 'If you do go to Montségur,' she says carefully, 'won't that make you feel worse? After all, you're not a Cathar and never will be so they are hardly going to welcome you. Raimon himself might turn you away.'

Yolanda rubs her other foot. 'Do you really think he'd do that?'

Laila scowls. She can still feel the bruises Raimon inflicted in the archer's hole. 'Who knows what he is capable of. And anyway, it wouldn't be up to him. It would be up to Metta Moonface's father and I can't think you want to be humiliated in front of her.'

Yolanda leans back and sees some shoes sticking out from behind the water barrel. 'Did the visitors leave those?'

'What?' Laila follows Yolanda's nod. 'Oh, I hadn't noticed. I expect so.'

'Bring them here.'

'Why? They're no use to you.'

'I don't care. Just bring them here.'

With bad grace, Laila collects the shoes. There are two pairs, one cloth pair with green ribbons to hold them on, and one sturdier pair, the leather once good quality but now hard, with the laces degraded and broken. 'They're hideous,' says Laila with heartfelt disgust. She thrusts them at Yolanda, who runs her fingers over them, noting the toe-shaped stains. 'Were these hers?'

Laila pretends to inspect them. 'No, no. They couldn't be. She had bigger feet than that. Much bigger. Really pretty huge,' she says, endearingly unconvincing.

Yolanda flings the shoes at the fire and Laila pokes at them until they are ablaze before hurrying off to the far corner of the hall. 'We pulled a barrel of wine in here,' she calls over. 'You could do with some.' She scoops out a panful and brings it to warm. Soon, the place is heavy with the aroma of grape and spices. Laila swills the wine about, pulls a phial from her pocket, glances slyly at Yolanda and tosses in the contents. The wine bubbles and gradually loses its acidity. 'Drink this,' she urges, ladling a scoop into an unwashed, slightly mildewed pewter mug. 'It'll warm you all the way through.' Yolanda drinks and gasps and drinks some more. It coats the back of her throat like warm velvet. Laila drinks straight from the pan, making small squeals as she burns her lips.

Yolanda leans back and holds out the mug again. Mouthful after mouthful flows sweetly down and in no time at all her jagged edges are soothed and softened. She takes more salve for her lips and offers some wine to Brees. The dog sniffs, takes a polite slurp and rubs his tongue against the stone like a child with a sour plum. Yolanda finds a laugh welling somewhere within the velvet. As Laila's ladles begin to slop unsteadily, Brees, getting a taste for it, cleans up the spills. 'I should have poisoned her,' Laila says confidingly, and Yolanda knows to whom she refers, 'and I should have poisoned him. I hope they both rot like fish, from the head down, and whilst they're still alive.' Yolanda wants to say something about poisoning Hugh, but it's too much effort. Instead, she has another drink.

The days are still short and when the shadows darken, neither girl gets up to light the lamps. Though they are not asleep, a noxious kind of comfort has descended, and they drowse, leaning half against each other and half against cushions that Laila, what seems like hours ago now, has pulled from trestles jammed against the wall. Gui and Guerau have not reappeared, preferring to sleep in the kennels than near Laila, who is not a relaxing companion. Above the girls' heads, the new wood creaks and settles amid the old wood's sighs. There is a faint howl, maybe a wolf, maybe the hounds dreaming. The girls loll lower and lower on to the cushions. Their breathing slows. Moving even a leg takes a long time and a good deal of concentration. Mostly they cannot be bothered even to do that. Water drips unevenly and forms a puddle somewhere they cannot see. The shutters rattle in the night wind. Doors bang, some quite close by. Yolanda raises herself with a supreme effort. 'There's nowhere —' she subsides.

'Nowhere,' Laila agrees, her voice dragging.

Yolanda raises herself again, and again subsides. All the words she wants are blurry. 'No . . . where.' Her eyes close.

'No,' Laila murmurs as her jaw slackens into sleep. Yolanda grunts.

Another door slams and a voice hurtles out of the gloom. 'Yolanda?

Yolanda is oblivious but Laila tries to snap her eyes open. At first she fails and sinks down again believing she is dreaming. Only when she is shaken violently by the hair does she jolt and jerk and try to peer into the fuzzy dark. Deep inside her head, in the small diamond whose clarity, whatever the state of the rest of her, Laila keeps alert as a dog's nose, she can hear her own voice berating herself for a fool. She and Yolanda are completely undefended apart from Brees, who is himself woozy with wine and even if he was not, is hardly a match for an armed intruder. *Stupid, stupid.* Now she is being dragged to her feet and finds she can barely stand. 'Stop it!

Stop it! Who are you?' She thinks that is what she says. It is certainly what she intends. The next thing she feels is a blast of freezing water. Her eyes fly open as her arms fly out.

'Wake up.' The voice hurtles at her again.

She senses Yolanda stirring.

'Hugh? Oh God.' Yolanda's voice is unrecognisable.

Hugh? Laila empties water from her ears.

'Were you expecting somebody else?' the voice asks.

'Expecting?' Yolanda can only repeat things as she rolls on to her knees.

Hugh fetches more water, aims it at Yolanda, hesitates, then throws it again over Laila. Instead, he takes a sliver of cloth, soaks it and thrusts it into Yolanda's hands. Automatically, she wipes her face and through the wine-fog becomes aware that her clothes are in a pile just where Laila dumped them. Hugh moves about, cumbersomely clad in leather, felt and steel against the twin scourges of the cold and bandit arrows. His shadow lies vastly across the floor.

Yolanda tries to pull her head out of the hole in which it feels stuck. She hardly knows where she is. Has she been whisked back to Carcassonne? 'Why are you here?' she asks with a great effort. She cannot ask where 'here' is.

'Why do you think I'm here?' Hugh knocks great clods of mud from his boots and claps his hands together, spattering icy droplets. 'Good God, Yolanda! You could have frozen to death in that storm. I had no word, no word at all. Nobody could find you.'

Vague memories of the journey flit through her mind. Brees groans.

Hugh fumbles for a flint, lights three lamps and pulls off his helmet. His hair sticks to his scalp and Yolanda can tell, from the way he scrapes his hand across his chin, that he is unshaven. His scar is livid where his helmet has rubbed against it and his eyes are puckered. She has an idea of time passing and the need to say something more. 'There's nothing for you here. Nobody and nothing.'

'Don't tell him that there's nobody here!' Laila has added to her soaking by dunking her head in the water barrel. Now she tosses it like a pony and glares blearily. 'You'll get no food here either, neither you nor your men.'

'I came alone.' Hugh throws his gauntlets down.

His words clang ominously in Yolanda's head. 'You're alone? Where are Amalric and Henri?' she says, though she has some difficulty with the names. 'You don't go anywhere without them.'

'They're with the army, on their way to Montségur.' Hugh's voice is very clipped in comparison with the girls'. 'Why is there nobody here?' Laila and Yolanda stand close together in silence. 'Has Aimery sent everybody away?'

'No.' Laila sucks air into her lungs and grips her hands together. 'Everybody's gone because Aimery's gone.'

Hugh bends to adjust the logs. 'Aimery's gone where?'

'To Montségur of course!' Laila slurs. Is Hugh stupid, or what? 'Isn't that where everybody's going? He's gone with Raimon.'

Hugh turns quickly and Laila can see his genuine surprise. 'With Raimon? You mean they've gone to fight at Montségur together?' He pauses as he tries to make sense of it. *Raimon does not belong at Montségur. He is not one of them.*

'That's about it,' Laila says and congratulates herself on speaking perfectly clearly.

'Raimon's gone to get the Blue Flame,' Yolanda interrupts, although she has to repeat it before Hugh can understand what she is saying.

'That's not really it at all. He's gone with a girl,' Laila contradicts, with alcohol's conspiratorial candour. 'She's called Metta and she's a scheming simpleton. He didn't wait for –' she gestures at Yolanda and shrugs.

Hugh discards his cloak and the bag slung round his waist. Though he keeps his dagger close, he also unstraps his baldric and without his sword his shadow lessens, although had Yolanda been entirely herself, she would have recognised the demeanour of a man who recognises an opportunity. As it is, she is alert to nothing.

'Raimon left you here because he understands that you're my wife,' Hugh says carefully, addressing her directly. 'He's accepted it and has found somebody else to love. I admire him for that.' He sees the pan of wine, tastes it and at once spits into the fire. 'For the love of Heaven, girl,' he says sharply to Laila, 'what have you put in it? Your tricks will kill somebody one day.' She wants to curl her lip at him but cannot find the right muscle.

Yolanda rocks on her haunches, holding on to Brees. This is just a dream. It must be. Nothing about it is real.

Hugh tips out his bag, unwraps a hunk of bread, some salted meat that has turned almost to leather and a round of cheese. He lays them on a table, out of Brees's reach. 'You should both eat,' he says. Neither girl moves. He brings the food over and tries to make them. Laila refuses point blank and Yolanda is like a ragdoll, her head too heavy for her body. Hugh lays her back down, eats a little bread himself and then sits, spreading his legs to the fire. Steam rises from his clothes. An hour passes. The night deepens. As Yolanda sleeps the sleep of the drugged, Laila watches Hugh. When he shifts, she shifts too. Eventually Hugh gets up and taps his foot. 'Go and find yourself another place for tonight,' he says. 'Yolanda and I have things to discuss.'

'Are you joking?'

'I've never been more serious in my life.'

'She's asleep.'

'She's more than that, thanks to you. But I'll wait and I want to wait alone.'

'I'm not leaving.'

'Shall I throw you out?'

'I'm not leaving Yolanda alone with you.'

He sighs. 'I could pick you up and pitch you through the door, and that dog too, but wouldn't you rather leave in a more dignified manner?'

Laila does not have to be entirely sober to be crafty. 'And why would I do that?'

Hugh takes a small pouch out of his bag. Laila fixes her gaze on it. He shakes it, holds it and shakes it again before, from a height, tipping it up. Into his waiting hand drips a starry waterfall of multicoloured gemstones set in a cascade of silver scales. Lastly falls the clasp, an emerald dragonfly with milky, opal-studded wings.

Laila's hand shoots out. Hugh dangles the jewel. She creeps forward. 'This necklace is priceless,' Hugh observes.

'Nothing is priceless.' Laila's answer is automatic. Her eyes are huge and hungry.

Hugh makes the necklace swing back and forth so that it dances and taunts in the firelight. He draws in his cheeks. 'Nothing that you know of,' he says. There is a long pause. 'Take it,' he says.

Laila's arm twitches. 'And in return?'

'Leave Yolanda and me alone for an hour, and take Brees with you.'

She shakes her head, but without conviction. The dragonfly is brilliant in the glow. Then it is gone, hidden back in the pouch. Laila almost cries.

'I'll just keep it and and throw you out then.' Hugh advances towards her. Yolanda sleeps on.

Laila skips back, her breathing quick. 'Don't touch me. You're not my husband.'

'No,' says Hugh wryly. 'God has some mercy.'

Laila cannot stay still. She darts about, towards Yolanda and then away. Her neck aches for the necklace, for its weight and glamour. She can feel its coolness against her skin. She can hear people sighing with envy. And after all, as Hugh says, he can pitch her out anyway. Indeed, that is just what he intends to do. A king's ransom for an hour he is going to have whatever she does. And he *is* Yolanda's husband.

She says not a word, but Hugh already knows he has her. He has barely pulled the necklace out again when fingers flash and briefly brush his as she snatches it away, seizes Brees and is outside the door. Hugh closes it behind her and she hears the key turning in the lock.

At once, Laila beats against it, though not very hard. 'Don't you dare hurt her,' she cries, cradling the necklace so as not to damage it.

Hugh does not hear her. In the swirl of conflicting desires, half determined to force his way and half ashamed that he has to, he is already bending down towards Yolanda. He speaks her name, low and urgent. Her lips part in an involuntary response. She has no idea who is calling. Perhaps it is Raimon. Hugh will not allow himself to hesitate, not now. He picks her up in his arms with rough tenderness. Only then does he look round, just briefly, to make sure he really is alone. As Laila's hammering ceases, he stops only to shrug off the covers before taking his wife away from the hearth, to a place where the fire's light does not shine.

Outside, Laila pushes Brees into the great hall, still roofless. She tries to put the necklace on but her fingers are shaking too much to fasten the catch. Eventually she sits, holding the necklace tight. The moon appears from behind a cloud and the necklace winks at her, the rubies glistening like drops of blood. With a tiny cry Laila's hand flies to her mouth in sudden revulsion at what she has done. But the dragonfly is so beautiful. She tosses it from hand to hand, sliding the silver scales over the curve of her chin. The weight and the even roll of the stones reassure her. She is not a bad person, she is just herself.

When she thinks an hour is up, she creeps back to the small hall. The door is still locked. Then she hears movement and for the first time in her life, loses courage. She cannot keep the necklace and face Yolanda. Which is it to be? Almost without thinking, she begins to slide furtively away, like a burglar taking advantage of the dark. Seizing an abandoned cloak, she sets off for the postern gate and then stops. Her box of tricks is still in the small hall. Is she really going to leave that behind? She paces back and forth. Surely she can still look Yolanda in the eye. She can do anything. Yet she finds herself pushing the gate open and flicking her hair with too much self-conscious vigour. Then she finds her excuse. She has unfinished business with Aimery. For the moment, she decides with her own kind of bravado, she will focus exclusively on that.

Waking Up

Though the dawn chorus is long past, it is still dark in the small hall. It is also very cold because the fire has gone out. Two shapes are humped in the corner under the window.

Brees has been lying by his mistress since Hugh departed, forced out by the knowledge that an army without a commander very soon turns into a rabble. As he dressed, Hugh toyed with the idea of taking Yolanda with him but the battlefield would be no place for his wife, particularly not a battlefield on which Raimon and Aimery would be fighting. Yet he could not force her to remain here or spare men to take her back to Carcassonne. In the end he left her in God's hands — and Laila's, except that she was not lurking outside as he expected. Fretting about the time but unwilling to shout out Laila's name, he eventually told Brees to keep good watch and sent the dog in.

And at first Brees had been delighted, but when his mistress refused to move, he grew worried. Now he sits unhappily, his tongue furred from his own kind of hangover.

Yolanda is curled with her arms round her knees, the side of her face crammed so hard against a cushion that its creases line her cheeks. Her back is crushed against the wall and the only things that occasionally twitch, quite involuntarily, are her toes. Whenever this happens, Brees looks hopeful. Perhaps she'll get up now?

She does not, and eventually a full bladder has Brees whining at the door. It does not open, so eventually he looses a stream against the table-leg. It does not please him, but there is nothing else for him to do. And it has one effect. Eventually, Yolanda has to rise to answer a similar need of her own. She checks carefully that the room is empty before she stumbles to the small corner urinal and then locates her heap of clothes. Ignoring their dampness, she pulls them on and gets straight back under the wolfskin.

She can see nobody, speak to nobody. Most particularly she does not want to see or speak to Laila because Laila will force her to remember and that she refuses to do. Her fists are clenched, and when they creep open, she clenches them again, tighter than before, as if they constituted some enormous bodily shield. When she can clench them no longer, she rises again, grabs a chair and drags it to the water-barrel, climbs up and plunges her head right in, soaking herself beyond her collar.

The water's icy skim is like sandpaper, filling her ears and scratching her neck. Nonetheless, she keeps her head dunked until she must gasp for breath. It has a momentary desired effect. When she pulls her head out, she can neither see nor hear anything. But as soon as the immediate hammerblow of cold subsides, shadowy memories seep in.

There is no pain, not any more, there is just a sawing ache that doubles her up, and behind the ache there is shame and fear and the worst thing of all, a halo of taint. A few hours pass. Gui and Guerau knock on the door, at first just the normal greetings of the day, but then increasingly anxious and afraid. She speaks only to tell them that she is perfectly all right and that Laila is not with her. The postern gate was open, they say. Somebody has been in. She reassures them, sends Brees out and tells them to leave her alone.

Just after noon, she longs more than anything for a bath but she cannot have one without help, and for help she must go outside and find Laila, whose absence only now begins to concern, except that her box of tricks is just where she left it and she would surely stir nowhere without that. Where is she, then? Another hour passes and a tight band circles Yolanda's heart. *Where is she?* Surely Hugh has not hurt her as well. He wouldn't. *But he's just hurt me,* she cries silently. *He could do anything.*

'Perhaps she's gone to Sir Aimery at Montségur,' Gui suggests, when at last Yolanda emerges. 'There was a closeness between them.'

'Why hasn't she waited for me? And why hasn't she taken her box?'

'Perhaps she heard that Sir Hugh's army is on the move and she wants to get there before he does?' It sounds a feeble reason but at the mention of Hugh's name, Yolanda doubles up. 'Hugh's not at Montségur,' she says, and Gui turns white as something of what has happened begins to dawn.

Yolanda straightens herself. 'Hugh must have made her go,' she says without any further explanation. 'He must have threatened her.' She is determined to believe it. She'll believe anything of Hugh now.

She goes back to the small hall and locks the door again, but then, agitated, re-emerges to demand that they ask the huntsman to empty the dogmeal from the old leather tub that her father had made for campaigns he never fought and drag it into the hall. With Gui and Guerau tasked to bank up the fire, Yolanda throws herself wildly into the task of pumping water to heat. Only when every available pan, jug and bucket is lodged in the hearth and the bath steaming and filled to the brim is she satisfied. Gui and Guerau exchange glances as she pushes them out. Before she closes the door, Gui lays a hand on her arm. She jumps back and slaps him smartly across the cheek. He gasps. She cringes. 'Oh God!' she cries, then, 'Go away! Please just go away!' They back off, their faces ashen.

When Yolanda has locked the door again, she pulls off her clothes and without looking at any part of herself climbs heavily into the bath and lies down. The leather feels scratchy against the skin of her back and the bath is not quite long enough to lie straight so her knees stick up. The water should soothe but at first it jangles and she cannot bear it seeping through every pore, reminding her in its insidious way that some barrier within her has been broken, not just the physical barrier that her friend Beatrice once told her about in breath-less detail, but some other barrier, much more intensely personal. From the breach, she feels everything beautiful about her is leaking away leaving only a dried-up and desic-cated shell. Terrified, she touches her lips to make sure they have not disappeared, as old women's do.

The rim of the bath digs into her neck, but now the water is her friend and she wants to stay in this brown pool for ever. Her reflection makes and unmakes itself and she stares at it as if she has never seen herself before.

Brees sits beside the bath, occasionally sticking his tongue in. The warmth of the water, with its faint tang of Yolanda, intrigues him.

He gets a terrible fright when she suddenly leaps out and flashes white across the room, her feet marking a wet trail. She has gone only to grab a small blanket and this time, when she leaps back into the bath, she attacks her legs and thighs, pummelling them, gouging them, to remove any last trace of Hugh. She goes over every inch of skin with meticulous care: the back of her neck, behind her knees, her nails, the palms of her hands and between her toes. She dunks her hair again and again, pulling at it, raking her fingers across her scalp. Finally, she turns to her stomach and by the time she is finished, it is scraped raw as a burned pan but she is triumphant. No des Arcis son could lodge in there now.

She uses the remaining jugs to rinse and after that the water is disgusting to her so she climbs out and lets the fire dry her, raising her arms and turning round like a joint on a spit. She gets as close to the flames as she can bear, drawing away just before her skin scorches. Brees whines his concern, but the scorching, too, is part of the cleansing process. Eventually, she lights a flambeau and rummages through

Laila's half-sewn garments, choosing not a dress but a loose tunic and some trousers that remind her of pictures she once saw in a book. The colours are inappropriately gaudy but she hardly notices. Lastly, she finds knitted leggings and hard-soled boots that have obviously been stolen from the visitors. No matter. She tugs them on. Her own clothes, the wet blanket and all the other bed covers except for the wolfskin, she burns. The smell is vile and the smoke billows, yellow and greasy. She runs from it. Brees presses close to her until they get outside when hunger makes him head for the kennels. She follows him for three paces and then stops. She has cleansed her body and before she speaks to anybody again, she wants to cleanse her mind.

She stands quite still and forces herself to remember exactly what happened. Does that seem strange to you? It does not to me, for Yolanda knows instinctively that every time she relives her ordeal, it will lose of a little of its potency. Only familiarity can rob nightmares of both their poison and their disconcerting ability to creep up unawares. However, though Yolanda takes a deep breath and braces herself, detailed memories elude her. The drugged wine Laila gave her, such a disabling enemy when Hugh arrived, now turns friend. All she can remember is Hugh's shadow, his weight and a long quaking shudder that might have been him or might have been her. Beyond that, nothing. She does not know whether to be grateful or not.

The troubadours approach tentatively. Her fingermarks are still red across Gui's cheek. 'Can you help me empty the bath?' she asks.

'We've already done it,' they reply. She blinks. She had no idea she has been standing still for so long. The troubadours say nothing more, only guide her to the kennels and sit with her in Farvel's empty set until, much later on, amid the normality of the hounds' routine, she decalcifies like a melting stone and becomes Yolanda again. They tend her as carefully as a mother, never touching her, always announcing their presence, asking no questions, making no demands. She feels safer here and does not return to the small hall.

Some days later, early in the morning, the huntsman smiles at her and places in her lap three mewling newborn hound puppies. At first she glares at them with dread, Hugh's demand for a son rattling her ears. Puppies! And what if? What if? She shakes her head and cannot speak.

The huntsman is not abashed. 'Farvel's offspring,' he says in his careful way, 'and the start of a new pack.' His eyes are bright. This is nature's answer to loss. Farvel's set must belong to others now.

'There'll be no need of a new pack here,' Yolanda says in a low voice.

'No new pack?'

'No. You must know that it's all finished for us. Aimery's gone and Raimon's gone. They're not coming back.'

'Is that right,' says the huntsman.

One of the puppies begins to scramble blindly up Yolanda's tunic and she sits without moving until its paws paddle with increasing desperation and finally, to stop it from falling, she has to put out a hand. Brees takes a fatherly interest and as more puppies arrive, Yolanda forgets her dread in the pleasure of seeing them wriggle and hearing the dogboys squeal with delight. The huntsman is right about one thing. There will be a new pack.

A week later, she is restless. 'I'm going down into the town,' she says. 'We need to know who's left.'

'You're not going back to Carcassonne, then?' Guerau asks. He is balancing four brindle bitches on his bull-like chest, and enjoying the jealousy that Gui, on whose chest only two puppies can fit, is trying unsuccessfully to conceal.

'No. Never.'

'Nor to Montségur?'

She hesitates. 'Do you think that's really where Laila went?'

'I don't know where else she'll have gone,' Gui says, plucking up a tri-coloured dog puppy and allowing it to bite his ear. 'She'll be after Sir Aimery, though. Those two are as thick as thieves.'

Yolanda does not want Aimery to know what has happened to her. She leans down and returns one of Guerau's puppies to its mother. 'I don't know what good I could do at Montségur and, anyway, I've no horse.'

'No,' the huntsman says, 'although the charcoal burner's got a sorrel on the other side of the valley.'

Yolanda shakes her head. Her desire to go into the town dissolves. She can decide on nothing.

In the end, as so often happens, something is decided for her.

Six weeks after Hugh's visit, heralded by a muted chorus of bells and ritualistic chanting, a group of three Inquisitors finally wends its way slowly up the disintegrating road to the château. After the snow, they spent Easter at Mirepoix before travelling further south, and because producing a trail of smoke, human ashes and misery takes time and effort, they are tired. Moreover, having been led to believe that the château would be rich hunting grounds for Saviours of Souls such as themselves, their exhaustion is compounded by the disappointment of learning that only a girl, two troubadours, a huntsman and some ridiculous dogboys are in residence. All that stony way just for this thin haul? These straight-backed, hollow-faced men of God feel a sense of anger on their Redeemer's behalf. Where are all the heretics? They chant more loudly, as if this might draw out sin as venom is drawn from a snake.

Yolanda greets them in the courtyard, with Gui and Guerau behind her. The huntsman locks the dogboys in the kennels to keep them out of harm's way. Only when the mules have stopped and the bells round their necks have settled are the Inquisitors' servants allowed to sink down and rest, although they never sit at ease for their masters' probing eyes are always upon them, boring into them, seeing thoughts they would rather keep secret.

The Inquisitors seem startled by Yolanda's appearance, about which she has almost forgotten. They mutter between themselves at her multicoloured tunic and rough, workman's trousers. They cannot place her at all.

The youngest Inquisitor dismounts and begins to walk about, his arms crossed in stern disapproval. The oldest one speaks. 'And where is Count Aimery?' he asks Guerau. 'We've heard he is now dedicated to the Cathar cause.'

'How should we know?'

Both the mounted Inquisitors lean forward, their feet pushing against the stirrups. 'Who asked you anything, insolent girl.'

Yolanda draws herself to her full height. 'I should be careful if I were you.'

'Careful? Oh really?' The dismounted Inquisitor picks up a stick.

Yolanda is not sure how she is holding herself so steady, but she turns round very slowly, removes the stick from him and breaks it in half. 'Don't you know who I am?'

All the Inquisitors at once are wary. They look at her more closely.

'I am married to Sir Hugh des Arcis,' Yolanda says, making her voice imperiously commanding. 'Do you know Sir Hugh, the chosen champion of Louis IX of France, the keeper of the king's oriflamme and a man whose career is of interest even to the Pope? You must know him, surely? And you'll know where to find him, too, because even now he's at Montségur, reclaiming the Blue Flame from the heretics.' She regrets throwing away Hugh's ring. At this moment it would have been good for something.

However, her announcement is enough to startle and the Inquisitors' foreheads crease. Of course they know Sir Hugh and they have no quarrel with him, nor do they wish for one. Indeed, the Pope has ordered them to pray every night for his success in capturing the Blue Flame and obliterating the last of the Cathars. Had they known Castelneuf was in the hands of Lady des Arcis and not Count Aimery, they would never have come here. Somebody will pay for this error.

The young Inquisitor, less judicious than the others, will not be thwarted. This is his first Inquisitorial tour and, so far, he has exterminated a heretic in every place. He does not want to spoil his record. He stabs a bony finger at Gui, Guerau and the huntsman. 'What about these three? They have the heretic look about them.'

His seniors flush with displeasure. The boy is assiduous and keen. He does not flinch when the heretics scream and he is imaginative, highly imaginative, when it comes to the extraction of answers. But he takes too much upon himself. One tries to silence him but Yolanda is already staring directly into his eyes. 'They are part of my household,' she says.

'But were they not also part of your brother's?' The young man clicks dirty teeth.

Yolanda regards him as she might regard a rat. 'I was part of my brother's household once,' she says. 'You must keep up if you ever wish to become as efficient an Inquisitor as my uncle Girald d'Amouroix.'

Even this young man starts at that name. Inquisitor Girald! He who was murdered so horribly! Why, he is almost an Inquisitorial saint! It is hardly believable that this creature is his niece. Nevertheless, he backs away a little.

The older Inquisitors are not unhappy at their younger friend's discomfiture. 'Knocked him off his perch, and not before time,' one murmurs to the other. The young man knows better than to retort.

Yolanda gestures round. 'As you see, we can offer no hospitality,' she says. 'You'll have to apply to my husband for that.'

'And we'll be sure to do so when we get to Montségur ourselves,' comes the answer. 'Now, get these servants back on their feet and mount up, Brother James.' Whips are flicked.

The young Inquisitor climbs resentfully aboard his mule, snagging his habit so that a very hairy bare leg is exposed. At once, with casual impudence copied from Laila, Yolanda unsnags the tunic and smoothes it down the leg, making the young man snort at unwanted sensations that erupt like fireworks. His leg flies backwards, his hands fly up and when he is thoroughly discomfited, Yolanda smacks his mule lightly on the bottom. 'There now,' she says, with unimpeachable innocence. 'You're decent again. What's your name? James, isn't it? I'll be sure to tell my husband to look out for you.'

After they leave, she is violently sick. 'Relief,' she says to the huntsman.

Four weeks later, when the late winter surge is long over and the bitches are basking with their puppies in the early summer sunshine, Yolanda runs down the steps and this time her eyes are filled with disbelief and terror. 'I was sick again this morning,' she says blankly. The puppies mewl. 'I can't be,' she cries to the huntsman. 'I just can't be. I scrubbed everything away. There was nothing left of Hugh, nothing, not anywhere.' The huntsman takes her hands. She cannot say any more, for she knows that what cannot be, is. And she knows that she has really known it ever since her mouth began to taste salty and her body to feel like a stranger's. Hugh has had his way and got his way. She is having his baby. 'I want that sorrel mare,' she says abruptly.

The huntsman does not move. 'Send for the sorrel mare,' she says.

'Where will you go?'

'To Montségur. To Laila. I know there's something in her box that can help me, but I can't tell what. I've got to find her.'

'The troubadours should go with you.'

Something in Yolanda snaps. 'There's only one horse,' she shouts, 'and don't you see, I've got to hurry. Brees will protect me.'

She turns on her heel, runs back up the steps and shoves a bundle together, with Laila's box at the top. Within two hours, the mare is collected and waiting. Gui gives her a leg-up whilst Guerau settles her pack. 'You do see, don't you?' Yolanda says to them all. 'Laila can fix anything.'

The huntsman speaks slowly. 'You do what you have to do, my lovely,' he says, 'but take care how you do it.'

She gives a wan smile and glances down at Brees. The dog is ready, undaunted by the prospect of another journey because he has almost forgotten the last one. 'If I ride hard and fast enough, maybe God will take care of it for me,' Yolanda says, although given that God seems already to have deserted her, she holds out no hope for that at all.

THE POG

We must go back, just a little, to find Aimery first up the path to what is known as the pog of Montségur. Set within a jostling pavilion of other mountains, its particular mix of cottage loaf, giant's nose and stubborn boil in need of lancing is quite unmistakable, though for the procession of Cathars something else marks it out.

At the base of the walls of the fortress, the eastern barbican thrusting up like a thumb, floats an uneven and occasional blue haze. The haze is, of course, a trick of the eye, a natural glow from the refraction of a sapphire sky against the glassy sun. To the travellers, however, it is the mark of the Flame and the sight of it makes every stomach lurch with both pride and fear. Here they are, ready to sacrifice their lives, and the Flame has seen fit to greet them. They ignore the plume of smoke that already rises from the kitchens at the back of the pog. Though this smoke is entirely benign, they need no reminders of what may be in store for them.

All except Sir Roger. He sees the smoke and at once regrets bringing his daughter. As they prepare for the climb, he allows his horse to dawdle. It is not too late. Even now he could order her cart to turn round or, better still, send it on through the Pyrenean passes to Spain where neither the French army nor the Inquisitors will follow. Raimon could take her. Raimon *must* take her. He pulls his skewbald round.

Raimon is riding alone, staring up like the others at the gauzy blue mist, when Sir Roger accosts him without apology. 'If you love Metta as you say you do, take her away from this. Take her to Spain.' Sir Roger pushes so close that their stirrups clink together and Raimon can smell the stale sweat on the old knight's woollen undershirt. 'She should never have come. What was I thinking? Please, Raimon. It's too late for me to take her back but you could take her forward.' He gestures at the peaks. 'That way lies life, and here,' he gestures at the fortress, 'lies death. I know it. We all know it. Who survives a last stand?' He drops his reins and wrings his hands.

Raimon heart sinks and he blames himself. How could he not have foreseen this? No man would willingly see a daughter perish. Look at how his own father has suffered at Adela's pointless decline. But he is in too deep to desert the Flame now. It is up there, waiting for him and he will not abandon it. 'Sir Roger,' he begins, and is at once rudely interrupted.

'Here we are! We must ride up together as far as we can,' cries Aimery, pushing Argos between them. 'The finest days of the Occitan are just beginning. Do you know, people will talk about this for centuries to come. Alain!' He stands in his stirrups and bellows. 'Take my standard out in front.'

When Sir Roger does not respond, Aimery reproaches him. 'Come, Sir Roger. Why the long face? This is surely a moment for all good Cathars to savour. The Blue Flame calls to us. Can't you hear it?'

Sir Roger makes an inarticulate noise and falls back, his eyes still boring into Raimon. Aimery, who sees it all, now bends Argos hard against Galahad so that the horses increase their step and leave Sir Roger behind. Scarcely is the old man out of earshot before Aimery winks. 'Well, *Sir* Raimon,' he jibes, 'I thought your prospective father-in-law might try to get you to elope with Metta. That would be tricky, wouldn't it? Still, I've saved you from trying to explain why you can't.'

'Go away!' Raimon forces the words through his teeth. 'Just go away, Aimery. You sully everything. You think you're a knight but you're nothing but a cheap opportunist.'

A loud crow issues from Aimery's mouth. '*Me*? *Me* an opportunist?' He leers into Raimon's face. 'Isn't opportunity what life's about, my friend? And I don't see you neglecting yours.'

The horses are sweating, their shoes scuffing sparks as the slope steepens. The glistening shingle provides no solid footholds. One horse falls and grazes its knees. Aimery shifts in his saddle, suddenly a soldier. 'Impossible for men to gallop up here at any rate,' he says. 'Hugh will be at some disadvantage.'

Raimon does not reply.

They climb on, the horses blowing and panting, and as

they get nearer to the root of the fortress Aimery suddenly begins to shout. 'Ho!' he bellows. 'Friends! Ho up there!' He jabs Raimon in the ribs. 'They'll see my banner and may think we're enemies. We must let them know we come in peace. You should shout too.'

Raimon wants to punch him.

Aimery shouts again and this time three arrows greet him in return, one landing in front of Argos's nose and the others in line with Aimery's toes. They bounce, for the ground is either too hard or too flimsy to get any purchase, but Aimery notes the barbed heads and jerks Argos to a halt. 'Ho there! I tell you we come in peace.' He squints up and is dazzled by the sun. Another arrow flies past. Argos treads on the shaft and snaps it. Aimery slowly raises his hands. They wait. No more arrows. Aimery grins. 'We'll have to walk from here on our own feet,' he says. 'I don't think the horses can come further even without riders. I suppose we just let them go.'

Raimon dismounts. Aimery swings a leg over and sits sidesaddle for a moment. Both of them look behind to where the procession has become uneven as a broken sentence. Many knights have already dismounted and the carts have stopped, the baggage slowly being unloaded on to human donkeys. The women hitch up their skirts to climb unhampered. Metta and Adela are together.

It is with true regret that Aimery lets Argos loose. Raimon hands Galahad over to Cador. The boy's chin is trembling. Just when he got his warhorse, he must lose it. Raimon draws him to one side. This is where they must part too. However brutal he must be, however much he must lie, he cannot let

Cador enter the fortress. He adopts his sternest face and his sternest tones. 'Now, Cador. Give me Unbent. I can manage for myself from here.'

The little boy sags, as if from a blow, even as he helps Raimon strap on the baldric. 'You said you wouldn't abandon me.'

'I'm not abandoning you. I'm giving you a different job. I don't want Galahad and Bors to wander off like Argos. You must take them and look after them.'

Cador is not fooled. Nobody else is leaving their squire behind. Raimon is getting rid of him. His voice rings out. 'You're my knight. You can't just dismiss me. I haven't done anything wrong.'

'A good squire obeys his lord.' Raimon will not relent. 'You can't come any further.'

'Do you want to end up with your stuff as tatty as Sir Roger's?'

Raimon gives the ghost of a smile. 'I don't think anybody will notice.'

The boy crumbles completely now. 'I don't believe any of it,' he sobs. 'You being a Cathar, or loving Metta – none of it. And don't try to persuade me because I never will.' Raimon has to look away. 'But the thing that's hardest,' Cador tries to find something on which to wipe his nose, 'the thing that's *really* hardest, is that you don't trust me any more.'

Now Raimon's fingers grip Cador's shoulders hard enough to bruise. The boy forgets his nose as Raimon shakes him. 'Remember what Sir Parsifal said just before he died?'

'He said we should live for the Flame, the Amouroix, the

Occitan and for love,' Cador gurgles.

'And then he asked a question. He asked which was the most important, and what was the answer?' Raimon draws their faces very close.

'"Love", Sir Raimon, that was the answer.' Their eyes lock together.

'And isn't trust part of love?' Raimon asks.

'I've always thought so,' Cador hiccups.

'And do you doubt that I love you as a knight should love a squire?'

'Not until now.'

'Now's not a time to doubt, Cador.' Their eyes are still locked. 'Not for a minute. It's because I trust you absolutely that you must do as I ask.' Raimon lets go of the boy's shoulders and, with sudden determination, slips off the baldric. 'Take Unbent,' he says, 'and wait for me. You won't know where or when I'm coming, but I am coming, Cador. Do you understand?'

There is no veil between them now. Neither moves. When, eventually, Raimon opens his mouth again, Cador puts his finger to his lips. He needs nothing more. Without another word, he hitches Unbent over his shoulder and begins to lead the horses down the hill. They take their time for the way is rough and though he does not look back, Raimon guesses rightly that for the first time in weeks, though his squire's eyes are wet with tears, they are shining.

After another hour, the fortress frowns directly above those climbing towards it, with the great keep to their left and the bailey to their right. Already they can hear the rumble of life within, and not only within. Beneath the walls, like a brood of chicks under a mother hen, lurks a collection of wooden huts, built and inhabited by those Cathars with monkish pretensions. However, faced with the threat of Louis's approaching army, prayer is not the only thing on their minds. Between every second hut stone slings have been erected with piles of hefty rocks beside them. Even these men of God will not be taken without a fight.

The main protection, however, bears no relation to either barbican or sling. Apart from the south-westerly path up which the visitors have just climbed, all the faces of the pog are either so sheer and unstable or so deeply and unevenly ridged that it would be physically impossible for an enemy force of any size to gain a firm hold. There is no need, therefore, for a bank of sentries, which is why Sir Roger's company is greeted by only four men standing on the wooden platform balanced on stilts in front of the fortress's gate. Their swords are unsheathed but, despite the earlier shower of arrows, they do not look alarmed.

'We're here to help defend the Flame,' Aimery calls up.

'Aren't you Count Aimery of Castelneuf?'

'Yes, that's me!'

The four men all peer down. 'Last we heard,' the tallest declares, tapping his sword on the railing, 'you wanted the Flame delivered to the King of France.' He twists his head. 'Cut the noise in there! We can't hear a thing.' The order is fired back. The noise subsides slightly.

'You heard right,' Aimery calls back, 'but perhaps you haven't heard that the king repaid me by firing my château and burning my villages. I owe no allegiance to him now.' The men consult.

Sir Roger, who has needed two supporting shoulders to make the last bit of the climb, now catches his breath. 'Is one of you Raymond de Perella?' he asks.

'No. I am.' A man with a face that has seen better days pushes through from behind. 'I control who comes in and out.' It seems an unnecessary statement and Raimon at once senses that there is tension up here. The White Wolf, no doubt, has put himself in charge.

Sir Roger plants his feet more firmly. 'We seek to come in.'

There is a pause. De Perella inspects the visitors and dwells on Aimery's banner. At last, he twitches impatiently. He is always impatient these days. 'Who vouches for Sir Aimery of Amouroix?'

'Oh, I do,' Sir Roger says in a slight fluster. He feels he should have made this clear without being asked. He is still thinking of Metta. He pulls himself together. 'The count provided hospitality when we were caught in the snow in the Amouroix and has travelled here with my blessing.'

'But he's a Catholic.'

'Was,' corrects Aimery, elbowing Sir Roger aside. 'As I say, the burning of my château by the French king taught me better.' His eyes are wide as the sky.

De Perella scrutinises him for a moment, then watches the procession slowly catching up with the leaders. The warhorses are wandering downhill, lipping the shoots lurking under last year's dead growth. Relaxed and unthreatening, they seem to offer reassurance. 'Wait there,' he orders.

'Not too long, I hope,' Aimery joshes. 'I hear Hugh des Arcis has already set out and we don't want to be caught on the wrong side of the wall.'

Nobody smiles but without much further ado, a small gate underneath the platform is opened and hands flap their willingness to draw the travellers in. This is the last possible moment. Sir Roger finds his daughter rosy with the unaccustomed exercise. 'Metta,' he says, catching her hands. 'Metta.'

'Come, Father,' she says, smiling directly at him. 'Journey's end.' He cannot make her stop and Raimon does not try. When she enters the fortress, the hearts of both men twinge.

It may seem odd to speak of claustrophobia when we are on the top of a hill where the wind is never still and where, from the ramparts, the vista spreads almost without limit, yet after an hour in the courtyard, Raimon can hardly breathe. The place is not just full, it is heaving with people, more people than the fortress was ever designed to hold, and, hemmed in by the high walls, the trapped air is overused and sour.

Like animals in a corral, men and women shuffle about, children playing between their legs and between the legs of three cows tethered next to two overflowing water cisterns. From makeshift lines, grey laundry hangs in dispirited flags and beneath the laundry lie several tightly swaddled babies shrieking their own complaints into the din. It feels more like a camp for refugees than a mustering ground for knights preparing for a final stand.

'For the love of God,' says Aimery, genuinely horrified. 'Let's hope we don't have to spend long in this pigpen.' Raimon cannot disagree.

The kitchens, banished to the perimeter to diminish the threat of fire, are shacks, with corn spilling from sacks lodged in doorways. Piles of half-uncovered and fly-ridden cheeses add to the general stink. Yet their particular stink offers some consolation: at least there is no shortage of food. The villagers at the bottom of the pog are clearly making good money through keeping the garrison supplied.

Despite this, the atmosphere is febrile. Rows flare over the tiniest things: disputed ownership of an egg, a stamped-on toe, an upturned bench over which somebody has tripped. Through this swirl, the new arrivals tread softly and though, as fellow Cathars and Occitanians, they are greeted ostensibly with joy, greetings are swiftly followed by clear reinforcements of small personal boundaries. 'I sleep there, and my wife beside me, so better to find somewhere else', or 'Sorry, we've been using that dip in the wall to store our clothes and armour, so can you find another slot?' The apologies are copious and some genuinely meant. Everybody is simply trying to live as best they can.

Only the keep, rising blackly on the opposite side to the kitchens with its bottom door firmly closed, is set apart from the general hum. Even the barbican tower seems friendly in comparison. 'The Flame's in the keep,' Aimery murmurs. 'Sure as you're not a Cathar.'

It is against the bottom of the keep, in a corner that has never, since building on the pog first began, been touched by the sun, that the household of Sir Roger de Salas eventually finds itself crammed. A few yellowing weeds are all that has ever flourished here and all that ever will.

Metta takes charge. 'We're lucky,' she announces cheerfully. 'At least we'll be sheltered from the wind.' The knights look about. Wind? They would welcome it down here. At least it would disperse the smell. 'And we're all together.' All together? In this discomfort, of what comfort is that? Despite Matta's best efforts, they mutter, angry and complaining. 'They don't need us here! There's no room! We shouldn't have come.'

Sir Roger loses his temper. 'What did you imagine it would be like?' he shouts. 'We do this for the Flame and the Occitan.'

The knights grumble more quietly.

Hours later, when the company has scrimped and squeezed and grudgingly shaken down, Raimon stands in the shadows, his head stretched back and his eyes glued upwards. Aimery is right. Though he can see nothing but a series of dark window slits outlining each floor, and the bottom door appears to be locked from the inside, the Flame must be in the keep. Nobody sleeps much. Raimon does not sleep at all.

There is a sudden buzz the following morning when de Perella's sons-in-law call everybody together. It seems that they are going to be addressed, and judging by the muted excitement, this is unusual. Nobody can really move very far, but eyes strain towards the wide wooden balcony that has been raised inside the curtain wall above the main gate. A narrow duckboard walkway leads from it straight to an upper door in the keep that Raimon has not noticed. The door at ground level must, Raimon thinks, be used for servicing domestic needs.

They are not kept waiting long. A man appears and at his appearance, Raimon's every pore prickles.

The White Wolf is just how he remembers him, his hair and beard still white as swansdown and his manner unassuming. However he is no longer wearing the clothes of a weaver as he was when he first appeared from Raimon's father's workshop. Now he wears a long black hooded robe like an Old Testament prophet. Nor is he alone. There must be two hundred Perfecti behind him, women as well as men, all dressed exactly the same, with sandalled feet protruding from rough hems. As the Perfecti process, everybody bows low, as is the custom, Aimery with a particular flourish. Raimon cannot bring himself to bow, so crouches as the cry 'Pray God to make a good Christian of me, and bring me to a good end', clearly well practised, goes up, and for a moment, all petty acrimony is submerged under a tide of devotion. The White Wolf stands as though he holds the key of heaven, and nobody questions or mutters because nobody wants to waste a second of the fix of hope he seems to offer.

'Cheat for not bowing!' Aimery hisses as Raimon rises again. Raimon does not answer.

The White Wolf is quietly accepting of all the adulation and when at last he speaks, he dominates this pulsating mass with the same soft voice that Raimon hears in nightmares.

'Good people,' the White Wolf says and watches his words settle like honey. 'How happy we are, here on this hilltop. God has given the Blue Flame into our hands as proof that we are his chosen ones.' He spreads his arms in a general embrace. 'Though our travails will be hard, there is no need to fear because we are the blessed. Here, at Montségur, we are writing the last and best chapter in the history of the

Occitan.' He smiles a smile of bliss. 'Is anybody afraid?'

The quality of the silence changes. The truth is that they are all afraid.

'Is there no honesty here?' His voice is gently teasing.

'I'm afraid,' a woman calls out. 'I'm afraid for my children.'

'Yes, I'm afraid too,' cries another.

The White Wolf laughs. 'It takes a woman,' he says, and everybody laughs until the White Wolf stops and at once the laughter is stifled. 'Do not fear,' he says, more loudly. 'Fear is the enemy of the Flame. Remember that, my friends. Good men have no fear because they have no need of it, nor good women either.'

The honest women at the back shrink, duly chastised.

Metta squeezes in beside Raimon. 'I'm not frightened because you're here,' she says.

'Metta —'

'Ssssh! He's not finished.'

The White Wolf grips the railing. 'Good people,' he says. 'I'm speaking today because we learn that the army headed by Sir Hugh des Arcis approaches, pitting the red oriflamme of the French king against the blue of our Flame. Very soon we are to be tested.' A groan arises. The White Wolf allows it to heighten before raising his hand. At once it diminishes. 'Now, I'm aware that though Sir Hugh carries the oriflamme in full sight of his troops, many of you have never seen the Flame, the symbol of the faith you have come so nobly to defend. Well, now it is time.' He moves to the side and there is a collective gasp from the crowd. Metta claps her hands over her mouth.

And there it is, in the hands of a black-robed acolyte, the tattered box that Raimon knows so well, with the Flame burning inside. The White Wolf takes the box and strokes it. Now his whole face glitters. He holds it up. The crowd sways and utters small ejaculations of praise. Then, just as suddenly as it appeared, the Flame is being passed quickly from Perfectus to Perfectus until it vanishes back into the keep.

Like everybody else, Raimon watches it until the last moment, feeling its colour wash up behind his eyelids, into his head and through his veins. The relief at just seeing it is intense. Though it does not make things better, it reassures. He has been right to come. The Flame of the Occitan does not belong here. This is not how it must be remembered.

The spell is broken by a question, and this time the White Wolf's voice is less gentle. He has been scrutinising the crowd and is amazed by what he has seen. 'You have gained entry here, Aimery of Amouroix?' he asks. '*You?* I can hardly believe it.'

Aimery clears his throat. 'Can't a man see the light?'

'A man might see the light,' the White Wolf counters, 'but seldom such a man as you.'

There is consternation. The crowd, re-energised by their holy icon, turns threatening. Some of the knights reach for their swords. The White Wolf intervenes. 'My dear friends, please! There will be plenty of blood shed by our enemies. Let's not do their work for them.'

Aimery, however, turns nervously to Sir Roger. 'You tell him,' he says, his breathing noisier than normal, 'and tell him that Raimon Belot is here too.'

But the White Wolf's eyes have already been raking the crowd. 'Fellow Cathars! There is another false friend here. Raimon Belot, step forward if you dare.'

Metta clutches Raimon's arm and moves forward with him.

The White Wolf peers. 'I am shocked at you, Raymond de Perella, for granting sanctuary to these creatures.' His eyes glint but his voice is as placid as that of a nun telling her beads. In such a place, this calmness is a weapon beyond price. Let the crowd do the shouting.

He is not disappointed. If there was muttering before, now there is uproar, and he lets it feed on itself before holding his hand up once again. 'My good people! You are right to be outraged. But Count Aimery is right too. A man may change. Perhaps Raimon Belot has changed, so I, for one, shall welcome him without suspicion if he openly declares, before God, that he is now a true believer.'

Raimon's mouth is dry. He imagined himself lying to the White Wolf. But to swear before so many! He struggles to say even one word. Then Metta's voice rises like a flute above the growling. 'Perfectus! You have forgotten the healing power of love! Has not Raimon already declared himself by coming here with me? We are here together and surely, in the face of such a blessing, we should trust, not condemn.'

Raimon colours violently. He has done this girl such a wrong as perhaps can never be righted.

'There can be no trust at a time of war,' shouts a voice from the back. 'And this is a time of war.'

'We must trust especially at a time of war,' Metta says

warmly, and every word is a nail in Raimon's heart. 'Isn't that right, Perfectus? Without trust, nothing can be won, because without trust we end up fighting each other.'

The White Wolf's smile shows strain. 'That's true enough,' he agrees, 'but it's also true that trust still requires caution. Can Raimon Belot prove that his past is truly behind him?'

'Do you trust me?' Metta demands.

The White Wolf fixes her with a kindly gaze. 'I have no reason not to trust you.'

'Then if I tell you that Raimon Belot is wearing my father's ring, will you trust him too?'

A wrinkle appears in the White Wolf's forehead. 'Your father's ring?'

Metta seizes Raimon's hand and holds it up, twisting the ring so that the sun catches gold and gem alike. She prods her father until he puts his heavy arm round Raimon's shoulders in a gesture of public affection. 'He wears that ring as a token of love for my daughter,' the old knight says. 'He put it on willingly and before witnesses. He has not taken it off since, nor done anything at all to make me suspect that he is not a man of honour.'

At the mention of love and honour, the murmuring has lost its growl. After all, are they not all Occitanians, and have they not, evening after evening, year after year, generation after generation, nodded and sighed as the troubadours have extolled the transforming power of these twin virtues in song and verse? Love is in their blood, honour in their souls. To them, this is not idle romance: love, particularly, can shift and transform as powerfully as the sun shifts the seasons. Some knights sigh. Some touch the hands of their wives. Others remain quite still as faces, unseen for years but never forgotten, rise up and meet them in secret communion.

The White Wolf watches carefully and steps back. He does not believe Raimon but he knows better than to challenge him again – at least not without evidence of treachery. He nudges the black-clad Perfectus behind him. 'Watch him,' he says.

He begins to walk along the duckboards towards the keep but now Adela is pushing her way through. 'Perfectus! Perfectus!' she cries. 'You haven't forgotten me?'

The White Wolf's demeanour changes at once. He moves swiftly back, the wrinkle vanishing from his forehead as he holds out his arms. 'Adela! God's most faithful daughter!' Adela worms her way through and is lifted by the crowd. For a second, as Perfecti pull her over the railing, the White Wolf wonders if she will berate him for having abandoned her when he fled from Castelneuf during the fire, and to pre-empt any such embarrassment, he hugs her to him with a joyous laugh as she bends low. 'Why, there's no need for that! You're already one of the saved.' By the time he lets go, she is positively bridal. 'Get her a proper gown,' the White Wolf orders a woman Perfectus behind him. 'She belongs with us.' Adela is handed down the line like a precious parcel. Only as she nears the keep door is there a frantic cry from below. 'Adela! Daughter!' It is Sicart's last appeal. For a second, the line of Perfecti wavers, but when Adela pretends not to hear, it closes round her again.

After the last Perfecti have vanished, Aimery finds

Raimon's ear. 'Easier than we thought, eh!' he whispers as Metta walks with her father.

'Don't come near me,' Raimon warns.

'Are you joking? We must stick together. If we're to wrest the Flame from this bunch of lunatics, it's the only way.'

'You want the Flame only for yourself.'

'Not for myself, my dear Raimon, not at all for myself. The Flame will go to King Louis of France. That's where it belongs now.'

'You're not an Occitanian, Aimery.' Raimon can hardly breathe.

'And you're not a faithful lover,' Aimery replies.

That night, to Raimon's surprise, he sleeps and as he sleeps he dreams a dream he neither likes nor understands. He dreams that he and Yolanda are together, not at Castelneuf but somewhere he does not recognise. Indeed, it is not really even a place, at least not a place that a map-maker might outline, for, like an unbounded melody, this place seems to have no limits. At first he thinks the Flame is missing and this alarms him. Then he sees his mistake. The Flame is here, only instead of commanding the landscape, it has become part of it, no longer a Flame to display on a hilltop to draw men to battle, no longer a Flame of sword and fire. Rather, the Flame in his dream pulses gently with the heart beneath.

When he wakes, he dismisses the dream wholesale as a fancy for old men whose force is spent. The real Flame is a call to arms. That is the Flame Sir Parsifal brought. That is the Flame the White Wolf has stolen. That is the Flame over which he and Yolanda forged their rings. That is the Flame of the Occitan. It is not dreams he needs but opportunities. He wonders if he is growing soft. But soon this worry is subsumed under a greater worry. How can he get the Flame when he is shadowed every moment by either the White Wolf's spy or Aimery? What is more, if he has no luck before Hugh's army spreads itself round the pog, even if he does gets the Flame, how will he get it away? Yet he cannot be precipitate. He knows he will only get once chance. So dreaming gives way to fretting until, when his moment does arrive, he is almost too wound up to grasp it.

THE ATTEMPT

It comes, naturally, when he least expects it. After dinner one evening, long after the bottom door is normally shut for the night, one of the Perfecti hurries out of the keep to fetch water and, for convenience' sake, does not slam the door behind him. Raimon, playing with his dagger, stares for some time before he jolts. His Perfectus shadow is nowhere to be seen. Aimery is nearby, though. Raimon bites his lip but does not stop. Aimery be damned. He jams his dagger in his belt. Here is his opportunity and he is not going to waste it.

Except before he gets anywhere near the door, he hears a sharp, familiar tone of complaint and a high voice behind the postern gate demanding entrance so loudly and persistently that all the sleeping babies wake and begin to wail.

And there is Laila swinging past the sentries, tossing her curls, flashing scarlet lips and shouting for Aimery. Raimon stalls, holding his breath. The door is wide open, the Perfectus is nonplussed. *Go, go*, his brain tells him. Yet he cannot. If Laila is here, Yolanda could be with her. He is paralysed and by the time he realises Laila is alone, the keep door has slammed and the opportunity is lost. Sickened, he watches how she throws off the hood of her cloak, and, just by that gesture, banishes drowsiness from every husband's eyes and alarms every wife. Sir Roger's company welcome her, however, recalling with pleasure her mimes and tricks. At last there will be amusement in this dreary hole. Last stands are not nearly as exotic as they sound. Only Raimon turns his back.

Aimery is half embarrassed, half triumphant. To be pursued by a lady, even if it is Laila – perhaps especially if it is Laila – marks him out rather enviably. With only momentary irresolution, he moves over to greet her. 'Well I never,' he says, waving to de Perella that Laila belongs to him. 'You must be keen. That's quite a climb in the dark.'

She shakes the pebbles from unsuitable shoes. 'A girl can do anything if she's determined enough.' She brushes against him deliberately.

'Ah, I think you're flattering me,' he says, herding her over to where he has staked his claim. Ignoring Raimon completely, she allows herself to be commandeered and seems more than contented when her shadow and Aimery's slowly settle into one.

The courtyard stills for sleep again, with only one baby still persistently crying. Raimon huddles by the keep door kicking himself primarily, then comforting himself that at least Aimery will, in future, be too distracted to follow him about. He wonders why Laila has come now when she would not come before, then dismisses this as of no consequence.

Laila just does exactly as she pleases. Trying to discover a motive is as pointless as trying to trap mercury.

Just before dawn he becomes aware of a woman threading her way quickly over the sleeping bodies. It is the mother of the persistent baby, though she is not carrying the baby with her. Instead, she begins to hammer on the keep door. 'Somebody!' she hollers, 'Somebody! Please come. My baby is sick! Come and lay your hands upon him. Please, one of you holy men, please! I beg you.'

The courtyard stirs again, at first with sympathy and then with increasing irritation as the woman's sobs become hysterical and her banging increases in fervour. 'For God's sake,' some burst out, 'answer the wretched woman at least!'

Eventually the door opens. A Perfectus is pulling his hood up. 'Yes? Yes?'

'My baby,' she says, clutching his arm, her voice ugly with fear. 'Get the Good Book and come to my baby.'

He asks her a few questions then vanishes inside and returns with a bundle. Before he has the chance to give the door more than a random backward kick, he is seized by the woman and dragged away. The door closes but the latch does not click. Once again, Raimon is poised and this time nothing will deflect him.

Hugging the wall, his hand is on the door, then he is inside, padding down a windowless corridor boasting only a single lamp. In the gloom, he can just make out doors opening off into what he imagines are storerooms. He touches his dagger then chooses an opening halfway up the corridor, pushes the door ajar and sets himself to wait.

It is a long twenty minutes before the Perfectus returns, but Raimon is ready. When the man passes, he grabs him round the neck and pulls him inside, jamming him face down into a sack of something soft. It is darker than pitch. 'Take off your habit,' Raimon hisses. The man half folds himself up as if to refuse but a timely prick with the dagger has him pulling his black habit over his head, quite forgetting about the rope belt that has bound it round his waist. Raimon clenches the dagger between his teeth and untangles the belt so that in a few fumbling seconds the man is reduced to his undergarments and Raimon, after tying up his victim's arms, has pulled on the habit himself, wrinkling his nose at the thick, sweaty smell embedded in its coarse weave. He feels about for an empty sack, finds one and tosses it over the man, securing it, for want of anything better, with a leather bootlace. Finally, he pulls off the Perfectus's sandals and slips his own feet into them. They are warm and clammy. His toes curl. 'I'm leaving somebody with you,' he lies. 'If you scream, he knows what to do.' The Perfectus is shivering. Raimon pretends to go out, closing the door with a thump. He hears the man exhale. Then Raimon coughs. The man utters a tiny groan. Raimon slips out again, pulling up the hood and this time closing the door without any sound at all.

The passage ends in a rough stone staircase that rises a long way before bending round and giving on to another floor. Raimon peers along. All the rooms here open on to each other and silver lances of light pierce the gloom. He hears the dull clink of pewter and some subdued chatter. Early breakfast before prayer. This must be the floor on which the Perfecti eat and conduct the daily necessities of living. It is also the floor with the door that gives out on to the walkway. The Flame will not be here. He continues upwards, meeting several Perfecti coming down. But though he is conscious that his ankles stick out, for he is much taller than his prisoner, nobody at this sleepy hour looks twice at him as he pushes past, head bowed. It is at least sixty steps until the next floor and here the doors are closed. He glances up. The staircase continues to bend round to the roof. Raimon goes no further. He steps off the staircase and into the first room. Something in his belly surges. The Flame is very near, and it is waiting for him. He is sure of it.

He strides forward, knowing that he will draw far more attention to himself if he looks shifty. He already has his hand on the handle when the door is opened briskly from the other side and he comes face to face with another Perfectus. At once he draws back, murmuring an apology which is reciprocated. A long line of black-habited men files through, most also with their hoods up against the morning chill. Their sandals slap against the bare flags. 'Are you not coming down to eat, brother?' one asks him.

He turns his body slightly, as though politely waiting to join the end of the line and only when the last flick of black has vanished does he press on through another door, and another, before he knows that the next room must contain the Flame.

He does not enter immediately. Instead, he sinks into the shadows. His plan is quite simple. He will wait and slip in with another Perfectus, sitting quietly until he sees how things are. There must be no hurry and when he strikes there must be no mercy. When he has disposed of anybody in his way, he must hide the Flame in the arms of the tunic, mingle again with the other Perfecti and hope he can get out before their loss is noticed. Even if the loss is noticed quickly, with all the Perfecti dressed the same and so many not really known to each other, it will take them a little while to single him out and anything may have happened by then.

There is not long to wait before he hears the slap of sandals again and now two Perfecti approach. He lodges his dagger in his sleeve and then slides in behind them. One turns and nods a greeting. He nods back. The first man opens the door and waits politely for Raimon to enter. To his consternation, Raimon finds himself not in a room but facing blank wood only two steps away. The Perfectus slips past him and slides another door that has been cut into the panelling.

The Flame is being kept in a small room-within-a-room and its box has been set to one side so that it burns naked as a lonely swimmer in its small sea of oil. It looks so vulnerable that Raimon wants to rush to it, cover it up and protect it. But he just bows like the other Perfecti, and bows again at the Perfectus who has been keeping it company through the night. This Perfectus is motioned away but takes no notice, so the four of them sit for twenty interminable minutes before the two who came in with Raimon rise and whisper to their colleague. When they glance over at Raimon, he sinks further into his hood, as if lost in prayer. They whisper some more, but not, he senses, with any suspicions about himself. It is domestic matters they discuss. Then they leave and he cannot believe his luck. Only one Perfectus between him and the Flame.

He shuffles on his knees across the floor. There is little distance to cover and the remaining Perfectus is bowed so low he has heard nothing. Raimon does not pause. With tight economy, he draws his dagger with one hand and slams the other over the Perfectus's mouth before the man even has time to gasp. His hood flaps back, though, and in the draught the Flame flares just enough to illuminate a set of thin-skinned, corpse-like features with which Raimon is horribly familiar. 'Oh God! Adela!' The cry breaks from his lips before he can stifle it and though he does not drop the dagger, his wrist refuses to tighten for the thrust.

The girl struggles in silence, her teeth showing green between Raimon's fingers. What hair she has left hangs lifeless from her head. There is no flesh on her bones. He could break her in half. Except he cannot.

'Aren't you going to kill me, Raimon?' Her breath comes at him in small mouldy puffs. 'If you don't kill me right now, it'll be too late. The White Wolf is always here directly after breakfast. That's why I wait here. I like to pray beside him.' She chatters and chatters, louder and louder, as excited as a child on the threshold of a party. Without killing her he cannot silence her and eventually the inevitable happens. As Perfecti begin to pour in, Raimon lets go of his sister and turns to the Flame. *Help me,* he cries silently. But it is crouched over its wick, almost folded into itself. If it summoned him, it has now forgotten him. As a tide of black habits seizes him and bundles him out, Raimon feels utterly deserted and when Adela raises her arms in a victory salute, he shudders. It is no use pretending that he is not afraid.

The White Wolf's studied mildness is thinner in the keep's council chamber than when he is outside, and the unnatural light dulls his swansdown hair to gunmetal grey. Close to, his certitude carries a pitiless rather than a charismatic edge. Yet despite his pleasure at being proved right about Raimon's treachery, he is preoccupied. Perfecti are scuttling in and out like cockroaches, whispering into his ear. Something else is happening and Raimon quickly guesses what it must be. During the night, the French army must have arrived at the bottom of the pog. Montségur has woken to find the oriflamme casting its shadow upwards. The last stand is beginning.

In the fuss, an order is issued and Raimon finds himself hustled out of the chamber, first down the steps and then up again. Perhaps he is to be pitched from the top of the keep. It is a long way to fall.

To his surprise, however, he finds himself back in the room-within-a-room. Something has changed, though. A solid iron grille, its open squares too small for a man to push an arm, has been dropped over the Flame's salver. The White Wolf is taking no chances. The Flame has been completely secured. It will be the Flame of the Cathars or it will be nothing. Tightly bound, Raimon is shackled in a corner, the last Perfectus closing the door and securing the lock.

Near the Flame yet unable to rescue it, surrounded by enemies but unable to fight, his imagination running hot with terrible visions of the fates of Metta and her father if the White Wolf decides they too have deceived him, Raimon finds that quite contrary to anything he previously believed, only now does he know the true meaning of torture.

STALEMATE

I forget the date, but I can be quite exact about the month Hugh arrives at Montségur. It is in the middle of May and he fully expects to leave within weeks, with the Flame safely delivered to the king and the defiant Cathars either in chains or reduced to ashes. To be fair to Hugh, the ashes would not be his choice, but the Inquisitors who joined his forces about ten miles from Montségur are implacable. When they take the fortress, those Cathars who refuse to recant and turn Catholic, together with those who are suspected of recanting only through fear of the pyre, will burn without trial because that is the will of the king, the will of the Pope in Rome and, most importantly, the will of God.

And there must be no mistakes. Though it is never quite said, Hugh understands perfectly clearly that if anything goes wrong the blame will rest with him. He does not question this. As the holder of the king's oriflamme, he commands the highest respect, and for a man commanding the highest respect, the only way to go is down.

Yet the Inquisitors find him rather distracted. Indeed, occasionally during the journey he has hardly seemed to be listening to them at all. They wonder if he is alarmed by the possible consequences of failure.

They could not be more wrong. Hugh is a soldier on campaign and, as such, cannot help thinking first and foremost of his knights, his strategy and his goals. However, alongside the permanent nag that is the lot of a commander, the memory of his night with Yolanda plays over and over in his mind. He can still smell her skin, taste her hair, hear her voice, and he can still feel the fury of her hurt and humiliation. All these things he can bear. Though he would have preferred her consent, she is his wife. What he cannot bear is not knowing whether his brutal gamble has borne fruit or whether he has sacrificed any small affection she had for him for nothing. This preys on him. He wonders whether to send back to Castelneuf for news but then wonders whether, unbearable as it is, not knowing is in fact better than disappointment. He lives in limbo.

And soon, as if to taunt him further, he finds that just as he could not force Yolanda to love him, so he cannot force Montségur to capitulate. The place is not the least as he expected. He knew, from scouts, that the fortress was on a mountaintop and from his visits to Castelneuf how steep the approach to such mountaintops in this region could be. What he has not expected is the sheer bloody-mindedness of this particular mountain, not just the scale and unassailability of its crags and overhangs, but also the impossibility of sealing off the thickly forested, ever-expanding necklace of ridges and gullies that spreads as deeply and widely round it as the sea round an island. Those whose advice is to 'storm the fortress' have clearly no notion that this would be possible only up the south-westerly face on the path taken by Sir Roger, and that since this path can accommodate fewer than five men in a row, and unmounted men at that, such an operation would simply be providing target practice for those manning the slings in the huts above. Nevertheless, Hugh does send fifty men up, and goes up himself at their head. Nobody should accuse him of not making an attempt. Fewer than twenty return.

Yet the mountain is not impregnable, as the occasional echoing shouts of welcome from the fortress walls reveal. Every day, local Occitanians reach the top and are welcomed inside. They, of course, do not go up by the main track. Slowly and reluctantly, over many years and through many generations, the mountain has been forced to yield up the unfathomable intricacies of its jagged and many-layered wooded skirts to those living beneath its shadow. To the people of Montségur, therefore, the pog has become a kind of monstrous friend and now it proves its worth. It is not impossible for a local Occitanian to find a way to the top, it is just impossible for a foreigner.

So, unable either to storm the mountain or, with his current number of soldiers, to cut off its supplies, since even to form the thinnest circle round the pog's full spread would involve virtually every knight not just in France but in Christendom, Hugh has no option but to send for reinforcements. As he waits for them to arrive, he can only settle in for the most unsatisfactory and permeable of sieges, deploying his men as best he can. His knights are angry. They should go home, they say. It is pointless hanging around when they can do so little. It makes them look foolish.

But Hugh stamps on such talk. The French king wants the Blue Flame and the Inquisitors want the Cathars. Both are on the top of the pog which, however unlikely it seems at the moment, will sooner or later have to surrender, if not for lack of food, which their friends may carry up those hidden paths, then for lack of water, which they probably cannot, at least not in sufficient quantities. Over the summer, the fortress will surely weaken. Meanwhile, they will continue to launch occasional assaults and block all the major roads out of the valley. Scouts and spies will try to map the mountain as best they can and all villagers caught selling the Cathars food or suspected of transporting it up to the fortress will be punished severely. Bribes will be offered to local guides. This, for the moment, is the best they can do.

I shall not bore you with details. Any siege is a tedious affair. There is no glamour, only a daily grind. There is no victory, except of having got through another day. Routines very soon become established. Every morning, at the bottom of the pog, the oriflamme is hoisted on a specially lengthened golden lance from which, when the wind is up, it flaps its red tails like bloodied fingers. Every evening, from the top, the White Wolf holds the Blue Flame aloft in reply.

This reassures Hugh. So long as he can see the Flame, he has not failed, and he also begins to understand that the White Wolf, who could clearly escape with the Flame should

he so desire, has no intention of doing so. Both sides understand that this will be a fight to the death.

Moreover, though the siege hardly threatens the lives of
those camped high above, for the mapping, punishments and
bribery yield no real results, just the presence of the French
army is certainly inconvenient. The very sight of the tents,
scattered as they are, puts off at least a few potential Cathar
recruits, and to reinforce the notion of French power, at
random intervals Hugh rolls the siege engines as far up the
path as he can and batters the pog. Though the catapulted
stones come tumbling uselessly back they make an alarming
noise and a good deal of dust. Above all, it gives the soldiers
something to do.

So much for the bottom of the pog. At the top, there is
much unhappiness for Sir Roger after news of Raimon's
attempt to steal the Flame is broadcast. Metta does not rant
and rage, she grows ever more silent because even she, with
her desire to see the best in things, cannot pretend she has not
been used. That Raimon has been unsuccessful somehow
rubs salt in the wound. However, she cannot help begging the
White Wolf not to hurt him and is reassured when she is told
that he is simply being kept near the Flame so that he can be
reminded every day of his great betrayal. The White Wolf
smiles secretly at Metta's obvious relief. How little this girl
understands. Raimon's suffering could not be more acute
were he to be flogged every hour. He has failed, and conspic-
uously so, as the Flame constantly reminds him. What is
more, the White Wolf will not allow him to discard the
Cathar habit. Raimon will wear it and, eventually, be paraded

in it. An exquisite punishment, and entirely within the Cathar precepts, for no blood will be shed, at least not by the White Wolf. He can leave that to the Inquisitiors.

He reveals none of this to Metta of course, just asks if there is anything he can do for her and when she requests to have her father's ring returned, returns it himself. She breaks down as he hands it over and when he gathers her to him, she barely resists. 'Let God take your pain,' he says pointedly. '*He* will not disappoint.'

Aimery, meanwhile, whilst telling everybody who will listen that he never trusted Raimon, privately has a go at Laila. 'Had you let me be,' he tells her, 'I would have gone into the keep with him and the Flame might be mine.' He has never bothered to pretend to her that his Cathar conversion is real. She responds by arching her back and when he asks, to tease, if she is sorry now that she believed Raimon to have thrown Yolanda over, since this is clearly not the case, she just shrugs. This makes Aimery smile. Though their backgrounds could hardly be more different, how similar they are! Laila's motto in life, so it seems to him, exactly mirrors his own: look after yourself and let all others go hang. Watching her sleep, curled up in his shadow, he feels quite tender towards this unexpected soulmate.

Time passes. The Flame and the oriflamme continue to flare at each other daily, the French soldiers occasionally rushing up the path only to be beaten back by the Cathar heretics. Hugh goes out with the mapping scouts himself but the sheer complexity of the mountain's natural defences continues to work against against him, leading him on, then suddenly presenting him with giddy drops or razor edges over which he cannot pass. Sometimes, following the trail of a sheep, a proper path between the trees is discovered. But it is of no use to an army. Nevertheless, Hugh maps it and sets up an armed sentry. Until reinforcements arrive, even such a tiny victory is better than nothing.

The day reinforcements do arrive is one for rejoicing. However, the rejoicing is only momentary. The numbers sent are far too small to make the difference required. The French knights are furious. Does nobody understand the difficulties they face? Hugh sets his lips. There will be no more men. Now it is up to him.

Summer settles in and sometimes, to those both on the top of the hill and those camped around it, it seems as though Montségur is the centre of the only universe that matters. Even the birds seem stuck here. Hugh could swear that the same five bone-breakers circle endlessly round the same patch of sky. As the heat intensifies, his men abandon their armour and leave it in haphazard heaps for others to trip over. It becomes hard to blame the sentries for yawning and dozing, for Hugh finds himself yawning and dozing too. Yet this heat is their friend. With day after day of cloudless sky, water must be running short in the fortress. Without water, nobody can hold out for long. Hugh also lets it be known in the village that anybody from within the fortress who wishes to parley with him will be granted safe passage. Nobody takes up the offer, but then, so Hugh says to himself, the water has not run out quite yet. If the rain holds off, all they have to do is wait.

High above, at the top of the keep and stuck between the Flame's grille and the suffocating wooden walls, a rope-bound Raimon can only sit silently, bolt upright, eating what is thrust before him, occasionally allowed to walk round the room-within-a-room and enduring the other humiliations of the captive. Every evening, when the White Wolf collects the Flame for the display, he tells Raimon how Metta is finding comfort in Adela's company and his own. As water becomes shorter, Raimon's ration is cut, along with his food.

Time stutters to a halt. The cisterns in the fortress empty. Mothers raise cracked voices as their babies' mouths crust over. Then the sun at midday is not so hot. The leaves fade to an exhausted green. People wake in the night, suddenly wanting blankets. And miraculously, just as the fortress begins seriously to parch, the rain comes. Hugh, woken in the night as it beats his tent, curses. The Cathar praise God and watch with childish excitement as the cisterns fill.

The rain galvanises Hugh. If he is not to be here next year and the year after, he must adopt a fresh strategy. The south-western path must be widened, the trees felled and the crags flattened. It will be a huge job and both knights and soldiers will object to being turned into labourers. They will simply have to be persuaded because there can be no more waiting and hoping. By the time the following winter is through, serious progress must have been made.

From the top of the fortress, the noise of sawing, dragging and rock breaking are easily audible. The White Wolf smiles. Soon it will be time for the ultimate sacrifice. God will be preparing.

The demolition galvanises Aimery because he senses that Hugh's new determination will not flag. However, he cannot be allowed to get the Flame. It must be Aimery who takes it to Paris. Only then will the king understand that he is quite forgiven the firing of Castelneuf as its count is still far more interested in a French future than an Occitanian past. Aimery sighs. He must stop being distracted by Laila, pleasurable as that is, and choose a moment likely to be more successful than Raimon's. He makes some preparations, hiding ropes in useful places and making sure his dagger and sword are fully sharp. He watches more carefully than he finds he has done for some months.

On the morning of the first frost, Hugh launches another sortie up the hill. This is not with any hope of success, but simply to reinforce the message sent out by the road-building: that however long it takes, he will win in the end. The sortie, in military terms, is laughable and easily countered by the Cathars with their slings. However, those within the fortress recognise something different in the demeanour of the French knights. They force their horses further and behind each knight lurks an archer. The Cathars, taking French impotence for granted, carelessly descend too far and one is pinned to a tree by an arrow. He is the first Cathar casualty and his dying screams elicit a shocked silence from the fortress. When another arrow narrowly misses another Cathar, de Perella orders the stone guns that, until now, have been sitting gathering moss, to be rolled into position between the fortress's crenellations. The men manning the eastern barbican dust down their armour and wear helmets.

After this, the mood on the pog turns very sober – too sober for the White Wolf's liking. He wants no despondency, for that might lead the knights to thoughts of a truce and the White Wolf will not countenance that. Martyrdom is what God wants and the martyr's crown is what they all deserve. When the fortress falls, they must all fall with it, taking the Blue Flame with them.

He calls them together. 'Why the long faces?' he cries. 'Our brother monk is in paradise, seized by the arrow of God's love. Come now. We should be rejoicing that the autumn rains have blessed us and that the oncoming winter will see us warm behind these strong and doughty walls whilst our oppressors shiver in their draughty tents. De Perella!' Raymond de Perella appears. 'It's time we had a celebration. We've plenty of food. Let's feast and afterwards open our hearts and sing.'

He lights a spark and after a little more persuasion, the cooks make preparations. With the smell of food and the promise of heaped plates, everybody relaxes and eventually, even amongst the Perfecti, a party atmosphere prevails. Having eaten and drunk more than usual, Aimery sees two of the brothers enter the latrine shack that overhangs the curtain wall at the back of the fortress. 'Come on,' he whispers to Laila. 'Now's as good a time as any.' For all his manifold faults, nobody could accuse Aimery of cowardice.

As the singing begins, they make their way together to the latrines. Aimery has a cursory look round and then they push their way in. When they are first interrupted, and even more when they see Laila, the Perfecti are highly affronted. 'Get out! Get out!' they bark. Only when Aimery draws his sword does their bark turn into a twitter. Their hands shoot out protectively and their bowels involuntarily empty. It is not difficult for Aimery to do just what Raimon did and divest them of their habits. It is more difficult to know what to do with the men themselves. 'Shove them through the waste hole,' Laila advises. 'That's the easiest.'

Aimery hesitates. The drop on to the rocks below is immense. One of the Perfecti begins to moan and the other, losing his head, yells for help. Aimery cannot afford to hesitate further. With a murderer's mercy, he cuts their throats before pushing them into the abyss.

Laila pulls on a habit but makes a face at the sandals. She'll not wear those, though her life depended on it. She drops the hem of the habit over her own shoes, purple today, with heels. Her green eyes glint. 'What now?'

Aimery grins. 'I've been busy,' he says, and pushes over a pile of stones to reveal one of his stolen ropes. 'After we've got the Flame, we can tie this to these posts and let ourselves down until we find a ridge. The rope's long enough, provided it holds.' He covers it up again.

They both thrill to the danger, infected with a madness in which there is no room for caution. They pull up their hoods and slide out of the privy one behind the other, folding their hands inside their sleeves as is the heretic way. With the company still singing and full from the feast, nobody gives them a second glance. The only people sitting glum are Sir Roger and Metta. 'Naughty Raimon,' Aimery murmurs in Laila's ear. 'Who'd have thought a weaver could break a heart?'

Laila's eyes harden but she does not reply.

The two of them walk freely into the keep behind a cook carrying the last of a large garlic pie. Keeping their heads bowed, Aimery and Laila follow the pie up the stairs. When the cook turns on to the domestic floor, Aimery and Laila continue up. On the next floor, there are three Perfecti sitting crosslegged, surreptitiously playing dice. When they see Aimery and Laila's hooded figures, they cover the dice like guilty schoolchildren. Aimery nods curtly and both he and Laila pass through the door and then through again, finally finding themselves outside the room-within-a-room, where two more Perfecti are sitting, empty plates beside them, and half dozing.

Aimery and Laila pass round them, turn the corner and settle themselves beyond the glow of any lamps. They wait. The door to the inner room is opened from time to time as Perfecti flow in and out. Laila leans very close to Aimery. 'Why are we waiting?' she asks.

'I'm thinking what's best to do when we get inside.'

'Oh, I dare say we'll think of something.' She raises an eyebrow and begins to move.

'Laila!' But she has gone. To stay with her, Aimery must move too.

The first thing they see is the grille round the Flame. Aimery's forehead puckers. The second is a Perfectus kneeling in a corner and the third, on the far side, with his hands, as always, bound behind him, is Raimon. Gaunt now, his Cathar habit stiff with sweat and his hair shaggy as Brees's, he is as pale as Aimery is flushed.

Laila quickly joins the black robed figures processing round the Flame's table and Aimery has little choice but to do the same. The Perfecti are usually silent, but today, in deference to the White Wolf's injunction to be cheerful, they murmur to each other and occasionally laugh. As he passes within Raimon's field of vision, Aimery raises his head so that his hood kinks back a trifle. When Laila next passes, she does the same.

Raimon notices nothing at first. The third time she comes round, Laila kicks out. Raimon's head jerks up and he almost chokes. Two Perfecti glance at him but pass on and then, with most of the others, pass back out of the door. Aimery and Laila keep walking round for what seems like hours before there is just themselves and the kneeling Perfectus left. Aimery and Laila grin.

Having killed two Perfecti in cold blood, Aimery finds it easier to contemplate killing a third, but another question bothers him. Should he kill Raimon as well? That would certainly show King Louis that the Count of Amouroix knows his duty, for Raimon is the most troublesome of the king's enemies. But he is uncertain how Laila might react and anyway, first things first. He moves fast, feeling his dagger, but as he yanks back the head of the kneeling Perfectus, Raimon bangs on his restraints and yells 'No!'. Aimery glances up, then down to see a well of sunken parchment into which a pair of colourless eyes have been carved. He can see no reason to stop. It is only as the hood falls completely away that he realises the stringy neck he has just slit is a woman's. It is a second longer before he realises he has killed Adela.

He drops her at once and makes for Raimon, unsure what he is going to do. But before he can decide, Laila is there cutting Raimon's bonds and helping him to rise. Aimery pauses. Perhaps she is right. They should keep Raimon alive until they have got the Flame away. He is entirely expendable and that might be useful.

Raimon does not want to lean on Laila, for he can never forget their fight, but he cannot stand without her. He limps and stumbles towards his dying sister. 'My God, Aimery! My God!' He can find no other words. Adela is lying face down, breathing her last.

'She hated you,' Aimery says quite dispassionately, 'and she wanted martyrdom. This is better than burning.' Nevertheless, he cleans his knife with unusual vigour before sticking it away. 'Come, come,' he says, as Raimon sinks down and takes Adela in his arms. 'She'd have killed you given half the chance.'

Laila is pulling at Raimon too. 'You can't help her now. Come on. We've got to get out.'

Raimon turns Adela over. In those seconds when life has gone but death has not yet taken its cold hold surely something about her will soften. Surely something of the sister he knew as a small boy will reappear. It does not. She might have been dead for months instead of seconds. He puts her down very slowly. The White Wolf killed her before Aimery did.

Laila is now pushing as well as pulling. 'The least you can do is hurry,' she says.

He swats her away. 'I'm going nowhere without the Flame.'

'And you imagine we would?' Aimery is searching the

room. 'Don't flatter yourself that we came for you. Now, where's the key to this damnable grille?'

Raimon does not move. 'The White Wolf has it,' he says. 'He never lets it go.'

Aimery shakes the grille and tries to break the lock with his dagger. He groans with frustration. 'What shall we do?'

Laila has found the ends of candles. 'We'll light one of these.'

Raimon leans against the wall. 'Don't be so stupid. The Flame's the Flame. It's not a toy to be shared.'

'How do you know?'

'I just know.' Yet he wants to get out, away from Adela, away from the White Wolf, away from here. The feeling is so strong. He goes to the grille. The Flame is still as glass. But he will never abandon it. For all these months, it is the only thing that has sustained him. Behind its grille, with unfailing brilliance, it has shone for him, keeping alive his faith in himself, and in the Occitan, when his soul and body ached in the gloom. He may die for it, but he would also have died without it. How can he leave it?

'You know nothing.' Laila throws a candle end at Aimery. 'Go on then, Aimery, you do it.'

But he, too, hesitates. Raimon is right. This is the Blue Flame of the Occitan. It cannot be treated as a plaything. And if he cannot bring the king the real Flame, perhaps he should take nothing at all. He does not want to be hanged for a fraud.

In the end, Laila grabs a candle herself and thrusts it through the grille. 'Stop it!' Raimon and Aimery cry together.

She takes no notice. 'I'll light it if you won't,' she snorts, 'and then you can blow this old Flame out.'

Raimon rushes at her as she pushes the candle through the bars. It just fits and she blows so that the Flame, light as a moth's wing, kinks and bends and touches the wick of the stub. Raimon dares not hit Laila's arm, although that is what he wants to do, for fear of putting the Flame out altogether. His tongue cleaves to the roof of his mouth and his legs shake as if the keep itself is quaking.

'There,' Laila says, with some satisfaction as her candle catches. 'The Flame. Now let's get out of here.'

Raimon can hardly speak. 'What have you done? What *have* you done?'

Laila straightens up. 'I've lit a new Flame,' she says, irritated, 'and I'll tell you something else. If your precious Flame really is everything you Occitanians say it is, it wouldn't be stuck in an old silver saucer and a decrepit wooden box. It wouldn't be stuck anywhere. A real Flame would be just as happy on this candle as on any other, and much happier with us than flickering away behind that stupid grille or with the White Wolf waving it about like some smug archbishop.'

But though something in Raimon stirs, he cannot believe her. After all, what can she know of the Flame, she who is, in essence, little more than a gypsy trickster? He seizes the bars of the grille again, and again tries to shove his own arm in, stretching every sinew to reach the silver salver that sits just out of reach. 'I can't get it!' he cries. 'I can't get it.' He rattles the bars wildly, straining and straining. There is heavy breathing beside him. 'Look!' Aimery says, 'just look.'

The Flame in the salver is subtly changing. Slowly, the rich blue that so intoxicated Raimon when it overflowed into the Castelneuf valley seventeen months before, fades. The Flame is still lit, indeed it is still blue, but all its charisma is gone. It seems quite hollow, its cone an empty shell. This is a flame, not a Flame, and it could neither intoxicate nor comfort anybody.

Raimon exhales slowly and tiny fragments of his dream return to him: Yolanda in the valley unbound as a melody and the Flame as the pulse of the land. He gazes and gazes at the silver salver, searching for reassurance. Has Laila done right, or is this the end of everything? He receives no answer. The empty flame bends neither to him nor away from him. He longs for Yolanda. She should be here now, not Laila. He closes his eyes.

They fly open again when Laila kicks him smartly and yanks at a convenient hank of his hair. 'Leave the dead with the dead,' she advises. 'That's what I always say.' And suddenly he is hobbling away from Adela's corpse and the empty flame and running as best he can with legs stiff from lack of use, through the door and towards the stairs.

'Pull up your hood and walk!' hisses Aimery, overtaking him, and Raimon slows. 'Give me the Flame,' Aimery demands of Laila, pulling up his own hood. 'I've taken a lamp. We can put it in there. We'll just have to hope nobody stares too closely.'

Suspicious of his rescuers and uncertain about what he has witnessed, Raimon's escape from the keep is the uneasiest of journeys. Aimery and Laila are almost running and Raimon's joints creak in his effort to keep up. He knows one thing for certain: that given half the chance they will leave him behind and the Flame will vanish with them.

They see light when they turn the corner on to the bottom floor. The door at the end is open though there is a knot of people bundled round it. The White Wolf is amongst them. Raimon can hear Perfecti running down the stairs behind him. They must have found Adela's body and perhaps also noticed the changes in the flame. He wants to hurry and has to force himself not to change pace. Ahead, Aimery and Laila are doing the same. He passes under the passage lamp and drops his head right into his chest as he is jostled so close to the White Wolf that he can smell the garlic on his breath. Then, at last, he is out in the teeming courtyard. Nobody catches his collar. Nobody is yelling 'murder'. They have a moment's respite. For a second he loses sight of Aimery and Laila, then spots them and is on their heels at the privy.

Unnervingly, the shack is occupied and when the door opens and an unknown man emerges, Raimon sags with relief. Had it been Metta or Sir Roger, could he have ignored them? He thinks briefly of his father, who will have to bear Adela's death alone. Laila prods him. He follows her inside.

Aimery locks the door and they are quickly working together, securing the rope. The wide slit through which the waste falls is stinking and slimy and if the urgency were not so great, all three would hang back. As it is, the moment the rope is knotted round the bottom of the doorpost, Aimery tumbles out the end into the low-lying cloud. Holding the lantern between his teeth, he lies down, his feet to the slit and his nose wrinkled against the stench. When he has wound his legs round the rope he is ready and begins to slither backwards. His legs vanish and suddenly he is at the tipping point. One inch further and he will be swinging in the abyss. His face is blotched red with effort. He had not realised he was so heavy. His back and stomach scrape through the muck and jam against the stone. He wriggles, grunts, gasps then is gone. The lantern is the last thing to disappear.

At once, Raimon and Laila are lying down and peering. They cannot see Aimery in the mist clinging to the fortress's walls but they hear him, his curses distorted by the clenching of his teeth as he crashes against the mountainside, clinging to the rope harder than he has ever clung to anything in his life. Swing, swing, crash, crash. But always he is descending, the rope scalds on his hands a welcome price to pay. In two long minutes, he has not nearly reached the bottom of the pog but he has reached the relative safety of a narrow ledge about sixty feet below. He is only halfway down before Laila is after him. As light as Aimery is heavy, she descends, deft hand over deft hand, more monkey than human. Her grin is enormous.

Then it is Raimon's turn. He wonders if his arms will hold him and finds it hard to push off though the smell is choking him. But he can hear a swell outside. The respite is over. Adela's corpse has been found. He takes a deep, repulsive breath.

The mist is moist and sticky, and he is sliding down quickly, too quickly, the rope flaying away the skin on the inside of his legs and arms, his muscles already shrieking. He forces his fingers to tighten as the wind flaps him like a flag, now into the cloud, now clear of it. Down, down, down he goes, all his nerves and ligaments stretched and howling. He cannot hold on longer, yet he does. He reaches the ledge so fast that his bones jar.

It is solid but only about half as wide as it is long, with crumbling sides stippled with old roots, from trees that have long since been battered and broken by the weather. His legs crumple. A sheer drop of more than a hundred feet lies behind him. In front, the ledge stretches like a crooked smile for about ten feet until it gives on to a wider, rounder space, almost a little plateau on which some grass and thin birches have managed to grow, but which then narrows again to a path that jolts its way unevenly through dense undergrowth to the very bottom of the pog.

Raimon steadies his legs and glances up. The rope, relieved of its burden, is swinging wide in the gusts, slapping against the clouds that begin to dump their burden of rain as it in protest. Raimon does not care. He cannot see the top of the fortress wall and if he cannot see it, then nobody in the fortress can see him.

Aimery is standing where the ledge widens, with the lantern in one hand and the other cockily on his hip. Laila is behind him, all alert acquiescence to the man she appears to have adopted as her lord. The rain stops falling vertically and turns into a persistent sideways sheet. Raimon walks forward with the exaggerated care of a tightrope artist.

Aimery spreads his legs further apart, his Cathar disguise beginning to drip. He holds out the lantern, saying nothing.

Raimon straightens up, although he barely realised he was hunched. He is almost within touching distance of the new Flame when he sees the knife that Aimery has raised heart height. 'No further for you, I think, Raimon.'

At first, Raimon does not hear clearly, for the wind is an unceasing moan and his hood is moulding itself to his head. But the knife is clear enough. He stops. The wind beats the rain against his cheeks as his eyes flick awkwardly between the Flame and the blade. He tries to speak and then realises he will have to shout. 'You're going to kill me now? Why didn't you just cut my throat along with the others in the keep?' It is hard to keep his balance. The skirt of the habit is moulding itself to his legs making every movement an increasing struggle.

Aimery shouts back. 'Laila and I thought we might need you. Isn't that right?' He tosses the last question over his shoulder.

Laila nods and gives a small skip. 'It is,' she says, or that is what Raimon understands her as saying.

The lantern swings and Aimery shoves it at Laila, motioning her to take it to the plateau, leaving just himself, Raimon and the knife poised between heaven and hell.

A strange dance is now performed on this narrow sill. Aimery jabs out with the knife, knowing he is too far away to draw blood but hoping to make Raimon jump. Raimon cannot jump but his feet splay and he hears a few pebbles of displaced rock tumble down, down and down again, like the distant rattle of timpani. His joints, shocked almost into paralysis by this sudden and protracted activity, hardly obey him. His head swims. Everything seems unreal.

Aimery laughs softly as his face shines out of the gloaming, his beard glistening in the rain that continues to sweep over them. Raimon shakes his head and is temporarily blinded by his hair whipping back and forth. The wind cannot decide in what direction to blow.

Now Aimery is speaking. 'There's really nowhere for you to go,' he says, and moves quickly, his fist gripping the knife harder. He is smiling. Raimon raises his arms – and oh, how heavy they feel. His shoulders can barely take the strain. A thought emerges. He must free his limbs, so he crouches and with an effort he can hardly manage, pulls the black habit over his head. This was a movement Aimery had not expected. His knife spins and misses its target.

Without the habit, Raimon feels as though a skin has been removed. Yet it is certainly easier to move. He does not drop the garment. Rather, burying his fists into the black wool he holds it out like a toreador facing a bull. Aimery is again disconcerted. He loses his smile and jabs with more ferocity. Raimon raises his black shield and the point of the knife rips it down the middle. The wind bites his ears.

Aimery creeps along and in an exact mirror image, Raimon creeps back as far as he is willing to go. Another thought forces its way in his head. If he tries only to defend himself, he will die. He must attack. If he cannot shove Aimery off the ledge, he must at least push him on to the wider plateau. They must fight properly instead of teetering like acrobats on the head of a pin. He whirls his arms so that the black cloth winds more securely around them and then moves forward adopting an aggressive stance. Automatically, Aimery sets his feet wider apart, one on each slippery edge, and begins to raise his knife once more. His mistake this time is to expect Raimon to hesitate. Raimon does not. Instead, smoothly dropping his shielded fists, he punches from underneath and causes Aimery almost to lose his balance. When the knife descends, though it cuts into Raimon's shoulder, it misses his neck. Raimon forges on, for to stop is to be lost. Whilst Aimery is righting himself, he drives forward and punches again from below. This time, however, Aimery is forewarned and his knife bites deep into Raimon's collarbone. Grinning, Aimery twists the blade and as the bone snaps, Raimon staggers. He feels no pain, only a terrible weakness.

Yet the thrust also loses Aimery the advantage, for as Raimon staggers, he hooks his right leg round Aimery's left bringing them both crashing down. They are barely six inches from the drop. He hears Laila scream as he crunches Aimery's elbow against unforgiving rock and watches his fist fly open. Neither hears the knife clanging its way to the bottom of the ravine.

The rain stops suddenly as both men struggle up. Now it is just a bare-knuckle fight and now Raimon drops his cloth shield. This time it is Aimery who is hampered by his habit, and he begins to pull at it as they swipe at each other like boxers.

Raimon, his strength fading, must find a new trick. He forces himself to believe that he is fit and well and fighting on the widest, flattest surface in the world. Ignoring the blood flowing down his arm, he squares his shoulders and lunges. Aimery lunges back directly. They briefly grapple but to no effect. Both men are breathing very fast. The drop is always waiting.

Laila places the Flame on the grass and stands poised, her eyes pinned on Aimery. Every time he threatens to topple, she gives small yelps of anxiety. Both men fall to their knees and now Aimery has begun to roar. There will be no truce. They each know that. They begin to slug at each other like exhausted pugilists, slipping and sliding as the stone begins to dry. Gradually, the cloud clears and they can see rocks miles below. Raimon can no longer pretend. He is losing. 'God help me!' he cries silently, though why God should he does not know.

Aimery launches a final assault. Raimon sees it coming and suddenly crouches. Aimery, pitched over, does a complete somersault. Raimon turns in time to see him fumbling and grabbing at one of the twisted treeroots, his legs punching out into nothingness. 'Help me!' Aimery cries, although he must be able to see that his opponent can barely help himself.

Nevertheless, without hesitation, Raimon offers Aimery his hand. In this dire peril, it is unthinkable not to. Aimery grabs the hand with fingers like wire and with the super-human strength of terror, hauls himself back on to the ridge. The agony in Raimon's shoulder takes his breath away. As soon as Aimery hitches a leg up, however, he lets go of Raimon's hand and seizes his ankle, trying to repay the favour by pitching his saviour off the other side. Raimon kicks out feebly, his strength is almost gone, but it is enough for Aimery, not yet quite firmly re-established, to be forced to let go and grab another root. Still on his knees, Raimon crawls away, dragging himself towards the relative safety of the plateau. He is barely aware of reaching it and the last thing he sees is not the Flame, though this is what he seeks, but a kite hovering, hopeful of an easy dinner.

Aimery's feet are still paddling and although his forearms are stretched flat against the stone, more of his torso is off the ridge than on and the strain as he inches himself up tears his tendons. 'Laila! Help me!' he bellows. Where is the girl, damn her?

A shadow falls. Laila is above him. He gives her a lopsided grin. 'Help me up and let's finish him off.'

Laila's hand is welcome. He finds a foothold and then the small slice of rock sheers off. 'Hold tight!' he gasps but her hand slips away.

'Can't you kneel so that I can get my arm round your neck? Then I can pull myself up more easily.' He is as angrily desperate for solid ground as a drunken sailor for a steady deck.

She kneels, just too far away. 'Come on!' he shouts at her. 'You need to be quick.'

'Quick?' says Laila in a strange voice. 'I wonder if Ugly died quickly.'

Aimery almost has one leg back on the ledge but the Cathar habit he never managed to discard is caught and he has to shake it free. His legs swing again. The drop is awesome. 'Ugly? Oh, that hideous dog. What on earth made you suddenly think of her?' His legs are scrabbling and his arms cramping. 'Come closer, for God's sake.' His grip loosens. He drops an inch.

'I think of her all the time,' Laila replies without moving.

'No you don't.' His toes can find no purchase.

'Yes, I do.'

'Lean down, damn you. She was just a dog.'

'And you are just the knight who killed her.'

It takes Aimery a long second to understand the implication of Laila's words. She sits prim as prim, quite content to wait. After all, she has waited many months for this moment, some of it terrified that it would be snatched from her. Now it is here she intends to enjoy it.

Aimery tries to find the authoritative voice that will command this guttersnipe to obey him. It has vanished. The wind ruffles his hair. He thinks of Laila's clever fingertips smoothing it in the night. She can follow his every thought and deliberately twirls her corkscrew curls as if they were on a picnic.

Aimery slips a little more, grunts and with a gargantuan effort, finds more solid treeroots. His legs stop flapping. He concentrates. He can do this. As he heaves himself forward, Laila stands up and he thinks she is going to walk away, but she does not. Instead, she smiles her cat smile, then flicks her skirt and displays ankles made more shapely by the purple shoes she is thankful not to have discarded. Now she comes very close to him. He does not dare move his hands again. His chin is lodged on a stone. Laila bends gracefully, touches her own knuckles to her lips and then touches his. 'Goodbye, Aimery,' she says.

'Christ in heaven, Laila! I didn't kill your dog.' He aims the words individually, like arrows.

'You didn't care!' She tosses hers like boulders.

'And nor did you, at least not for long. My God, girl, but you're a demon.'

'Well then, I'll look forward to seeing you in hell.'

Aimery feels one treeroot loosen and his voice pulses to a shriek. 'All right, all right. I apologise for Ugly. It was my fault. I'll build a church for her. I'll ask the Pope to make her a saint. What else can I do?'

Laila smiles almost sadly. 'Nothing, Aimery. Nothing at all.' She begins to walk away.

The treeroot loosens further. 'Please, Laila. Don't go. After I've delivered the Flame, the king has promised to make me a great man at the French court. I'll marry you! You can be a great lady. The greatest. You can have castles and servants and jewels. You can have a whole pack of ugly dogs. Anything you like. Anything.'

Her hand goes to her breast, where Hugh's necklace is secreted. She keeps walking.

'*Laila!* We can have such a future together.'

She walks three more paces.

'*Laila!*'

She turns and then she is running back. 'Aimery of Amouroix! There's no need to plead. Of course I wouldn't leave you like this. What do you think I am?' The sun turns her eyes turquoise. His face is luminous with relief. 'There's only one trouble about the future, though,' she says. 'Yours is behind you.' And then, sporting her most unreadable smile, she raises her hem again, only this time Aimery has no time to admire her ankle before, taking deliberate aim, she plunges a high heel first into the back of one of his hands, then the other.

The effect is instant and dreadful. Aimery's fingers cannot

hold. The final slide is surprisingly slow which gives Laila ample time to witness the appalling contortions of his face. *It's as it should be*, she repeats to herself in her hardest voice as she braces herself for the final catastrophe. *A death for a death.*

Nevertheless, the unearthly shriek that is forced from Aimery's lungs as, at last, his back arches and his head tips into the chasm, has her cringing. She thought she would continue to look but she cannot. She tries to listen but she cannot do that either. She tries to rejoice. But in the event, all she can do is fold herself up and chant Ugly's name like a mantra until the wind has whipped Aimery's last rasping sob so carelessly from mountain top to mountain top that there is nothing left to toss into the valley.

After that Laila does not dally. Pelting back to Raimon she yanks off her habit and her shoes, for both are repulsive to her now. 'Hurry,' she urges as she rips Raimon's shirt into bandages to bind up his wounds. 'Hurry!' But he is dead to the world and it takes her an age to raise him. Even then, he has to lean so heavily against her that their progress is too slow for her liking. She pinches and hits him, sometimes with her arms, sometimes with the Flame's lantern, until the ridge and the plateau disappear as if they never were. Only then does she slow. She has had her revenge, yet instead of basking in it, she finds herself angry, furious even, that it does not taste nearly as sweet as it should.

FACE TO FACE

Days later, Raimon and Laila sit together in a clearing in another valley some way from the pog, hidden from both the fortress and Hugh's soldiers – hidden, indeed, from everybody who does not chance upon them. Laila has managed several small miracles of theft from a hamlet and a travelling pedlar, but though Raimon is now in marginally better shape, his bone does not mend and his wound festers. If only Laila had her box of tricks he could be good as new in no time but without it she can do very little. Not that she gives any indication of worrying. They sit silently because when they are not silent they argue. Laila has recounted with pride the details of Aimery's death and Raimon has not bothered to mask his shock and revulsion. 'It was inhuman, Laila. Inhuman.'

'What he did to Ugly was inhuman.'

'Ugly was a dog.'

'Don't insult dogs.'

He still seems almost unable to believe it and cannot leave

it alone. 'You flirted with him, followed him all the way here – I believe you'd even have married him – and all for that?' He shudders.

'Well, do you wish he were still alive?' This is always her final, tart defence because she knows it is impossible for Raimon to say that he does. Aimery was a schemer when he should have been a knight, a stoat when he should have been a stag. Who could mourn such a creature? Yet he was Yolanda's brother and Raimon cannot help wondering how it will look to her that he, with all his pretensions of knighthood, was there when Aimery was killed by a girl yet was too enfeebled to prevent it. Occasionally, he is aware of a fleeting shadow crossing Laila's face and this alone affords some relief. Perhaps deep in Laila's multicoloured soul there is a dirty smudge of shame. What he cannot know, of course, is that Laila's shame has nothing to do with Aimery at all and rests entirely in a necklace Raimon has never seen and she will never show him.

They cannot remain at odds, however, for Raimon depends on Laila for everything. As a respite from her, he gazes at the Flame. Its regal intensity has gentled like the face of an old king whose uncompromising certainties have been tempered by time and the experience of loss. At night, in a rising fever that Laila cannot control, he thinks he hears snatches of the Flame's Song. He wants to join in but the Song turns into a lullaby that his mother used to sing and which he once taught to Yolanda when they were sleeping under the stars. Hot and uncomfortable, one morning he blurts out, 'Where's Yolanda's ring?'

Laila does not bawl at him as he expects, but fiddles. 'I haven't got it any more,' she says finally.

'You've thrown it away!' Does this girl's heartlessness know no boundaries?

'No, of course I didn't.' She pauses. 'Yolanda has it.'

'What?' He at once suspects her of lying. 'You sent it to her?'

'No. I saw her. She came to Castelneuf.'

He is motionless. 'When?'

'Before I came here.'

'You mean she's at Castelneuf right now?'

Laila begins to plait her curls very fast. 'I've no idea where she is now. All I'm saying is that I last saw her at Castelneuf.'

Raimon tries but fails to get up. 'She let you come here alone? Why? Not so that you could kill her brother.'

'I'm not going to talk about Aimery *again* and don't be so stupid. I told her Ugly was dead but of course I didn't tell her what I was going to do about it. I just — I just told her I was coming here and she didn't try to stop me.' She is as hot as Raimon, and knows she is blustering.

Raimon says nothing until she has finished. His eyes are narrow and accusing. 'Why didn't she come with you?'

'She didn't want to. And why should she? You'd gone off with Metta Moonface. She was hardly likely to want to congratulate you.'

Raimon winces, but something still is not right. 'You came without your box and you've stayed with me although you don't even like me.'

She tries to shrug his questions away. 'What I do with my

box is my own affair. And why not stay with you? I only hated you when I thought you'd thrown Yolanda over.' Now she is angry with everybody and everything for conspiring to make her feel guilty. She is not guilty of anything! 'What does it matter anyway? It's all over now. You've got the Flame. We can go back to Yolanda. Everything's perfect.'

'Perfect? Are you mad? Perfect, with the French army battering the pog and all those people holed up in the fortress?'

'So? Let them fight each other. This isn't your war any more.'

He longs to agree. He longs to pick up the Flame, carry it back to Yolanda at Castelneuf and build a huge wall to keep the rest of the world out. But how can he? 'My father's up there, and Metta and Sir Roger. Sir Hugh's still Yolanda's husband.' He speaks slowly and pulls the Flame towards him. 'Of course it's still my war.'

'You can forget about your father, and that girl and Sir Roger. They've chosen their fates, poor ninnies.' Laila wriggles her bare toes before she adds, with studied guilelessness, 'As for Hugh still being Yolanda's husband, I don't think she thinks of him as such any more. I don't think she even likes him.'

'Is that what she said? Is that why she came home?' His face flushes.

'Why else?' Laila says grandly, and then she expands, making circles with her ankles. 'She understands everything, you know. I explained when I gave her your ring.'

'She didn't get my message?'

'What message?'

'I sent a message.'

Laila shakes her head. 'Well, it doesn't matter now, does it?'

There are two bright spots in Raimon's cheeks. 'Why didn't she come with you?'

'A girl has some pride, you know. Why should she come tearing after you? And anyway, as the wife of Hugh des Arcis, they would hardly have welcomed her into the fortress.'

'But she chose to stay with Hugh before. Why has she suddenly changed her mind?'

Laila stops twiddling her ankles. Something so obvious occurs to her she cannot imagine why she has not seen it before. She has absolutely no need to feel uncomfortable or guilty about leaving Yolanda with Hugh and taking the necklace. The truth is that she has actually done Raimon a favour. Yolanda is too soft-hearted. That's why she stayed with Hugh when he was injured. If she was ever to leave him properly, she needed to hate him, and after the night at Castelneuf, she will certainly do that. Raimon need have no fears. Never again will Yolanda think of her husband with anything other than loathing. And she, Laila, played her part! Far from feeling guilty, she should be blowing her own trumpet. Her fingers creep up her bodice. She has been far too fastidious. She can wear the necklace with pride. Yet she does not draw it out. Instead, she changes the subject. 'Where's Cador?'

Raimon answers shortly. He is still thinking of Yolanda. 'He's waiting for me.' Then he pays more attention. 'Or perhaps he's gone back to Castelneuf. So much time has passed. He may have given up hope.'

'Don't be an idiot,' Laila says. 'If you told him to wait, he'll still be waiting somewhere round here. He's like a faithful dog, that boy.'

She gets up, wanting to be busy because as sometimes happens, the echo of Aimery's howl has begun to throb again in her ears. She rattles her curls, hating Aimery even more now that he is dead than she did when he was alive. She thought she would be rid of him. Instead, he haunts her. 'I'm going on the scavenge,' she says. 'We need food and I should collect more garlic for your bandage. You're still too hot and you need to sleep better.'

Relieved to be alone, Raimon lies down. Yolanda is at Castelneuf. She has come there for him, and surely she will wait for him. If only his neck would stop throbbing. He pulls at his clothes as his temperature rises. Why are the leaves golden when surely it is still high summer? His mind begins to drift and this time when he sleeps, he dreams of nothing at all.

Laila is good at hiding and scarcely needs to do so, for the terrain, being so uneven and bulgy with rocks and so chequered with trees and bushes, some alone, some in clumps big enough to secrete an entire village, is entirely on her side. Only somebody with a real familiarity with the look and shape of the land would detect anything moving, and the russet abundance of the autumnal colours absorbs and complements her red hair. Laila still curses every time she slips and her bare feet tear, but, after the enforced inactivity with Raimon, she enjoys moving quickly, leaping and bounding, wriggling and looping. On impulse, she winds back and ventures nearer to the Montségur pog than usual, partly because she needs medicines a French knight may have in his possession and partly to see if she can find Cador. If he is still here, which she is certain he will be, he will have the horses.

She is systematic in her search. Cador will need water and shelter and would probably choose somewhere where he can see the main highway leading from this valley and back to Castelneuf. If Raimon were to appear, Cador would want to be familiar with the routine movements on their easiest and quickest route out. Now, where would she choose? Here? Or here?

Two hours later, she works her way with some difficulty to the top of a small crag overlooking an indent similar to the one in which she and Raimon are hiding, but broader and longer. Directly below her, crammed against the crag, she can just make out the stone chimney of a shepherd's thick-walled shelter. This would be perfect. And then she laughs. On the far side is one shape she does not recognise and two she does, all three cropping grass.

She has every reason to be pleased with herself. 'Hey! Galahad! Bors!' She hitches her skirts and begins to negotiate a way down, though even this takes some time, for the land conceals and reveals as it pleases and just when you think you really must have reached your goal it conceals again.

Cador is waiting when Laila finally approaches, and does not seem nearly as surprised to see her as she thinks he ought to be. In fact, his demeanour is a peculiar mixture of relief and anxious caution. 'Is Sir Raimon with you?' His first question is as predictable as Laila's evasive reply. 'Can you see him?'

He flushes. 'Have you come from the fortress?'

'I might have done.'

'Is he still inside?'

She ignores the question. Something about Cador's stance makes her wary as a hare. 'What's going on here?' she says, and advances on him with menaces. 'Is this some kind of trap?' She reverses at speed towards the horses, ready to vault on to Bors and gallop off.

Cador glances back at the hut. Another figure emerges through the wooden door, holding hard to a huge shaggy dog. 'Cador? Who are you —'

Laila leaps as though stung. 'Yolanda!'

Yolanda gives an inarticulate shout, lets go of Brees and runs straight, her arms wide. 'Laila! Laila! Oh, at last! Thank God!' She throws herself at the girl.

Laila is amazed and not a little disturbed. 'Steady!' she says, hardly knowing how to respond. Tentatively, she proffers a hug. 'You're wearing my clothes!' She pats her. 'I didn't expect to see you.'

'No,' Yolanda says, when the first tempest has died down, 'and I didn't know if you would really be here. When you disappeared, I thought Hugh — I thought — I don't know.' She takes a deep breath. 'I thought something terrible might have happened to you. Then I needed you, Laila, so I came here just hoping and hoping and I've been waiting and waiting. I didn't know what else to do or where else to go. And here you are. I knew you'd come if I thought about you hard enough.'

'So you find you can't live without me?' Laila's uneasiness makes her brittle. Yolanda looks different. Laila pales. She will not think why this might be.

'Come,' Yolanda takes her arm so that she cannot escape. 'Please.'

Cador watches as she ushers Laila inside, Brees following, his tongue hanging out. The boy has only a hazy idea about what is wrong with Yolanda. When he saw her on the road months ago, recognising not her but Brees, and, at some risk to himself, went to warn her that she would be taken by Sir Hugh's soldiers if she ventured much nearer to Montségur, she said very little. Nor, since he led her here, has she said much more, except to ask if he knows where Laila is. To start with she was so restless that every day he expected her to mount the sorrel mare and leave. But she was also constantly sick and as the time passed, though she carried on asking about Laila, she became listless and barely moved. He wanted to go for help, fearing she might die, but how could he leave her unprotected? Now, though he neither likes nor trusts Laila, his relief outweighs everything else. If she can restore Yolanda to health, he will forgive her much. He runs inside himself. 'I'm going for food,' he says and Yolanda nods.

She is sitting in the back room of the two-roomed shelter, where there are matching stone beds built into the walls, the fireplace between them. When Cador has gone, she sits down on one bed. Brees hauls himself up beside her, taking up the post he has adopted during the long, dull stretch of time that has passed. Laila glances about. Scavenged blankets, furs and food are set tidily about. Amongst the domestic clutter, she spots her box of tricks. 'Oh!' She leaps up and seizes the box, stroking it and inspecting the clasp for signs of interference. 'You've brought it with you! I've missed it!' She folds the box into her arms, instinct telling her to keep talking. *Whatever's happened it's not my fault*, she repeats endlessly to herself, feeling the necklace bump against her breast. 'Now look.' She is brisk. 'I've good news and bad. Which do you want first? I think you should have the bad because although it *is* bad, it's not so bad. I mean, it would be worse if —'

'Laila!' Yolanda is rocking, Raimon's ring and her own swinging. 'Laila! Laila!'

Laila's briskness increases. 'I'm wondering if —'

Yolanda interrupts. 'First of all, did Hugh hurt you?' She looks at Laila straight.

'Hugh?' Laila's tone is quite innocent as she gathers her wits. 'Tell me, Yolanda, how much do you remember about that night?'

'I remember arriving at home and I remember us sitting in front of the fire. I remember the wine.' Yolanda grimaces, then shudders.

Laila allows no more. She is safe. Yolanda knows nothing of Hugh's bribe. She rushes to reassure. 'But it's over, Yolanda. Here we are, and do you know something? Raimon is up the hill. Yes! Raimon! We can go and get him. In fact we must, because he's injured and needs medicines from here.' She sits down opposite Yolanda, opens the box and buries her head inside it. 'Let me see. Let me see.'

Yolanda leans over and smacks the box shut, making Laila

yelp. 'Why are you being so stupid, Laila? You, of all people. Don't you understand? I'm having Hugh's baby.' Laila cannot avoid anything now. She puts down the box. 'Help me!' It is a cry from the bottom of Yolanda's heart.

Now the necklace cuts like a dagger. 'I'll kill him,' Laila says quietly. 'I'll kill him.'

Yolanda remains seated. 'Oh, for goodness' sake. That's not the answer.' Her voice is cold.

'It would make me feel better,' Laila says.

'But how exactly would it help me? It's not Hugh who needs to vanish. It's what he's left behind.' Yolanda begins to punch her stomach with ruthless mechanical fists. 'You can do it, Laila, I know you can. You can do anything.'

'You want me to –' Laila tails off.

Yolanda stands, surging with disappointment and anger. Why is Laila being so dim? 'Do you need me to spell everything out? I want you to help me get rid of the baby.' She enunciates each word very clearly. Brees whines and glares at Laila with frustrated sorrow. 'Under this tunic of yours I'm about six months gone.' Laila kicks the stone bed. 'Is that all you've got to say? You're not normally so squeamish.'

Laila rises, her anger equal to Yolanda's. 'Have you any idea how dangerous that would be? For a start, it's much too late.'

Yolanda will not back down. 'Just give me a potion and I'll drink it. You don't need to do anything more.'

Laila shakes her head to and fro, to and fro. 'It's not that easy.'

'I never said it was easy!' Yolanda speaks with what she feels is extreme patience, 'But it's certainly possible. It has to be. I can't have this baby. Surely I don't have to explain to you why not.'

'I've seen it done in Paris. It's horrible.' Laila shudders. 'Horrible.'

Yolanda's jaw sets but her voice does not waver. 'Horrible things are done every day. You've done plenty of horrible things yourself.'

'I've never done that.'

'But you know how.' Laila bites her lip. 'You do know. And anyway, you've got enough bottles and possets and sheeps' horns full of powders in your box to kill anything.'

'You've rifled through my things! How dare you!'

'You left me and you didn't come back.'

'Hugh told me to go.'

'And since when did you do what he told you to do?'

They are both quivering now.

Yolanda cracks first. She takes Laila's hands. 'Don't you understand, Laila? Raimon mustn't see me like this. Please. You're my only hope. If you don't help me, everything will be over. Everything.'

'Yolanda —' Laila takes a deep breath.

'If you don't help me, I swear I'll do it myself. I've thought about it so often whilst I've been waiting, but I just hoped — I just hoped —'

'Yolanda,' Laila repeats.

Yolanda stares at her with a dawning contempt. She drops Laila's hands and hits her own head. 'Oh, of course! How stupid of *me*! I know what you're worried about. Well, don't be worried. I've brought money. I can pay for your services.'

Laila looks blank.

'Well,' says Yolanda sharply. 'That's what you're waiting for, isn't it? You want to know that you'll be paid?'

For the first time in her life, Laila feels something inside her crush rather than explode. 'It's not about money.'

Yolanda laughs, a wild, hard laugh. 'Oh, come on! It's always about money with you.'

'Not this time.'

'Prove it then. Do this for me.'

Laila throws back her curls. 'I don't want to.'

'Don't make me beg.'

Laila jerks. 'No, don't beg. Don't *ever* beg.' She can hear Aimery begging. She can hear Aimery howl.

Yolanda seizes her hands again. 'Then you'll do it?'

Laila wants to say no. She wants to refuse. But how can she? 'Yes, I'll do it, I'll do it,' she shouts suddenly, making Yolanda jump backwards.

'Today?' Yolanda insists.

'I'll have to get things ready.'

'Tell me that by tomorrow morning, this thing —' Yolanda jerks her head down at her stomach — 'will be gone.'

Laila can only nod. 'It may take a little time to work, but soon. Certainly by tomorrow night.'

Yolanda lets go of Laila's hands and sits down heavily. 'Thank God.'

Laila pulls her box to her. 'Don't thank him yet.'

Now Yolanda is calm again. Now she can speak of Raimon, although when Laila tells of his wounds and his fever she walks quickly from the fireplace to the stone partition and back again. 'Hurry back to him. There's no need to wait. Just give me the potion and I'll manage perfectly well on my own.'

Laila begins to pull things from her box. She fills a mortar. 'Is there water here?'

Yolanda pulls out a leather bucket. Laila talks as she works. 'Raimon does love you, you know,' she says. 'He never loved that girl I told you about. You were right. He did just want to get the Flame back.'

'I never really believed you.' Yolanda stands very close. 'Tell me what happened, only don't delay with what you're doing. Don't delay for a second.'

Lailas hands are full of phials and soon her fingers are stained. As she mixes and pounds, she restricts her story to what she considers its essentials, and tries to make sure it tallies up with what she has said to Raimon. Soon, however, she realises that it hardly matters what she says for Yolanda is not really listening. She takes a deep breath before giving her an even more highly edited account of Aimery's death. This elicits a gasp. Yolanda has to sit down. Laila works on in silence.

At last an evil-coloured liquid is swirling in a globe. 'I could go back and bring Raimon here.' Laila is suddenly filled with dread. 'Wouldn't you like him with you?'

Yolanda jerks, Aimery temporarily swept away. 'Are you mad? Don't you dare bring him and don't you dare tell him anything about this – ever.'

'You did nothing wrong. He might understand.'

Yolanda pitches her a glance of unremitting scorn and

puts out her hand for the globe. 'If you tell him, I'll never see you or speak to you again. Now, is that it?'

'It should be,' says Laila, letting go with great reluctance.

'Off you go then. Go on. Hurry.'

Laila snaps the box shut, then opens it and snaps it again.

'Go on! Go!' Yolanda puts the globe behind her as though frightened that it might be snatched back.

Laila wipes her hands, tucks her box under her arm and heads for the door. A moment later, she returns once more. 'If you decide you don't want to go through with it —'

'Why would I? Get out!'

But still Laila hangs on until, framed by the light and in a deadpan voice, she begins to recount something she swore to herself she had forgotten. Yolanda tries to push her away but Laila clings to the doorpost. Her story does not take long. 'And that's how my mother died.'

Yolanda is aghast. 'But when we were in Paris, you said your mother was a princess. You said she sold you and your sister. You said that if we passed her in the street, you would spit at her. You never said she was dead, or dead like THAT.'

'Well, that's the truth.' Laila thrusts her chin in the air.

'But why tell me now?' cries Yolanda, the globe rattling in her hand. 'I don't want to know that NOW!'

'When would you want to know then?' Laila shouts back, her face dissolving in a maelstrom of emotions, none of which she wants to feel. 'Exactly when?' Then she turns on her heel and runs, sending Cador, who has just returned, flying.

Yolanda stares after her as the boy picks himself and his booty up. He has bread and more wood for the fire. Yolanda eventually takes the fuel but motions the food away and says not a word. Disappointed and confused, Cador takes refuge with the horses and, with the rough comb he has fashioned from a branch, begins quite methodically to groom them.

Yolanda spends five minutes dissecting Laila's story. Is it true or is it not? How can she know? She feels a lurch in her stomach. *This* is true. *This* is what she does know. She holds the globe to the light. Its contents are sticky. She sniffs at the neck. There is no smell. Brees also sniffs it and turns away. Yolanda goes outside.

Cador is now hunkered down, his hair fallen over his face as he polishes Galahad's hoofs with a cloth. He looks up. 'I don't want to be disturbed,' she says. 'Will you keep guard?' Her voice is shaky at the edges. He nods. She turns to go in, then turns again. 'Thank you.' She shuts the door.

Night falls and passes. Dawn breaks. The place is silent save for the munching and sighs of the horses.

It is midday when Laila reappears, her box strapped to her back. The horses are dozing now, a crisp sun glancing off flanks shiny as a set of pewter plates. Cador lies near them, exhausted, for he remained awake all night. He sleeps deeply, as children do, with Unbent underneath him, its point sticking out below his feet. But he is not unconscious. When an adder slides silently over Unbent's tip, his eyelashes flutter. Laila is quieter than an adder. Cador sleeps on.

The girl does not know what she hopes to find in the hut but sees at once how things are. The globe is empty. Yolanda is sitting bolt upright, her face pinched and pale and her shoulders tense. For a second, she regards Laila with horror.

'You haven't brought —'

'No, of course I haven't brought Raimon. I haven't even told him you're here. He thinks I'm away finding more food. I only managed to steal a tiny bit on the way back up the hill.'

Yolanda's shoulders sink a little. 'How is he?'

'He'll live.' Laila's tone is sarcastic.

'I'm glad you're back. Why hasn't it started yet?'

Laila sits beside her. 'You feel nothing?'

'Nothing.'

Laila opens her box, slowly shakes out two more potions and pours them into a wooden bowl. 'Perhaps I didn't get the mixture quite right.'

Yolanda drums her heels with frustration but Laila takes no notice. She keeps hold of the bowl for a moment. 'Are you still sure, Yolanda? Really sure?'

Yolanda gives the bowl an angry tug, almost spilling the contents. 'Perhaps you forgot the spell last time.'

'I'm not a witch,' says Laila shortly.

'But you're a magician.'

'This isn't a magic trick.'

Yolanda is too busy gulping to answer. The taste is vile but she drinks every drop.

'Now it will start,' Laila says, throwing the bowl on the fire, 'though it still may take a few hours. It should be over by morning.'

Yolanda gives a tight nod. They wait. Occasionally the baby kicks but Yolanda resolutely takes no notice. It is towards evening when she crosses her arms hard against her stomach. Here come the cramps. After an hour, she is finding it hard not to cry out. She was braced for sharp stabs but this is a dull monotonous thud, as though two strong men are wielding mallets. Thud, thud, thud, thud, and though she is clutching her stomach, the pain is actually further back. She wants to get into a bath, feeling instinctively that heat would ease the bruising. However, even in her distress she rejoices. This is the end. This is it. After tonight, she will never think about Hugh again.

Brees whines and pushes his head under her arm. Another spasm. She tenses hard and afterwards pushes Brees away, fearing that she could hurt him. 'Tie him up outside,' she orders.

The real torture is the great racking spasms that begin far apart and then run into each other. From somewhere beneath them, she vaguely hears Laila calling her name. A covered twig is pressed between her lips and Yolanda bites down so hard that her teeth puncture the leather. Now the pain is neither mallet nor spasm. It is a serrated sword twisting in her gut.

'God alive, Laila,' she suddenly screams, dropping the twig, 'how can this be right? It's just a baby!' She sinks again, but the words bang around her head as she convulses. 'Just a baby!' Did she not once say that Raimon was 'just a weaver'? The pain changes. Now heat rises from her toes and descends from her scalp. She is certain that when it meets in the middle she will erupt like an earthquake and the baby will be ejected like a missile. She finds herself looking for it, and then, in the panting space between spasms, at her arms. They are no longer clamped round her stomach. Somehow, without her noticing, they have raised themselves. But why? She tries to force them down but nothing obeys her. She is entirely at the mercy of her body. 'I will not catch the baby,' she shouts out, absolutely convinced that it is about to hurtle into view. 'I must not.' And surely here it is, rising in front of her. It should look like Hugh. After all, she's expelling Hugh. But it just looks like a baby, any baby. No. That's not true either. Another dagger twist. Her groans are low, like an old man's. *It looks like her baby.* Suddenly the heat drains away and there is nothing in front of her. She can see no baby at all – at least nowhere except inside her head. It doesn't vanish from there.

Her teeth begin to chatter and she is freezing despite Laila piling on blankets and banking up the fire. Is that her howling she can hear? No, no, it's Brees. Or is it the baby too? *No,* she implores, *please don't let it be the baby. The baby must die but it mustn't suffer.* She can torture herself but she does not want to torture it. She grabs Laila's arm. 'Has it come? Has it come?' She cannot hear her own voice for the roaring in her ears.

Laila shakes her head.

Yolanda's spine contorts. She can feel such movement now, the movement of a thousand legs. The baby is fighting her, fighting her for its life. 'Stop! Stop!' she begs it. 'Don't fight! Just go quietly!' But it is marshalling its strength against her and she is marshalling hers against it. *'You're of the north and I'm of the south. You're French and I'm an Occitanian. Don't you see? You tie me to Hugh and I love Raimon.'* She knows her mistake at once. She should not address this child personally. But how can she help it when its face keeps appearing? It's just a baby. A baby. Her baby. Yet it is too late now. It must be too late. The baby kicks again, and this time she seems to see it opening its mouth to cry. 'No!' she shouts urgently, 'don't do that. It's too late. Don't you understand? It's too late. You're gone.' But it kicks again, and suddenly it is she who is crying.

Laila is with her, holding her shoulders. 'Don't die on me, Yolanda. Don't.'

'I don't want to die! I don't want to die. I don't want it to die.'

Laila crouches. 'You don't want it to die?' She shakes her. 'Is that what you're saying?' Cador is standing in the doorway, terrified. 'Get out! Get out!' Laila bellows at him.

Yolanda is babbling. Brees is barking and barking to be let loose. Laila cups Yolanda's face hard enough to crack her jaw. 'Listen to me. Do you want it to stop?'

'No! Yes! I don't know!' Yolanda rolls over, curling up and moaning, yanking at the blankets. 'I don't know anything. God help me!' She feels herself shoved flat back and then her head pulled up. 'Drink this,' Laila orders her, forcing open her mouth. 'Come on, Yolanda. Drink it.'

Yolanda flips her head from side to side. Laila rams the cup against her lips, brooking no refusal. Half the stuff slides down Yolanda's front and her stomach heaves to reject the rest but Laila never lets up. For an entire dreadful hour, she forces her to drink and drink and drink. Now it is Laila who is shouting prayers and imprecations at her own dark gods, for Yolanda's struggles grow fainter, until finally as dusk falls, she lies limp. There is no more to do.

Well after sunrise the following morning, Laila emerges, haggard and shaking. Cador is lugging a wooden bucket for the horses. She does not speak to him and at the sight of her, her curls flat, her hands red and her legs dragging, he drops the bucket and rushes towards the shelter. Laila is in front of him in a second. 'Don't go in there.'

'Why not?'

The question is not Cador's. He has not spoken and the effect on the boy is electric. Giving a shriek, he launches himself at the figure slowly easing down the rocks. 'Sir Raimon! Oh, Sir Raimon! I've been waiting.' He darts about, half wanting to get Unbent and half wanting to offer a shoulder to lean on.

It is the first time Raimon has ever seen Laila look frightened and that is more frightening to Raimon than anything else. 'I knew you were keeping something from me. I followed you as long as I could, then lost you, but I saw smoke and heard barking. I knew it was Brees. I just knew it.' He is struggling to hurry, the Flame in his good hand, whilst he flings the other arm out of its sling. All the wound's healing and more is ruined but he does not notice and would not care if he did. He will get into that shelter if he has to kill Laila. He holds the Flame before him as though it were a talisman.

Laila recovers herself. 'If you go in, you'll regret it.'

'If you try and stop me, *you'll* regret it.'

Raimon is at the door now, Cador cowering behind him. They both blink, seeing nothing in the sudden shadow. Raimon fumbles forward through the arch and into the back room.

The fire is burning low and he can see no movement of

any kind from the blankets heaped on the stone beds. He holds the Flame high. 'Yolanda?' There is no response. His eyes fix on the box of tricks. He lowers the Flame and hears Laila come in behind him. 'What have you done to her?'

'Only what she asked.' Laila tries to bypass him but he grabs her and thrusts her back through the arch. He does not want her here. 'Yolanda?' Still nothing, except from outside Brees's noisy unhappiness rises and rises. Raimon stands above the blankets, stares down and then grits his teeth before pulling them away.

Yolanda is lying on her back, her eyes closed. The Flame is superfluous, for her face is so white that it illuminates itself. Her lips are half open so that he can see the familiar chip in her front tooth. Round her neck are the two rings they forged by the river to cement their love. He bends down, wanting so much to touch her, but not daring. 'Is she dead?' His whisper is barely audible but Laila hears it.

'She's unconscious.'

'Is she dying?'

'Maybe. I don't know.' Laila's voice is without expression.

Raimon spins round. 'What's been happening here?'

Laila says nothing. 'Cador! Cador!' Raimon shouts. The little boy comes running. He repeats the same question.

Cador's eyes are irresistibly drawn to Yolanda. He claps his hands over his mouth. 'Lady Yolanda came,' he stammers, 'then Laila came and now you're here.'

'Yolanda came with Hugh?'

'No. She came on her own, on the sorrel horse outside. I saw her and I was waiting for you, so we came here. Sir Hugh doesn't know she's here, at least I don't think so because if he did, he'd be trying to find her.'

'Was she hurt?'

Cador hesitates.

'Was she hurt, boy? Tell me!'

'I don't think so,' poor Cador offers, 'but she was different.'

'In what way different?'

'She wouldn't really talk to me. She was like –' he struggled – 'like one of those actors you see at fairs, who paint themselves and pretend to be marble. She seemed very sick.'

Raimon tries to calm himself. 'Come, hold the Flame,' he says to Cador, and kneels down.

'That's the Flame?' This is not the reunion of which Cador dreamed. 'It doesn't look like it.' But he takes the lantern all the same.

Raimon does not explain. He still cannot touch Yolanda for fear of finding her stiff and cold. He has no idea what he would do then. He gives a long shudder, his face almost as white as hers, then suddenly, unable to bear the suspense, he seizes her hand and holds it for a long, long moment. The fingers flex. He is suddenly squeezing it very hard. 'Yolanda! Answer me!'

Only one cheek twitches, just a tiny twitch as if from a fly, but it is enough. He drops her hand and tries to pick her up. Laila darts forward. 'For goodness' sake, Raimon, you'll kill her yet.'

He barks as loudly as Brees but lies her down again. 'I'll save her from you. *What have you done?*'

Laila begins to hop from one foot to the other, tucking

Yolanda in again. In her relief she lets loose a torrent of abuse. 'So, Sir High and Mighty, what makes you think she doesn't need saving from *you* and not *me*? We wouldn't be in this mess if you'd really loved her. What sort of lover gallops off into the sunset in a huff, I'd like to know? If you'd stayed with her, none of this would ever have happened so I'll have none of this "what have you done to her" because if anybody's to blame for this mess it's certainly not me. I'm just the poor sap who's been forced to help her out of it.'

'But what's the matter with her?' Raimon is terrified. '*What is it?*'

'Nothing that need concern you. Now, get out of my way. She's not out of danger yet.' Laila berates him all the time that she fetches water and sends Cador for more water still. Now she is rough with Yolanda, pulling her away from Raimon and scrubbing her face and wrists with cold cloths. Cador holds the Flame for light until eventually Laila dries Yolanda off and goes outside to release an increasingly frantic Brees. The dog rushes in, rears up and licks and licks at his mistress's face before pulling himself completely on to the bed and settling between her inert body and the wall, his tail beating a persistent tattoo against her legs. Cador places the Flame's lantern beside Raimon and goes outside. Somebody must still stand guard and that somebody must be him.

Laila moves silently, bundling up soiled blankets and only when she is convinced that Yolanda is sleeping more peacefully does she too venture back into the sun. She takes a dozen deep breaths before beckoning to Cador. 'We'll bury these,' she says. He nods, averts his eyes and does not ask why.

Sometime in the late afternoon, Yolanda speaks. 'Did it work?'

Raimon leans over. 'Did what work?'

Yolanda's eyes fly open and her expression is not what Raimon expects. 'Where's Laila?'

'Does it matter?'

Yolanda's lips are flaky and her mouth tastes of ashes. Raimon finds an old flagon of wine. She turns her head away. 'I need Laila,' she says.

'Are you in pain?'

She considers. 'No.' She does not seem to know whether to be pleased about this or not. 'I just want Laila.'

Raimon tries not to let his hurt show. 'Why do you need her? I can get you anything you want.' He touches her forehead. 'Yolanda, your ring. I didn't –'

'I have both of them,' she murmurs, and now she turns to him. He strokes her forehead. 'The worst of whatever it is is over, I'm sure of it,' he says.

A tear slides horizontally over the bridge of her nose. Raimon wipes it away. 'What's the worst?' she whispers. 'I don't know any more.' She drops her chin on to her chest. 'I really need Laila. I need to ask her something.'

'Why Laila?' Raimon suddenly cannot bear it any longer. 'Why not ask me?'

'I can't, Raimon. Please.'

He gets up. 'I'll fetch her.' His voice is dull.

'Raimon?' He is back by her side at once. 'You got the Flame?'

'Yes,' he says, 'I got the Flame. It's here. But oh, Yolanda, the price was high.'

She moves her fingers against his and closes her eyes.

He goes outside. Laila and Cador are returning, their faces streaked black. 'She wants you,' he says to Laila.

'Yes,' she says, giving him a funny look he cannot interpret. 'I expect she does.'

He does not follow her but goes to Cador and makes much of him, allowing the little boy to return Unbent to him with formal ceremony. All the time, however, his ears are pinned for sounds from the shelter.

At last Laila comes out, and to his alarm, Yolanda is beside her, walking with difficulty. Laila settles her on a flat stone and comes, whispering, to Raimon. 'She wants you now. If you make her cry, I'll punch you.' She skips to Cador. 'Come on. Let's find the horses some new grass. This stuff's got no goodness left in it.' They disappear into the trees.

Just the fact of being together in the sun and with Brees beside them is a joy. Raimon and Yolanda lean against each other, just as they used to, except that they are no longer as they used to be, nor will be again. That part of their life is closed. Yet Yolanda can still rest her head on Raimon's shoulder and feel everything he cannot say. She can have these few moments, surely, for once she has told him what she has to tell him, they may be the last. The sun shifts quite some distance before she forces herself to move. She sits independently now, tightens every muscle and looks at him directly. 'I'm having a baby,' she says and does not know any longer if she is horrified or exultant.

Raimon flinches and then slams backwards as though somebody has physically hit him. There is a long pause.

'Hugh?' It comes out as a retort.

She nods. She knows he is trying not to look down to where the baby still lodges, despite all her efforts, and though she cannot explain the turmoil she feels, she knows she must try to help him. 'Raimon, please just listen without saying anything.'

Her injunction is unnecessary. He is mute.

'Hugh knows I can't love him,' she says, trying to keep everything unrealistically matter of fact, 'yet he wants a son. He came to Castelneuf.' Her words come more quickly. 'I will not, will never, speak of that. But he got his way. He may not have a son, of course, but he has a child. I thought to get rid of it. I asked Laila to help. She didn't want to but I more or less forced her and I wanted it to work and then I didn't and I shan't try to be rid of it again. I can't explain why I shan't, except that it has nothing to do with Hugh.' She laces her fingers.

Raimon's voice comes from far away. 'When will the baby be born?'

'January.'

'Will you go back to Hugh?'

'No.'

'What about the – the child?'

Now she trembles. 'I suppose I shall have to give it up to him. It's a des Arcis.' She wants to make everything clear, expose it all so that nothing festers in a corner.

'I hadn't thought he'd stoop so low.' Raimon's voice is nothing more than a metallic hiss.

'None of us knows how low we can go.' Yolanda puts out

a tentative hand. Her crisis has passed as Raimon's is just beginning. He does not take her hand. Instead, he gets up because he cannot stay still. The muscles of his face shift and roll. 'Raimon, stay with me.'

He avoids her eyes. 'I'm going to murder him.'

She stands as best she can. 'And if I say I don't want you to?'

'I won't believe you.'

'For God's sake, Raimon, I've tried killing. I know it's not an answer.'

'He's a common ra —'

Now she leaps. 'Don't say that word! Don't say it! Don't you think I've said it enough times for all of us?' She crunches her arms round herself, protecting herself from everybody and everything. 'Now he's just a husband I once had and the father of this baby. Can't you see? I must think of it like that because it's the only way I can survive without going mad.'

Her face is so open to him, so pleading, so trusting, that despite himself he begins to melt. Now he can take her hand. More than that, he clutches at her as he might if she were drowning or about to fall off a cliff. He wants to gather her up, to reassure her, to hold her so tightly that their skin is welded together. Then he hears Laila's laughter. She and Cador are returning with the horses. And the laughter, which has nothing to do with him, still seems to mock him, ridiculing all his cradling instincts. Before he can stop himself he draws back and Yolanda is left stranded.

Immediately, Raimon curses himself, but the moment cannot be recaptured. Yolanda's face is closing. Her hand has dropped. She is folding herself away. He backs towards Bors. 'Where are you going?' Yolanda's voice is tight.

His response is clipped. 'I told you. Hugh doesn't deserve to live.'

'And I'm telling you again. This is my business. Mine.'

His soul feels as though it will burst through his skin. 'How can you say that, Yolanda? What happens to you happens to me. Don't you understand that? And this –' he gestures to her stomach – 'is just –' he struggles – 'not us. It's nothing to us. *It's nothing to do with us at all.*'

She moves towards him, but is frightened to open herself up again. Doesn't *he* understand? Never has she felt so raw and muddled. She loves this man with all her heart. He is her. She is him. Yet though she resents this thing inside her with every fibre of her being, there is no denying that it is part of her too. Not part of Hugh. Part of *her*. She claps her hands to her head. She longs to be at Castelneuf, somewhere that's theirs, so that Raimon can feel what she cannot explain. Then she sinks. It is impossible now that Raimon will ever come to Castelneuf again. How can he, knowing what Hugh has done there?

She feels Raimon's gaze on her, repulsed by her, as though she has some huge blemish running from her head to her toes. Though he may not mean to, he is making her feel dirty when she was just starting to feel clean. In a last effort, she breaks the thong round her neck. 'Here. Your ring.'

He scrapes out some kind of sound. He wants that battered black circle so badly. It seems to him that the best of his life is soldered into it. But even as he extends his hand, Hugh's child intervenes. *Yolanda was to be yours completely*, the child crows. *Now a bit of her will never be yours, and if you can't have all of her, do you really want any?*

He hesitates and then it is too late. Yolanda slowly withdraws the rings, although even now she cannot help making one last, punishing effort. 'Raimon, listen! Listen to how lucky we are. We have each other. We have the Flame. We can leave this place to Hugh and the White Wolf and find another home for ourselves. We can build a new Castelneuf, a new Occitan even. Let's go back to the Amouroix. It's where the Flame belongs and where we belong. I'm ready! Aren't you? We can go together.'

She has a magnificence about her, yet Laila's laugh and the child's imaginary crowing are still a barbed barrier between them.

'I'm going for Hugh,' he says, choking. 'Don't deny me that, Yolanda.'

She breaks down suddenly and shockingly. 'I deny you nothing,' she cries, flinging out a final appeal she does not want to have to make, 'and I'm offering you everything. Can't you take it?'

'How can I take something that's already taken?' It is half an agonised whisper, half the roar of a wounded bull. Raimon rushes passed her. He vaults on to Bors and, stopping only to sweep up the Flame, thunders out of the valley with Cador on Galahad behind him.

Sometime later, an errant gust of wind swings the door of the shelter wide. It swings so hard that its hinges twist, but nobody rushes to secure it because there is no longer anybody there.

SILENCE

The first Cathar casualty, on the day that, unbeknownst to those either in the fortress or below, Aimery meets his Maker, together with the impetus of the road widening, marks a turning point in the French fortunes at Montségur. They are no longer despondent. The labour is hard, but there are fewer complaints from the knights about being used as workhorses. The Cathars are not invulnerable and though it may take some time, the French can at least now see a time when this siege will end and they will be able to go home. As Hugh predicted, however, progress is slow. Every inch gained from the pog is backbreaking. With the onset of winter, progress will be even slower. However, as he reminds the knights and soldiers on a daily basis, now that they are taking decisive action, sometime in the spring the king will get the Flame and the Occitan will be part of the French kingdom. One great remaining irritation is that the villagers continue to grow fat on the proceeds of the Cathar trade they ply up paths that Hugh will never discover. 'How much money do you suppose is salted away up there?' some of the knights ask him, staring up at the fortress hungrily, imagining a fountain of treasure. 'The only treasure we are commissioned to secure is the Blue Flame,' Hugh always repeats in his most curt military tones to cut off further comment.

He has aged during this deeply unsatisfactory campaign. He sleeps badly and though he has charts and maps and plans to keep him more than fully occupied, finds himself permanently counting off the months. Any possible baby must be due in the New Year. The New Year! He will still be here then. Of that he is sure. And afterwards? Will he be lauded by the king for a fine achievement or disgraced because it has taken so long? Will he remain the keeper of the oriflamme or find himself the ex-lord of Arcis? Stuck here, he has no idea about either Yolanda's condition or the French king's mood and no way of finding out. He finds this burden frustrating. He begins to count the days, cutting notches in his tent pole. *I'm counting for nothing*, he tells himself, but carries on doing it.

Raimon, too, is frustrated. He does not want to kill Hugh surreptitiously, like a thief in the night. He will settle for nothing less than single combat, sword against sword, knight against knight. He will fight Sir Hugh des Arcis as Sir Raimon de Maurand, as Sir Parsifal would wish, not as weaver Raimon Belot. He cannot do this today or even tomorrow because he will only get once chance, and to maximise that chance his collarbone and wounds must be properly mended and he must be properly fit. So he spies, reassures himself that the siege is unlikely to be over before the winter has blown itself out, and forces himself to bide his time.

Parted from Laila and her box of tricks, Cador has to add the role of doctor to that of squire, groom and forager. On Raimon's instructions he binds his master's shoulder tighter and tighter, as if the bones can be forced to knit together. Hunched round the fire that provides some protection against the encroaching frosts, Raimon turns the lantern this way and that. The Flame is still small and, when its colour is not disguised with leaves in a trick Cador learned from Sir Parsifal, its blue still intense and rich. Yet often, hardly realising what they are doing, both Raimon and Cador use it as a real lantern, even carrying it on the end of a pole. Once, this would have felt disrespectful, like using the Bible as a mudscraper. Now it seems natural, as though the Flame has become part of them rather than apart from them.

But as Raimon waits for his body to heal he cannot accept the kindly comfort it offers. Consumed by an isolating anger – at Hugh, at himself, at the circumstances in which they find themselves – in the Flame's homely glow he can see nothing but a future that has been snatched from him. It is unfortunate too, though unsurprising, that Cador's ministrations make Raimon's wound worse, not better. Had Raimon been in the best of health, things might have been different. But weakened from his lengthy captivity and in worsening weather, his condition deteriorates. This adds to the daily bitterness. Yet when, sometime after Christmas, an unhappy and frightened Cador suggests going to find Laila again, or if not her, somebody with some knowledge of medicine, he receives a curt rebuff. The wound *will* heal. They only have to wait a little longer.

In the end, when it becomes clear even to Raimon that waiting is not enough, and after Cador asks directly what he must do with the Flame if Raimon dies, something finally breaks. Is he really, through his obstinacy, going to condemn this faithful boy to wander alone with the Flame as Sir Parsifal once did? When Cador goes for food, he sits with the Flame a long time, never looking away as it burns steady as a father's eye. Three days later, he bids Cador bridle the horses. He knows what he must do.

They return to the shepherd's hut in a February snow-storm and when they find it empty, head without further discussion towards Castelneuf, the lantern lighting their way and the horses' hoofs padding noiselessly in the deepening white. Cador gives up ministering to the wound which, left to breathe, finally begins to settle itself. The days are uneventful and as the pain begins to ease, Raimon finds himself less tense. Now he tries to face the future as it is. Yolanda will give birth to the child. He must accept that. But once it is born? He stiffens again. It must already be born. Well then, now it is born it will be a separate thing from her, and anything separate can be removed. Did not Yolanda herself say that Hugh would claim it? Perhaps it is already on its way to the des Arcis château and, once there, they need never refer to it again.

And if she still has it? Even that is not a disaster, for she will know, just as he does, that no des Arcis child can ever live at Castelneuf. In his wilder moments, he imagines somehow giving the baby to Metta when the siege is over, for even Hugh will surely not allow the women and children to burn. As the horses eat up the miles, he feels he was foolish to despair. This thing need not hang over them for ever. With the child miles away and Hugh killed in the single combat Raimon will shortly be demanding, that will be the end of it. And if Hugh kills him instead? Raimon does not countenance that thought.

As they reach my boundaries the journey for Raimon becomes a journey of memories. Though snow had fallen, everything seems blue-lit as the Flame guides them over the mountain where Aimery once went to kill a bear and nearly killed Raimon instead, and illuminates the familiar outline of the high plateau on which Raimon was himself besieged. Yet how quickly nature reclaims her own! There is no evidence of those hard months now. It is as if they never were. Raimon rides on. Only when the Flame floods the opening of the cave in which Yolanda once, blindly and unforgettably, traced the contours of his face with her fingers in the dark, does he stop. The memory of her touch is so strong that he puts up his own fingers as if to catch hers before they slip away.

They arrive in the Castelneuf valley in a chill, windless dusk, with the château's lights shining honey-coloured through the pearly gloom. As they ride up the road down which Raimon sledged with Metta, both he and Cador are aware that the town, though not empty, lacks all those cheerful, thriving sounds through which it once sang. Raimon touches the lantern. He has the Flame whose advent brought both hope and dereliction. Now it must be the key to restoring life in this place, which had such life before.

He slips off Bors round the side of the château walls, near to where, in his childhood, there had always been a hole. After the old count's death, Aimery had had it stopped up. Raimon has not forgotten, but hole or no hole, he knows this bit of wall well and wants to enter unnoticed. Cador is horrified. 'You can't climb with your arm in that state!'

'No, but you can. We'll get you in and there'll be at least one horse in the stable — that sorrel that Yolanda was riding. She knows you. Bring her out and tie a rope round her neck. She can haul me over. Then you wait with her in the stable.'

'What are you going to do?'

'I'm going to do what has to be done.'

'I want to come with you. You're not strong enough to wield Unbent. A squire has his duties.'

'And one of them is to do as he's told.'

Twenty painful minutes later, with the roan returned to the stables, its absence unmissed, and scuffing their footprints as best they can, Raimon is standing at the bottom of the keep steps with the lantern in his hand. The hounds begin to sing but nobody appears to take much notice. Their song tilts from warning to greeting as they realise that their visitor is no enemy. Raimon loves them for that.

He secretes the lantern behind his back and climbs swiftly up the steps to the great hall, still half roofless and quite empty. It feels a long time since it rang with the sounds of hammer and mallet. A different time entirely. He will not think of that time. Instead, he knocks the snow from his boots and silently makes his way through to the small hall. There he stops short. Laila is standing with her back to him, slightly bent over, preoccupied because overburdened. She has not heard him and without thinking he edges backwards into the shadows. He wants nothing to do with Laila. He must see Yolanda alone. The girl puts something down – her box, so it turns out – and leaves the room.

At once Raimon pitches forward, sets down the lantern and fumbles with the box's catch. He gives a wry smile. The inside is crammed full of tinted bottles and oddly shaped stones, old teeth, thin straggles of hair tied in ribbon, various dented coins, an amputated finger, endless phials of hair dye and, lined up like autumn leaves, elegant, pointed pouches fashioned from goats' ears. Holding the Flame closer, he rummages underneath until, next to a bone jar marked 'poison', he finds the small sheep's horn filled with wound salve. He takes it. Cador will be pleased. He replaces everything else very carefully. Laila will notice but he does not care. He hears her returning, closes the box and retreats.

Outside in the courtyard again, he collects Cador and hurries him up the steps into the old pigeon loft. The steps are slimy with disuse and they find nothing but the desiccated remains of those birds who waited too long for food that never came. Everything of Aimery's has turned to dust. What sympathy Raimon feels is restricted to the birds.

The following morning is crisp and cloudless and the sun is blinding on the snow. Raimon, his shoulder plastered with salve, stretches. Despite everything, he has slept well and this seems a good sign. His shoulder takes longer than usual to resume its normal throbbing. He is not going to die of his wound, at least.

Both he and Cador are relieved when the hounds are let out, for they will scuff any remaining tracks, although they also worry that they may show some interest in the loft. But the loft is tame when what you long for is a chase with the promise of blood. The older hounds pad directly to the gate and sit, their sterns swaying in expectant hope. The young ones, having larked around for a few minutes, slither after them and sing until the air pulsates.

Then there is different barking, and down the great hall steps bounds Brees. He glances at the pigeon loft and his tail momentarily pauses mid-wag. However, scent is not carrying today and when the dogboys, also released from the kennels, tumble about, his tail resumes its thumping and, with more joyful barks, he tumbles with them. Gui and Guerau are suddenly outside too, shouting for quiet. The reason is soon apparent. Helped by a crimson-curled Laila, Yolanda emerges. She is carrying a bundle.

Raimon's every nerve crackles, every fibre of his being focused on the bundle which he has thought about for so long but never, so it seems to him now, really visualised. Here it is. Beneath those blankets Hugh's child is. Of course it will be a son. Raimon knows that instinctively. What Hugh wanted Hugh has got. Raimon finds he is shaking.

Yolanda holds her bundle awkwardly. She is very white apart from her eyes. They are huge black holes. Laila hovers over her. There is something so unusual – no, more than unusual, downright odd – about seeing Laila so tender that

Raimon's stomach pitches and rises in his ribs. He leans forward as Yolanda begins to walk towards the mounting block and sits down. She still stares straight ahead, deaf to whatever it is Laila is saying, and Raimon's stomach rises further, filled with something akin to triumph. Yolanda sits too still for joy, too still for care. The baby is dead. He wants to punch the air. There is a God.

He begins to move, unable to stop himself, until he hears Cador's warning exclamation. He looks again, and now there is something — Raimon cannot see what — but some kind of movement from the bundle. His stomach sinks like a stone. The baby is not dead. Indeed, it is very much alive and it is wriggling. Yolanda is suddenly alive too and begins to adjust the blankets. A tiny fist shoots out and she folds it back in. Raimon watches as a hawk watches a rabbit. But it is not the care she takes that sends all his insides and not just his stomach crashing like a dying horse: it is the way her neck is curved. Such a tiny curve, but so revelatory, for it is not the curve of somebody performing a chore for an unwanted monstrosity. The curve flows down Yolanda's whole body forming a perfect arc of love and protection. When she raises her face again, even from this distance he can see, shining through the exhaustion and the memory of pain, an awkward wonder, quite new and clearly not altogether welcome, but so strong that she cannot help but accept and submit to it.

That night, Raimon enters the keep again. With the Flame held before him, he goes up the stairs quietly and this time opens the door to the small hall without pausing even to listen. Yolanda is lying in a bed that has been pulled near to the hearth, with Laila in a smaller cot slightly to the side. Brees shoots up, but Yolanda does not move and Raimon pacifies the dog until he settles back, head on paws.

Then, ignoring Laila, Raimon gazes down. Yolanda is fast asleep, one arm thrown up, one leg half hanging out of the blankets, her hair a bird's nest and her mouth slightly open. She is exactly the girl he has always known except that in a wooden crib next to her is a creature whose life, he understands now without a shadow of a doubt, she would choose over his not because she wants to, but because she would not be able to help herself.

He puts the Flame on the floor, unable to stop himself imagining the night Hugh came here, to this very room, and though he has not really meant to, he picks the child up. He is rough. The baby's eyes open and they contemplate each other, himself and Hugh's son. How easy, Raimon thinks, to dash the soft skull against the hearthstone. How easy to stamp on this unwanted creature and bury it. How easy and how impossible, because unwanted does not mean unloved. Raimon wants both to laugh and to cry because this tiny, dribbling infant has won a battle it is not even aware of fighting.

He returns the child to its cradle. He had thought to speak to Yolanda, but what can he say? He tries to construct a few phrases. No words come. But they will, of that he is sure, only not here and not to Yolanda. Everything he has to say will go into his challenge to Hugh. Nothing is over yet. By depriving this baby of its father and Hugh of the chance to see his son, Raimon will have his revenge.

He holds the Flame above Yolanda, leaving the baby in darkness. With the tip of his index finger, he traces her face, gently tidying her hair. The two leather rings, back on their thong, are nestled in the small indent at the bottom of her neck. He places the lantern on the table, pressing his thumb against the hot glass as a man presses a branding iron against a cow. He does not wince at the pain. He rejoices in the mark. Then he leans over. He wants so badly to wear his ring but cannot bring himself to take it. As long as it remains with her, he can believe that he is with her. 'I leave you the Flame that burns for the Occitan, the Amouroix and for love,' he breathes. She sighs. He holds his breath. She sleeps on. He breathes again. 'But love is the most important and oh, Yolanda,' he touches her lips, 'how I've loved you.'

Only then is he aware again of Laila, limbs taut and ready to spring. They observe each other for a whole minute before, with a murmur, Yolanda rolls over and Raimon has, from somewhere, to find the strength to tear himself away.

THE CHALLENGE

By the end of February, morale amongst the French besiegers has sunk again. The winter has stretched out like a long penance with the wet now joining the cold. Progress on the road construction is, some days, impossible. Men are injured by falling stones. They squabble about digging rotas and declare the whole project misconceived. Who can blame them? The skin between their toes cracks in boots that are never dry. Fingers are painfully raw. Armour is rusting, noses run and though Hugh insists they still respond with a thrust of the oriflamme when the White Wolf holds up a flame he does not, or will not, realise is empty, they do so in dispirited silence. Even the threats of the Inquisitors, who have now taken it upon themselves to harangue them, in God's name, whenever they threaten to desert, go unheeded.

Only one thing keeps them going and it is the thought that up in the fortress the Cathars too must be tiring, for Hugh, with a mixture of persistent bribery and the threat of brutality, has had some success in cutting off their supplies.

Now the villagers sell to the French. At least that means the food is better and every mouthful a Frenchman eats is a mouthful less for the heretics.

If they could see inside the fortress, they would be more heartened still, for shortage of fresh vegetables has brought disease. It would not be so bad if the Cathars could bury the bodies, but there is nowhere to do that so they must tip them unceremoniously over the walls. To see loved ones dispatched like this saps the soul. Sicart is amongst the dead, though never having recovered from seeing Adela's stiff, spidery frame being carried shoulder-high along the walkway on the day Raimon escaped, he is happy to go.

Left to himself, and despite all the 'last stand' rhetoric, Raymond de Perella might have tried to come to an accommodation with Hugh. He knows as well as Hugh does that despite the current halt, the spring will bring renewed vigour in the road building, and though those Cathars still strong and able-bodied could slip away down the hidden paths, the weak and sick could not and it is unthinkable to leave them behind. Everything, therefore, points to a truce. However, de Perella is no longer master of this fortress. The more desperate their position becomes, the stronger runs the White Wolf's writ. Reinforced by the 'Flame', without which he is now seldom seen, this most ardent of Perfecti encourages, cajoles and inspires. Though there are corpses stacked, he somehow keeps the Cathars believing that God is in the fortress with them and will not desert them. He never tells them that God will smite their enemies. They must not expect such an ordinary miracle. The miracle is that their sacrifice, even unto death, is a victory beyond price, a heavenly victory, a victory for which God will shower them with praise and reward when they meet him face to face.

Sir Roger and Metta are amongst those listening. In the brouhaha following the murder of Adela and the disappearance of Raimon, Aimery and Laila, they were hauled into the keep and questioned with threats. Sir Roger roundly and furiously condemned Raimon. Metta tearfully defended him. In the end, however, the White Wolf had a Bible brought. 'What has happened is an abomination,' he said. 'I shall not forget that, but we have a great struggle ahead and it is not good if we are divided amongst ourselves. So, Sir Roger, we will gather the brethren together and you will publicly swear, and your daughter too, that you have not and will never betray the Cathar cause.'

Sir Roger had been outraged. That he and Metta, stalwart Occitanians and lifelong Cathars, should have to swear loyalty is beyond insulting. But when the Bible, heavy in its wooden jacket, was laid on a table, both father and daughter repeated the words they were told to repeat. What else was there to do? Metta simply seemed glad to end the matter, though she is not unscarred. There is a stoop in her shoulders that was never there before and when the White Wolf comforts and instructs her, she listens to him without demur.

The real beginning of the actual end comes through a combination of five consecutive days of better weather and a piece of luck. Handing out bribes in the village, Hugh is approached by three men from the Basque country who volunteer, for a triple fee, to lead a small group of Hugh's best climbers up to the eastern barbican. The path is so sheer and precipitous that they suggest the climb should take place at night to prevent disabling fear and dizziness. Climbing in the dark will have its own dangers, but also advantages. The heretics in the barbican will be taken so completely by surprise that if the French are clever, they might take possession of it before the rest of the fortress even realises what has happened.

Hugh rejects the offer outright. To pay for the privilege of sending his men straight into a death trap seems an unlikely strategy for victory. The Basques do not argue, they just begin to load their donkeys. This is not their war. They seek only money and if it is not forthcoming here, there will be other opportunities. Hugh watches, and after they have moved out, sends men to usher them off the road and to his council tent where he makes them repeat their offer in front of witnesses. There is disagreement amongst his knights as to the trust-worthiness of these unlikely allies, but eventually ten men volunteer to climb.

The night passes slowly. Hugh paces about and at dawn, as work resumes on the road, strains his eyes upwards. He sees nothing at first. It is only as the sun breaks through that he gives a long, low whoop. From the top of the barbican, Cathar blue has given way to des Arcis yellow and crimson.

Now French spirits soar. They redouble their efforts on the road, but there is hardly any need, for not only can they now turn the barbican's stone guns on to the Cathars without any danger to themselves, but the villagers finally agree to send nothing more up to the fortress. The Cathars inside it are on their own.

Hugh waits for an emissary. Surely now the heretics will give up, for though they are still defended on three sides, the fall of the barbican is a fatal breach. At first, no message comes. Instead, the White Wolf's empty flame is thrust higher and higher. But Hugh is patient and eventually, as the French manning the barbican's stone gun deal out death inside the fortress with monotonous thumps, de Perella, unable to bear the screams of the women and children any longer, crawls between the corpses and holds up a grimy cloth that was once white. Hugh's men peer at him. After what seems like an age, a knight shouts. At last, the bombardment stops and despite the White Wolf, negotiations begin.

In all the excitement, not much notice is taken in the French camp of a lone rider in the early morning with only a squire in tow. Though Raimon feels for Unbent, he and Cador ride through unmolested. Once in the main camp, however, Amalric and Henri recognise the horses. 'Whoa there! Bors? Galahad?' Their reins are seized as Henri peers at Raimon with peeved surprise. 'We thought you were up there with them.'

'I want to see Sir Hugh,' Raimon says.

'In irons is the only way he wants you.' They drag Raimon from the saddle.

'I demand to see Sir Hugh.' And there is Hugh in front of him, not seeing him for a moment because he is reading. Even when he looks up, his gaze is quite uncomprehending. Then he starts. 'You! Have you come from the fortress?'

'I want to speak to you.'

'Is it about this?' Hugh brandishes the parchment. 'Have

they sent you to negotiate in person? A strange choice, if you don't mind my saying so.'

'I'm throwing down a challenge.'

'A challenge?' Hugh's lips twitch. 'To me? Here? Now?' He raises his eyebrows suddenly. 'Oh, I see. Is it de Perella's idea that the fate of the Occitan should be decided in some kind of spectacle? You and I with the Flame between us?'

'No,' Raimon says, his blood boiling at Hugh's mocking tone. 'My challenge is nothing to do with the fortress or even the Flame. It's to do with Yolanda.'

Hugh involuntarily crushes the message. 'You've seen her? How?' Then, in dread, 'She's not up there, is she?'

Raimon stands like a mutineer. He will tell Hugh nothing. Amalric administers a hefty slap across the face, which Raimon receives unflinching. Hugh scrutinises him. 'Come,' he says at last, his mocking tone vanished.

Raimon hesitates, conscious of Cador's danger.

'See that this boy and the horses are safe and fed,' Hugh orders a passing squire. 'Come,' he repeats, and when Amalric and Henri move to flank him, gestures them away. 'I can defend myself,' he says, 'and rest assured, I won't hesitate.'

They pass by the oriflamme. The air is too still for it to flap, so it hangs, a dew-drenched, heavy threat, its red tails stained and tattered. Against the memory of the Flame's small, fresh vigour, the banner of France soiled and worn out. Raimon regards it with contempt.

He ducks his head beneath a tasselled awning. Hugh's belongings are neatly stored, with his good armour still laid in its chests and covered with an oil cloth, his long, two-handed sword gleaming on top. Raimon is suddenly glad that before they entered the camp he had Cador cut his hair and clean his boots. He does not want to feel like a vagabond.

'A challenge,' remarks Hugh, tracking Raimon's every move. 'It's a while since I've had one of those.' He may no longer be mocking but he never forgets that he is a French knight, the keeper of the king's oriflamme, and that Raimon is a weaver's son. If Raimon wants to meet him on equal terms, he must earn the right. Yet Raimon is also possessed of one great advantage. He already knows what Hugh longs to know.

'I've come to kill you,' Raimon blurts out.

Hugh sets his legs a little wider. His eyes bore harder into Raimon's. 'She's had a baby,' he says very slowly. 'That's it, isn't it? She's had my baby and it's a boy.' He cannot control the leaping of his heart.

Raimon will stamp on that leap. 'She was having *a* baby but she got rid of it.' He spits the lie straight out.

But Hugh is already shaking his head. 'Don't take me for a fool, Raimon. If she'd got rid of the child you wouldn't be here because she'd never have told you. Do you think she would risk you doing just what you're doing now and losing your life as a consequence? You see, she may not love me but I know her just as well as you do.' Without thinking, he smoothes and folds the parchment again and again.

Raimon is telling himself all the while to keep calm, that losing control will get him nowhere, but his fury rocks him. 'You forced her. She was unprotected and you just took her like an animal. You claim to be a knight? Why, you're nothing but a common criminal.' Abandoning his knightly challenge, he throws off Unbent and springs forward like a market-place boxer. Never mind sword thrusts and parries, he will grind every ounce of Hugh's flesh and every hair of his head into the dirt.

The parchment flies into the air as they wrestle, muscle against muscle, bone against bone. More heavily built and less blindly livid, Hugh pins Raimon against the armour chest, strong and triumphant. 'You'll have to do better than this, my friend.'

'I'll murder you! I'll murder you!' Raimon bellows.

Hugh gives him one last shove and then lets him go. Raimon rushes for Unbent but Hugh does not pick up his own sword. Instead, he retrieves the parchment and holds it out like a shield. 'Can you read?'

Raimon raises Unbent.

Hugh searches for something. 'Metta,' he says suddenly. 'Isn't that her name?'

Raimon is stopped in his tracks.

Hugh straightens the parchment and motions to it.

Raimon hesitates, then snatches it. He cannot make out the words at first for his eyes are hazy with hate. Suspecting Hugh of a trick, his gaze keeps darting from parchment to Hugh and back. Eventually Hugh retreats and when Raimon looks properly, he can see that what he holds is a treaty. He frowns. Hugh is motionless. Raimon lowers Unbent and reads.

The words are quite clear. The Blue Flame of the Occitan is to be handed over to Hugh, the keeper of the oriflamme. Then, all the knights in the fortress will be spared if they give up being Cathars and Occitanians and instead embrace Catholicism and swear allegiance to King Louis. This they must do in front of witnesses and any who refuse will burn. After that, the fortress of Montségur will pass to the French crown. As for the Perfecti, they must give themselves over to Hugh, who will pass them on to the Inquisitors as he sees fit.

Raimon's whole self tightens with revulsion at the humiliation for the Occitanian knights. He begins to raise Unbent again. 'What's this to do with Metta? You're surely not going to burn the women and children.'

Hugh feels for a stool and sits down, his sword within reach. He cannot suppress the joy the thought of his child gives him, but he tries to keep his voice grave. 'Listen to me. The Perfecti holed up in the fortress are as determined as any Inquisitor. The White Wolf seeks the martyr's flames not just for himself but for them all. I cannot save the women if they won't save themselves.' He pauses. 'Don't you also have a sister? And then there's Aimery.'

Raimon is trembling. 'They're both dead.'

'Aimery's dead?' Hugh exhales hard. He seems to forget Raimon for a moment. 'How?' Raimon says nothing. 'May God have mercy on his soul.' Then Hugh is brisk again. 'Listen to me. I'm in charge here and as long as I'm in command, I can make sure the terms of the treaty are upheld.' Raimon makes a disparaging sound. 'Don't be a fool, Raimon. Don't you understand? This treaty is the best the Cathars can hope for. Better than the best. Don't you realise that there are people within my own camp who want everybody in the fortress to burn whether they recant and swear allegiance to the king or not? But de Perella has sent a message that he will not sign it.'

Raimon is groaning inside. He already anticipates what is coming. Hugh shakes the parchment. 'This may be your last challenge – apart,' he adds drily, 'from your challenge to me.'

Raimon grips Unbent again, but Hugh has been clever. The thought of Metta burning undermines Raimon's single-minded focus on Yolanda. He cannot just pretend he never knew her.

Hugh scrutinises him. 'And you still want the Blue Flame, don't you?'

Here is a victory that Raimon will not hide. 'I have the Flame already,' he declares.

Hugh's smile loses a smidgen of its sparkle. 'The Flame's still on the pog,' he says curtly. 'We see it every night.' Raimon raises his eyebrows. Hugh speaks with care. 'How would that be possible if, as you say, you have it?'

Raimon ignores the question. 'Without the Flame you're finished,' he says. 'The king doesn't really care about anything else. That's the prize he wants.'

'The Flame's on the pog,' Hugh repeats. He gets up and walks to and fro. Raimon *must* be bluffing. The White Wolf would never allow it to be removed. In his fury and upset over Yolanda, Raimon is reduced to fantasy. Hugh decides not to mention the Flame again. He taps his fingers. 'There's not much time left. Though we have not yet agreed terms, tomorrow, at the latest, de Perella will surrender and the prisoners will be paraded before the Inquisitors. That's the moment they will have to decide whether to bow to France and Catholicism and live, or die as miserable heretics.' The two men are now face to face. 'You have knowledge of the pyre yourself, Raimon,' Hugh says more softly. 'You cannot want more people to suffer than have suffered already.'

Raimon pales and shifts. Hugh presses his advantage. 'Your challenge to me must wait because this is my treaty and if you kill me, another will be drawn up dictating terms much more unfavourable. As it is, you could take this back to them and see if you can get at least some to listen. Naturally, I cannot save the Occitan, but I can compose an oath of allegiance to the king that the knights can swear with honour before being freed to go home.' He shakes his head. 'The Perfecti, whatever their sex or age, are different. I am told to hand them over to the Inquisitors as I see fit.' He swallows. Burnings! Executions! The thought sickens him. This is a time for life not death. He goes to his table and touches the box in which he keeps the ring he gave Yolanda, then he comes back to Raimon. 'Listen to me very carefully. The Cathars must renounce the White Wolf and all his works. Do you understand? They must renounce *the White Wolf*.'

At first Raimon does not listen. Hugh repeats himself twice more until Raimon cannot pretend not to understand. The words are clever, offering a lifeline to Sir Roger and to Metta and to the Occitanian knights now contemplating their fates. Such a lifeline, once rejected, will not be offered again. Yet the thought of acting as Hugh's messenger boy whilst his fury burns so hot against him is almost impossible. He fights for time. 'And if they won't renounce the White Wolf?'

There is a short silence. 'You know what will happen then.' Neither man moves. 'Will you go?' Hugh asks.

A flicker crosses Raimon's face. He raises Unbent again. Hugh reaches into the armour chest but Raimon is not aiming for him. Instead, as he strides from the tent, he cleanly severs two of the Orimflamme's damp crimson tails and tosses them into the mud. With a cry, Amalric and Henri draw their own swords but Hugh, looming in his tent's entrance, harshly commands them to hold off. He has a child. Raimon does not. It suddenly seems to him unnecessary to punish a man who is punished so much already.

FACING THE ENEMY

It takes twenty minutes or so for the group of twenty French men-at-arms to mount and gather at the bottom of the half-widened road, with Raimon in their midst. They will ride as far as they can and leave the horses with armed squires. A phalanx of archers flanks them, for Hugh is still taking no chances. The stone guns may be silent but the heretics will have other weapons.

The journey is conducted in silence and without incident, and in two hours they are at the fortress gate, Raimon walking behind. Once again, he sends Cador back down the hill with Bors and Galahad, although this time he tells him to stay close to the French camp. 'And don't let go of the horses,' he tells him. 'Whatever happens, don't let go.' Cador nods. He will not let go.

The day is dull, and in the grey sheen that might be November rather than March, the keep looms over the walls as though the place were still impregnable. Only the fluttering des Arcis pennant and the welcoming shouts from the barbican signal the Cathar defeat.

Still, as they approach, it occurs to Raimon that they might be ignored and have to retreat. However, even as he thinks this, the gate opens, with de Perella emerging first, the White Wolf stalking serenely behind him, and, shuffling in their wake, a huddle of others, their forced bravado both admirable and tragic. Above, between the crenellations, Occitanian archers are poised to trade arrow for arrow with the French archers now setting their arrows below. Hugh was right to be wary.

Raimon can see Sir Roger but not Metta. The White Wolf glances behind only once and, like children in a game of Grandmother's Footsteps, the shufflers cease to shuffle. Raimon knows the White Wolf will be smiling. Montségur may be finished but his power remains intact.

De Perella coughs and when Raimon moves through to face him, his cough turns to a choke. Even the White Wolf's face blackens. 'You!' De Perella shakes his head. 'God will punish the trouble you cause.'

Raimon does not try to explain. He demands to speak to de Perella privately and when this is finally agreed, shows him Hugh's terms, repeating, word for word, what Hugh has told him. It takes some time to persuade the knight to read and listen, for de Perella's anger with Raimon keeps spouting forth like a capricious geyser. When he finally understands, he shakes his head. 'They'll not give in, not one of them,' he says, and seems glad at this slight to Raimon until his attention is drawn to movement at the bottom of the pog.

The French camp is moving, but not away. In the time it

has taken for Raimon to climb, the Inquisitors have ordered the tents to be shifted so that on the flat land they have been occupying until now, a large square, as though for the proposed foundations of a not insubstantial farmhouse, can be marked out in chalk. Nearby, the trees cut down during the widening of the road are being dragged and split into faggots, and straw is being brought in great bundles from barns in the village. In the middle of the square, the red cross of the Inquisitors has been hoisted. 'God help us!' De Perella clutches at Raimon's arm. 'They're preparing an inferno.'

'Never mind God. Help yourselves,' Raimon urges. 'Look at the treaty again and listen to what Sir Hugh said. You can save yourselves without dishonour. There need be no inferno. Talk to your knights. Talk to the Perfecti. Please.'

De Perella closes his eyes momentarily and opens them to find Raimon leading him back into the fortress and everybody following behind.

The White Wolf joins the Perfecti on the walkway above. Everybody else remains below. De Perella sends a page for an old wooden box, climbs on and removes his leather hat. A sudden gust of wind whips his thinning hair into whirligig straggles. 'My friends,' he says, when he can fix his nerves, 'you have all acquitted yourselves with great distinction during this last heroic siege. The Occitan will not forget you. But now the siege is broken we must decide how to respond to the terms that are offered.'

'Pin them to his back with a dagger,' somebody shouts, pointing at Raimon. 'He tried to steal the Flame. If there are to be terms, let's hear them from Sir Hugh des Arcis himself.'

'Even King Louis'd be better than a thief,' calls out another. Raimon winces.

De Perella stands taller, his courage returning now he can no longer actually see the makings of the pyre. 'You're right,' he says. 'For myself, I'm a true Occitanian and I'll never swear allegiance to King Louis of France. They may hang me for that if they want. Nor will I renounce my Cathar faith.' There is wild cheering. He raises his voice. 'I'll go down from this pog a Cathar and an Occitanian and that's what I'll remain.' More wild cheering, although mothers clutch their children to them. Smoke from the kitchens billows. The cheering dies away and de Perella's courage with it. He coughs. 'But we can remain Occitanians and Cathars and live!'

There is uncomfortable muttering. 'And men will go to the moon,' comes a shout from the back.

'No,' says de Perella. 'There will be an oath, but I'm told it will be one that we can swear without dishonour and then all knights can go free.' A small buzz follows this. The women lean forward, and the knights too, though they pretend not to.

'How? And who will guarantee it?' The question is repeated loudly, then more loudly still.

At de Perella's invitation, Raimon climbs on to the box and speaks very quickly. 'Just hear me out! Please! It's guaranteed by Sir Hugh des Arcis.' There is general derision at both Raimon and this proposition, yet there is a shifting about too. When the women shout for quiet, with hidden relief the knights give way.

'Women and children can go home at once, and knights

can disperse after they have taken the oath,' Raimon tells them. As for all you Perfecti —' he turns and stares upwards — 'so long as you renounce the White Wolf and all his works, you'll also be spared.'

The knights are now silent but the Perfecti are not. One or two cry out. The White Wolf licks his lips. The smallest ruffle creases his forehead. Ah, this is a different game. He touches his smooth beard. He should still be able to win.

One Perfectus, either braver or more cowardly than the others, and who is standing far away from the White Wolf, peers over the walkway railing to address Raimon directly. 'You mean,' he says slowly, 'that in order to escape the pyre we don't actually have to renounce our Cathar faith?'

'Sir Hugh said "renounce the White Wolf",' Raimon replies. 'Make of that what you will.'

The Perfecti rock from side to side as though the information has unbalanced them. 'And do you trust Sir Hugh des Arcis?' The brave one speaks again.

Raimon trembles as everybody leans to hear his response. He would swallow if only his throat had not constricted. He still cannot see Metta but there is only one answer to make if these people are not to burn. But oh, how hard it is to get the words out. 'I do,' he says at last. 'Over this, at least, I think Sir Hugh will keep his word.'

The White Wolf claps his hands as though Raimon were a fairground act. 'Was divide and rule not an old ruse of the Romans? Renounce me and all my works? It makes me sound like the devil.' He stops clapping and walks down the line of Perfecti, forcing each one to meet his gaze. 'But you will already have seen straight through this trick, just as I have. The words Raimon offers on behalf of the lackey of the King of France are weasel words. Renounce me? What nonsense is this? For the love of God! How can I, a humble worker in God's vineyard, be important enough to renounce! But let me tell you something that is important. However alluring the fancy words and phrases our enemies concoct, they are a snare, because you know as well as I that renouncing even the humblest worker is tantamount to renouncing not just our Cathar faith, but the Blue Flame, the Occitan and even God himself. Do you really want to do that?'

His voice, so soft and still, penetrates like a needle. As he draws them back to him, touching an arm here, settling a hood there, such irresistible confidence and peace emanate from him that shoulders visibly sink and faces smooth. At those who resist, he smiles a smile of such openness and joy that it is impossible not to smile back. Without any semblance of hurry, he walks down the whole line and then back and then down again until he knows he has them safe in the palm of his hand. Then his voice softens further, though he makes sure that now it reaches not just the Perfecti but the knights below. 'Don't be frightened, my children. Stay strong! Are a few more years on this earth really more valuable than eternal salvation?' Nobody replies. He comes to a halt and, richly satisfied, leans over the rail himself. 'There, my treacherous friend.' He throws his words at Raimon. 'There is our answer to Sir Hugh's offer. Nobody here will renounce the Cathar faith. Now get off this mountain. You dirty it.'

'Let me repeat. Sir Hugh said nothing about the Cathar faith. He said they must renounce you.'

A hubbub arises. Suddenly everybody is anxious and perplexed. The Perfecti turn to each other. Renouncing their faith is impossible. But for all his persuasive words, is the same really true of the White Wolf? He is, after all, only a man. Could they renounce him? Should they? A seed of doubt is sown.

As nervous and uncertain as everybody else, but praying he has done enough, Raimon leaps down from the box and tries to find Metta. Why is she not near her father? He shoves his way through the crowd. Nobody seems to know whether to embrace him or lynch him. He uselessly calls her name. Somebody grabs him. He tries to fight them off but they are pointing. He stops fighting, raises his eyes to the walkway again and then he sees her. No wonder she was invisible, for she, too, is dressed in black. She has taken the consolation. She is a Perfectus herself.

Raimon fights his way back through the crowd and swings himself up by the walkway's wooden struts. The hubbub is lessening as de Perella quiets his knights and the White Wolf his Perfecti. He places a hand on Metta's shoulder and she turns. Peering out from the black hood is exactly the same girl he first saw through the snow at Castelneuf, the funereal cloth only accentuating the fair smoothness of her cheeks, her round eyes and the untroubled stillness of her forehead. He fumbles for words but she does not. 'Hello, Raimon,' she says and now he sees how appearances are deceptive. She has changed. Her voice has sunk and her tone is graver. Her cheeks may be smooth but her lips are dry. Her joy in life has not vanished but it is thinner. Raimon is horribly reminded of Adela. 'Metta!'

She blinks. Only her mouth trembles slightly.

'Metta. I can't – I don't –'

Her eyes are slightly veiled. He does not know what message his own are sending out. 'Listen to me,' he says, gripping her tightly, 'I promise on my own life that Sir Hugh des Arcis will keep his word. You really can remain Cathars.'

'Yes.'

'Come down to your father.'

'I'm happy up here.' She bows her head and eases herself away.

'Metta!' His voice rings out.

'I don't believe she's listening any more.' The White Wolf's voice is a snarl in his ear.

Slowly, Raimon swings himself over the railing and makes his way back to de Perella. This is not over yet.

The White Wolf addresses the whole company as he tries to regain the initiative, this time choosing a tone of mildly disappointed reproach. 'It's hard to believe, after we've been through so much together, that in exchange for a few years lived in subjection to King Louis you're willing to abandon the Flame and break the promise you made on the Bible.' He pauses, then throws up his hands in genuine horror. 'You are happy to break your word to God?'

He judges it perfectly. The Perfecti stall and look at their feet and once again the White Wolf strides up and down, not cajoling them this time but unfurling his confidence like a banner. 'My beloved friends! Let's be steadfast! Surely that's how you want to be remembered: as one of those who refused to fail the Flame, the Occitan or God. Could there be a more glorious epitaph?'

The force of his words has the Perfecti easing back into a ragged line, their faces full of shame.

'You no longer have the Blue Flame,' Raimon shouts.

The White Wolf laughs gaily. 'In your dreams, Raimon. The Blue Flame is as safely here as the mountain itself. Nobody need take my word for that. They see it every night.'

'What you have is not the Flame.'

'Oh no?' The White Wolf hardly bothers to listen. 'Even for a master of lies that's a little far-fetched.'

'You don't understand the Flame. You don't understand anything.' Raimon will not be silenced. 'Listen to me!' He appeals directly to the Perfecti and out of his mouth tumbles a jumble of Laila's words. 'You think the Flame is unchanging, that it must always be the same and I thought so too. But I was wrong. Don't you see? Things that don't change are nothing but a trap. If nothing changes then we just end up going round in the same circle of fire and war and death.' He takes a deep breath. He tries to lower his voice but it will not be lowered. 'Before I left here I lit a new Flame from the old one and the one that remains here, the one on which the White Wolf stakes his life and yours too, is just an empty shell. Don't be under any illusions. If you die for that, you'll die for nothing.'

There is an odd, uncomfortable groan.

'And where's this new Flame, then,' the White Wolf mocks. 'Is it hidden in your sleeve?'

But the Perfecti are disturbed. Raimon sounds sincere. And his words provide yet another oh so enticing escape route from the pyre.

De Perella steps back on to the box. He has made up his mind once and for all. 'Perfecti,' he urges, 'Look over the walls.' They hesitate. 'Go on! Look!' The Perfecti look and reel back. The square below is more like a house than ever now, as it has been divided up into smaller squares, like rooms, using neat stacks of faggots, each square carpeted with straw. Such a pyre has never been seen before. Like the wicked castle in some infernal fairytale, it will consume them all at one sitting. Two Perfecti faint. 'Just look at it!' de Perella urges again. 'Do you want to give the Inquisitors the satisfaction of setting it alight? Surely it would be much better in God's eyes as well as our own to mutter a few words before disappearing into the countryside. If you're alive, you can continue your preaching and good works for many years to come. You can hardly do that if you're dead.'

'Cowardly talk!' The White Wolf stands in a shaft of sunlight. 'The pyre's agony is momentary whilst Heaven's joy is for ever. Die for God and the Blue Flame.' He is transfigured.

Raimon bangs Unbent against the box. 'It's time!' His voice is commanding. 'Those Perfecti who wish to renounce the White Wolf and continue to serve God, take off your habits. Take them off and live.' He does this entirely for Metta. Once her habit is removed, she will not be able to change her mind.

'No! No!' the White Wolf rejoins. His teeth are now

gritted. 'Keep on your habits and die. It's what the Blue Flame wants. It's what God wants.'

Everybody freezes, waiting to see what everybody else does. In the end, six black habits are laid on the rocks and four men and two women, shivering in long cotton shirts, come down from the walkway.

The rest remain still, Metta amongst them. The White Wolf has more than a partial triumph. Raimon cannot bear it. 'Metta! Metta!'

His arm is locked in a huge grip. 'Keep away from my daughter.' Sir Roger is shaking him. 'Keep away, do you hear?'

'Do you want her to burn? For God's sake, Sir Roger, help me persuade her.'

'You persuade her? How dare you! She only became a Perfectus because of you. If you'd been true, she'd have been your wife, not one of these wretched ghouls.'

'Can you persuade her then? Can you?'

Sir Roger suddenly looks very old. Raimon wrenches himself away and swings again on to the walkway. This time when he seizes Metta he is not gentle. 'Take off the habit.' She does not move. He tries to sound less peremptory. 'You can remain a Perfectus, you know. Just take off the habit for now.'

'And renounce the White Wolf?'

'Yes.'

'I don't want to renounce him.'

'Come on, Metta. When we spoke of him at Castelneuf, you said outright that you didn't find him praiseworthy. How can you follow any man who thinks he knows God better than God knows himself?'

'I see the White Wolf's faults,' she says. 'I probably see them better than you. But to renounce him is to cast him off, to say that his whole life has been a sham. That's a cruel thing to do, Raimon.' Her eyes are clear and frank. 'I don't like cruelty, so though it's true that I disagree with some of his notions, when I took the consolation from him I accepted them. That was the nature of my promise.'

'Metta, listen. I did a terrible thing to you. How can I blame you for listening to the White Wolf when I proved so faithless. But you know why I did it.'

'Yes, I know,' she says. 'And I've often thought that you tried to warn me the day we went sledging. Do you remember that day?'

'Of course I remember it!'

'You told me then that you'd do anything for the Occitan.' She smiles a little sadly. 'I suppose I just didn't think it would be to abandon me.'

'I don't know what to say! I don't know what to say! Only that martyrdom isn't for you. It isn't!'

She looks at him straight. 'I gave the White Wolf my word on the Holy Bible. I can't take it back.'

'You wouldn't be breaking your word! You can remain a Cathar! Don't you understand that?'

The terrible, familiar voice interrupts. 'She's not stupid, Raimon. She's just loyal, not a virtue by which you set much store.'

Raimon spins round. 'You want her to burn?'

'That's not the right question,' the White Wolf observes. He is gaunt with effort. 'I want her to remain true, unlike these others whose weakness you have so cleverly exploited. What you and Sir Hugh des Arcis offer is nothing but dust. Isn't that right, Metta?'

She nods but her eyes never leave Raimon's face.

'Come,' the White Wolf chides her gently. 'As I so often say to you, the enemy appears in many guises.'

'Leave her!' Raimon is shouting.

The White Wolf pauses. 'What are you going to do? Rip the habit from her body without her permission?'

'If I have to!' He makes a sudden move but Metta shrinks away from him and now he shrinks back from her. He cannot use violence against her and the White Wolf knows it. He watches her being ushered into the group of the doomed and sinks down to bury his head in his hands.

PARADISE RED

The fortress gates do not shut again, though it takes until the next day before all the preparations are made. The Occitaninan wives busy themselves stuffing packs for their journeys home as their husbands decide whether the remaining animals should be slaughtered or driven out. At last, an hour before noon and leaving a great mess behind them, the heretics begin to file down the mountain, the persistent Perfecti moving like a black bruise at their side. Sir Roger rages impotently all the way: at himself, at his daughter and at Raimon, who has stayed on the pog all night and now walks silently a little way from Metta, taking Sir Roger's abuse as a man takes a lash he knows he deserves. The White Wolf walks behind them all, and though the way is rough, he holds his flame shoulder high.

The Inquisitors are standing in a huddle, condemning Hugh for presenting terms of surrender they consider far too lenient. As the Cathars pass, they make a great show of crossing themselves.

The women and children are sent away at once but the Occitanian knights are forced into pairs and file in front of Hugh, now seated on a regal chair. Though the oriflamme hanging behind him is mutilated, nobody witnessing this scene can be in any doubt that it is the French king's justice that is being administered, or that Hugh des Arcis intends to keep his word. As each pair of knights kneels, they find that Hugh sticks closely to the letter of the treaty. They must acknowledge the sovereignty of the King of France but they are not required to surrender either their castles or their titles. Sir Roger takes the oath last.

You may feel, as the Inquisitors certainly do, that Hugh has been weak, but I can tell you that he has been wise, for Hugh knows, as the king does, that magnanimity is a far more powerful weapon than subjection. Each knight will return home grateful for royal mercy and his future behaviour will be constrained by it.

It is different with the Perfecti. Hugh has offered them all he can offer. They must surrender the Blue Flame, and those who will not renounce the White Wolf will die. There are no alternatives. He watches them coming towards him with some surprise. So many? He thought more would take advantage of the proffered escape. He sees Metta, so young and so misguidedly steadfast. Raimon lurks in the background.

The pyre is now virtually complete, a roofless house, with the faggots, some piled up to four feet high, marking out the inside rooms and a high palisade serving as the outside walls. The youngest and keenest Inquisitors do not like this design for it will block their view of the burning heretics and ruin the spectacle. The older Inquisitors disagree. Mass burnings – and this will be the biggest ever organised – are not spectacles, they are cataclysms to which nobody can tell quite how they will react. Better to herd the heretics inside and then hide them from view. They appease the younger Inquisitors by sending them off through the 'door' to ensure that the straw 'carpet' is layered thickly enough and the builders have remembered to leave openings into all the internal 'rooms'. These walls will provide the essential fuel. When the enthusiasts emerge, few are still complaining about a spectacle.

The builders work steadily and by mid-afternoon, the monstrous palace is ready to receive its guests. There is no point in further delay, so as the last plank in the palisade is secured and with the Inquisitors kneeling in public prayer, the victims, young and old, sick and healthy, are pushed unceremoniously inside. Raimon cannot bear it. Abandoning all self-control, he hangs on to Metta until, right at the door, she extricates herself. Sir Roger, roaring, tries to follow his daughter and is taken into custody by two French knights who are ordered to tie him to a horse and accompany him home.

The White Wolf is kept back and brought before Hugh, who finds him neither frightened nor regretful, not for himself and not for those to die with him. Only his oddly childish clutching of the flame betrays any human chink in his armour of religious fervour.

'I'll have the flame,' Hugh says but does not reach out for his prize at once. 'You could save these people, you know. Why not tell them that you'll bear the whole punishment for them. The

Inquisitors will be angry, but that won't matter to you. Your Perfecti will still be under sentence of death, of course, but I could refer the matter of their execution to the Pope and that could take years.' The White Wolf just smiles. How little these Frenchmen know him. Hugh presses him again. 'Do you want them all to burn? I can hardly believe that.'

'You can believe what you like.' The White Wolf is his usual mild self, his face pure as a child's. 'But we know what we believe. We are martyrs whom God will welcome into paradise with loving arms.'

'And what if you're wrong? What if God views you as a murderer?' Hugh will not give up yet.

'Me? A murderer?' The White Wolf seems genuinely amused. 'Who is building the house of death, Sir Hugh? Who will give the order to fire the straw? There are certainly murderers here but I am not of their number.'

Hugh tries one last time. 'Save these heretics! Or at least save the young ones. They'll listen to you.'

The White Wolf glances towards the palisade, from which the prayers of his followers are rising in direct competition with the prayers of the Inquisitors. 'We Cathars do not want to be saved,' he says pleasantly. 'As I have already said, what's there to cling to on earth when God awaits us in heaven?'

'And I repeat, what if God doesn't want the likes of you?'

'Oh, I'm prepared to take the risk.' Not a flicker of doubt crosses the White Wolf's countenance, not a twitch of apprehension.

Hugh stretches out for the flame. Only now does the White Wolf blench, finding that at this moment of greatest trial he does not want to lose it. His voice exhibits the tiniest of cracks. 'You know that the Flame will be ours whatever you do with it, wherever you take it.' His fingers are tight round the box. 'Long after we are all ashes, people will say "that was the Blue Flame of the Cathars".'

'They will say it was the Blue Flame of the Occitan,' Hugh replies equally forcefully, 'if, that is, they speak of it at all. Now give it to me.' The White Wolf takes half a step back, recovers himself and hands the box over. 'We do not need its physical presence,' he says with masterful loftiness, though his eyes linger on the salver. 'God lit it for us and he won't forget that.'

'But did he?' Hugh fingers the box. 'Raimon says that there's another Flame, one that supersedes this one.' He speaks with a carelessness he does not feel, for notwithstanding anything the White Wolf might desire, his own future in the king's service depends on this flame being the real Flame.

The White Wolf throws back his head. 'What else do you expect a weaver to say?' His tone is now contemptuous.

Hugh wants to be convinced. 'How can we tell?'

The White Wolf speaks slowly and very clearly. 'I'm telling you, the Flame can't change. It's our anchor. It binds us to the past.'

'And what about the future?' Hugh thinks of Yolanda and his son.

'The future?' For once the White Wolf looks nonplussed. 'The future must be the same as the past. That's what the Blue Flame tells us.'

Hugh stops fingering the box and looks directly inside, to where the flame sits dully in its drying oil, casting a shadow that even on this grey afternoon does not transfix. A cold thread begins to wrap itself round his heart. If the White Wolf is wrong and Raimon right, he is doomed. The king is a holy man. He will not be duped by a false relic. He raises the box and brings it close to his eyes. It is just a box. It is just a flame. With jolting certainty, he finds he knows where the truth lies. He lowers the box in a sudden fury. 'You've made a mistake that's going to kill us both,' he rasps. 'Look at it, man, just look! Flames light the way into the future. The one you've been hanging on to is fit only to light the way to hell.' He stands up and throws the box back. 'You fool. You're going to the pyre for nothing and I have nothing to take to the king.' And now, inexplicably, he begins to laugh at the stupid, pointless pity of it all. He watches the White Wolf caressing the box as though it were alive. 'There's something of an irony here, don't you think?' Hugh says.

The White Wolf's voice has no crack now. 'There's no irony. I have the Flame.'

'You have your flame but not God's.' Hugh shakes his head. The Inquisitors are muttering, wondering what Hugh is doing. He sits down and collects himself. 'Look. If you must die for it, I can't stop you. But die by yourself and send all these others home. Do that one good thing.' The White Wolf smiles that demented, complacent smile. 'Go to hell, then,' Hugh says violently and gets up again. 'This is not the Blue Flame,' he shouts at the Inquisitors. 'The Flame is gone.' Then he steps away leaving the White Wolf to carry his spent talisman into the place of no return.

Even with all the care that had been taken, the palisade takes some lighting. The wood is still damp and the wind light, so it is almost dark by the time patches of it can really be said to have caught in any way at all. In a slow cadence, the prayers of the heretics rise an octave, though as the smoke swirls they soon dissolve into coughs. They have spread themselves through the rooms, holding hands as much as they are able. There is an eerie silence apart from the crackling of the brushwood with which the builders begin to line the planks in an attempt to hurry the firing process along. When this is not immediately successful, they begin to toss lighted torches over the palisade to fire the straw carpet. The pyre/house is too broad for any torch to reach the middle so when it does begin to burn properly it is from the outside in.

Now there are cries as well as coughs, for the entrances to the rooms are narrow and when a torch hits its mark, people are crushed in the scramble for a safer spot. Some Perfecti panic and begin to scream, and once they have started screaming find they cannot stop, while those villagers who have gathered to watch, unable to bear the ear-aching and increasing volume, grab their children and flee. As the terrible chorus rises, even the horses, though tethered behind the French tents, grow restive and finally throw up their heads and break free. Many of the French knights rush after them and not wanting to witness anymore, gallop away.

Only the Inquisitors remain apparently unmoved. Though their eyes begin to stream as the smoke becomes more brackish and whips out of the pyre/house as well as in, their prayers are still intact. They gather on one side of the square and Hugh and Raimon on another, though not side by side.

It would be untrue to say that, visually, this reluctant bonfire is hideous. Rather, its size and careful construction confer an awesome beauty once the planks really start to burn and the brushwood turns to loose fountains of fiery confetti. Not that Raimon thinks so for one moment. It is not the smoke that has him only able to breathe in short sharp snatches, it is the thought that he should never have let go of Metta. He lunges forward and is grabbed from behind. 'That's suicide.' Hugh's arms are strong.

'I've got to get her out,' Raimon's teeth are chattering despite the heat. 'She thinks she's dying for the Flame but she's not.'

'I know.'

Raimon twists. Their eyes meet. Raimon pulls away. 'Leave me alone! You're as responsible for this horror as if you'd chucked in a torch yourself.'

'I do the king's work.' Hugh will not let go.

'That's a disgraceful answer.' Raimon is still trying to shake Hugh off.

Hugh shakes him back, then says abruptly, 'If we're to get her, we must go now.'

A tiny pause. 'You?'

'Call it my challenge.' Hugh finally lets go and without even pausing to take off their swords, they rush towards the palisade together.

The outside has well and truly caught now and the fire-raisers have retired, their job done. The flaming brushwood helps Hugh and Raimon, for it has burned a hole in the bottom of the palisade through which, kicking the brushwood aside, they can push.

Inside, they find a bizarre scene. The rooms in and out of which the Perfecti are surging are still largely intact, and the straw underfoot lit only in patches. Were it not for the smoke and the rising heat, you could almost believe yourself to be in a fairground maze. Raimon and Hugh join the surge, pushing and searching, the latter made far harder because most of the Perfecti have covered their faces with their hoods. Then there are those who fall as the surge quickens.

'Work your way to the middle,' Hugh cries, but this is easier said than done, for as the straw gradually erupts, it lights the faggots, and in trying not to be knocked over by Perfecti flailing about as their habits smoulder and their feet scorch, it becomes difficult to gauge in which direction they are going.

Now, through the smoke, comes the smell of roasting flesh, and suddenly the straw is beginning to bubble like a cauldron. Then, like a singer waiting for his cue, the fire begins to roar.

At once, all vestiges of human dignity evaporate. There is no room for it. As the fire fastens to hoods, hair and sleeves, the Perfecti are terrifyingly quickly transformed into half-naked creatures, yowling and hopping on all fours, crawling over and buffeting against each other in their hideous agonies.

Raimon and Hugh have to cling together to survive, batting out the flames that seize their legs and arms. 'This way!' Hugh cries and they batter their way through towards what they hope may the centre of this vortex, where the straw and faggots may not yet be convulsed. It is a fearsome journey, much worse than Yolanda's in the snow, but they are rewarded. In the very middle room, even through the wild and pullulating noise, there remains a semblance of calm. The White Wolf stands there, shifting his feet as the hem of his habit smokes. Though his beard is still white, his shoulders are speckled with ash. Uncannily tranquil in the apocalypse erupting around him, he is holding up his empty flame and reciting, like a mantra, 'We are the Flame's martyrs. Rejoice at how glorious we are! See how the Flame burns with pleasure at our sacrifice!'

But he is wrong. The flame is not burning with pleasure. It is barely burning at all. Nothing about it dances. Nothing about it inspires. In its battered box it looks what it is, the insubstantial remains of an old icon whose time was glorious but has now passed.

Those round the White Wolf try to rally to his call, but all they can do is cleave to one another. The White Wolf shakes the box as his feet grow hotter. 'The Flame! The Flame!' He is begging it – ordering it – to rise to the occasion, but instead it sinks lower still, not blue at all but the palest of reds. The White Wolf bites his cheeks. He shakes the box again, and then, as though heavenly music has just broken out, raises his voice in a triumphant shout. 'Look at the colour! Just look! Of course! Now is not the time for blue but the time for red! And not just any red! Rejoice, my friends! This is the red of paradise! Paradise red!'

Those around, half crying, now try to take up his call. 'Paradise red!' they echo, but their hearts are not in it. Indeed, as the flames begin to flicker through the faggots, paradise red seems no colour at all.

Metta is nearest to the White Wolf as the straw shifts and, in this last redoubt, the fire blazes through. The screaming rises yet another pitch as the heat hits them in huge billows. Coughing and stamping and with one hand over his mouth, Raimon yanks at Metta's sleeve and keeps hold when she pulls away in terror, as though expecting the devil. 'You!' she cries. 'Go away! Get out of here! You don't have to burn. Let it be over! Just let it be over!'

'Nothing's over.' Raimon hangs on grimly.

'I'm not leaving. I promised.'

'Are you deranged, girl?' Hugh is on her other side.

She is pleading. 'I can't give in. I'm not a coward! I won't leave the Flame —'

Raimon lets go of her arm and roughly seizes her shoulders. Fiery tendrils are sneaking up their legs and he can feel Unbent hot on his back. They begin to choke. 'Die if you must,' Raimon splutters, 'but don't die for a fraud. Look at the flame. Just look.' She looks. The White Wolf is holding it high, like some fantastical magician about to perform his best trick. 'What do you see?' She shakes her head. 'What do you see, Metta? Answer me! You *must* answer me!'

'I see nothing, *nothing!*' she sobs.

'Exactly,' Raimon shouts in her ear. '*Nothing.* But I have a Flame and that's not nothing. It's far from nothing. I have the true Flame of the Occitan.'

'Don't believe them, Metta,' shrills the White Wolf. 'What are they doing here, the Flame's two enemies together! Get them out! Out! This is *our* moment.' He shakes the Flame some more. 'Burn strong for us!' he begs. 'Burn strong and blue and paradise red!' But in answer, the wooden box collapses and in seconds the White Wolf is left only with the salver, really just a tiny and very scratched silver plate. 'NO!' he shrieks as the flame shrinks into the oil. 'NO!' He clings to the salver as it scalds his fingers. There is a momentary lull, as though everybody is taking a breath, and then quite suddenly, in the midst of this furnace, the old flame goes out.

Now the White Wolf staggers like a man whose leg has been lopped off, but for Metta a chain has snapped. As the White Wolf loses every last ounce of self-possession and joins the screamers, she clutches at Raimon, sobbing and groaning, and then Hugh is hauling them both away from the collapsing walls and back towards the remains of the palisade.

The journey out is worse even than the journey in for though the flames are leaping, the air is now so thick that every step is a step in the dark. They feel the White Wolf behind them as they struggle, all of them bent double. But he is not trying to escape. He is still trying to pull Metta back. 'Metta! Metta! Don't desert me. We'll go to heaven together. Together!' His eyes are rolling, his beard just a bristle and the skin is peeling from the back of his head. 'This is what God wants! Our suffering is his greatest delight. Don't you want to please God, Metta? Don't you? You disappoint me! You dis-a-ppoint me.' His words lengthen as he begins to disintegrate. He seizes her hood.

She turns. He is a repulsive sight. Now it is she who tries to pull him with her. 'Come out. Come out of here, please. Let Raimon save you. I'm begging. How can dying like this possibly be God's will?'

The White Wolf is almost completely alight now. He bares his teeth and pushes her away. 'You question God's will? You dare to? God knows his own, Metta. God knows his own. Perhaps I was mistaken in you. Perhaps you're not one of his own after all.'

You think there is a limit to pain? Not for the White Wolf. His greatest torture comes as he draws his last breath, and the pain is not the searing sensation in his chest as the fire collapses his lungs. It is far deeper pain than that, for it is only when it is far too late that he sees something more appalling than any sight on earth. As he stretches what remains of his arms towards the starry comforts of heaven and begs God to gather him up, he sees God slowly turning his back. The sight burns hotter than the hottest fire. It burns so hot that it burns away the point of him. His arms drop. 'Sweet Jesus,' he whispers but nobody hears him.

Raimon will not let Metta look or even think as he keeps her sandwiched between himself and Hugh. Kicking in front and behind, they beat their way back to the palisade, most of which is now just a hollow heap, and cry out with relief when they feel the flames behind them. Their relief is momentary. Instead of being met with cooler air, they are confronted with bristling swords.

Though there are not enough of them to form a complete chain, the Inquisitors have fanned out like sentries to drive any escapee heretics back into the flames. To reinforce his authority, the Chief Inquisitor has also seized the oriflamme which, with the wind now rising, is flourishing its six remaining tails as though they were flames themselves. It takes a moment for them to recognise Hugh as he appears before them, blackened and raw, but as soon as somebody shouts his name, the Chief Inquisitor cracks the oriflamme like a whip. 'You? Sir Hugh des Arcis? You, the keeper of the oriflamme, presume to cheat God of his rightful revenge? *You presume to save his enemies?* Oh, Sir Hugh, you presume too much – far too much.' The man's fervour almost lifts him off the ground. 'Seize him!' he orders.

'Run, Metta, run!' Who knows who shouts? It might be Hugh, it might be Raimon. All that matters is that she finds herself stumbling obediently away, trying to put as much distance as possible between herself and the hell from which she has been rescued. There is no such relief for Hugh and Raimon, for within seconds the French knight and the Occitan weaver are fighting side by side. Hugh will not be taken without a struggle and Raimon cannot leave Hugh to struggle alone. 'The other is a heretic too,' the Chief Inquisitor bawls. 'Never mind bringing them to me! Push them both back into the fire. I'll answer to the king!'

Though Raimon thrusts and parries like a cornered jackal and Hugh lunges like a stag at bay, little by little they are forced to retreat. The Chief Inquisitor edges nearer and tries to hit Raimon with the oriflamme but instead finds himself grappling with Hugh and forced to let it go. Now the Inquisitor pulls out a sword and lunges. Hampered by the banner, Hugh cannot defend himself. At once, Raimon pushes Unbent between them and the Inquisitor turns on him too, raising his blade for the killer blow. Hugh uses the oriflamme as a huge swat, and, in two simultaneous giant leaps, he and Raimon catapult themselves back into the furnace where they know neither soldiers nor Inquisitors will dare to follow.

The fire has consumed everything in its wake – faggots, hair, bone, flesh and cloth, and is roaring with less intensity. Now it is the smell that is unendurable. Raimon gags as it invades every vein, every muscle, every pore. It is the smell of pure evil. Underfoot, through an all-pervading viscous slime, unidentifiable splinters push between his blistered toes. This mulch is all that remains of the two hundred human beings who, hours before, had been part of God's creation. Hugh is not moving well and at last he falls, the oriflamme slapping hard down beside him. Raimon wrenches him up and feels a sudden gush of blood. For a moment he cannot tell whether the gush is from himself or from Hugh.

Hugh supplies the answer. 'Get out of here as best you can.' His breath is uneven. 'The Inquisitors can't be everywhere. Find Metta and get her back to her father. That's what you can do for her. It's what you must do.'

Raimon gazes wildly about. How can he leave a dying man in this devil's cauldron?

Hugh's eyes are wide and the pupils already glazy. 'I'm afraid there'll be no single combat now,' he whispers, 'but I still have a challenge for you.'

'Come on, get up!' Raimon jerks at Hugh's legs. 'Get up!'

Hugh groans vastly. Raimon tries to force him but Hugh is a dead weight. He tries again. Hugh struggles to hold on to Raimon's arm but finally gives up. 'I'm done,' he says. 'I'm done.' He is gasping. 'But here's my challenge, Raimon.' He searches for Raimon's eyes. He wants to say something about Yolanda, Raimon knows it. He does not want to hear it. He will not meet Hugh's eyes.

Hugh's gaze begins to dim. He can hardly see Raimon at all now. His chest heaves as he gathers himself to speak slowly and clearly. 'Take my sword to my son and look after him for me.'

Raimon claps his hands over his ears. 'Don't ask such a thing! I won't take it! I don't want him!'

'You must take it. You must have him. You must.'

'No! Aren't you listening? Never. Not your son. Why do you ask something so impossible of me?'

Hugh gives a faint, exhausted half-smile. 'What a silly question,' he murmurs. 'Why do you think I ask?'

'I don't know! I don't know!'

'Oh yes, Raimon, you do.' His cheeks spasm. 'I ask you because Yolanda loves you. I ask you because you're a brave man. But most of all –' the words come hard now, and not just because his lungs are filling – 'I ask you because I've nobody else to ask.'

Raimon roars and bends over Hugh, sometimes holding him, sometimes shaking him until Hugh's eyes roll and he gives a last, faint and wistful sigh as death rattles his throat.

Years later, Raimon is glad about what he does next. At the time, though, he has no idea why he does it except that it is suddenly unthinkable to leave a man, any man, to the unforgiving mercy of the elements and the Inquisitors. Placing Hugh's sword to one side, he smoothes out the oriflamme and swiftly rolls his enemy's corpse into it before binding it up as tightly as he can. Then he runs for a flaming plank and sets the banner's edges alight. Hugh will have his own pyre. He waits, holding his breath, and only when the fire is white-hot does he exhale, and even then he waits a moment longer, trying to find some fitting words of valediction. But what should they be? He has no idea, so simply seizes Hugh's sword, plunges it into Unbent's scabbard and makes once again for the palisade. Behind him, the oriflamme loosens and the folded tails flutter until, at last, scorched and torn but freed from all constraint, they stream in one red silken salute straight up to heaven.

THE VALLEY

Raimon sits quite dumb on the journey back to Castelneuf. The Blue Flame is saved but he feels lost. The White Wolf is dead but the Occitan is defeated. Despite all Raimon's efforts, the south has bowed to the north and Raimon mourns for the land he loves. And then there is Hugh's challenge, over which Raimon's soul is in turmoil. All is over and nothing is over. He wishes he had the Flame with him, that he could hold up the lantern to guide him as it guided him before. Yet he knows, too, that over Hugh's child he must make his own decision.

Cador looks after Metta. He hung on to Bors and Galahad during the burnings, just as he was bid, and it was he who, searching for Raimon, found the desolate, desperate girl hopelessly crawling up the pog again, seeking sanctuary in the empty fortress. When Cador shouted Raimon's name, she flung an arm towards the pyre and, in return, he flung her the horses' reins. With the Inquisitors driven away from the palisade by the stench and the unbreathable, greasy residue coating every particle of air, the boy held his nose and plunged in. It was he who pulled Raimon out. It was he, too, who took charge of their escape, calculating the safest route away from a place that, at an infamous time, was already achieving a special infamy all of its own.

It takes three days for Raimon to feel even partially clean. Even when the mountain pavilions amongst which Montségur is secreted are long out of sight and there is nothing above but larks and spring sunshine he shudders, for the pyre seems glued to him, ready to engulf him again at any minute. Only Metta riding pillion protects him. She makes no demands and he hopes she knows that he is glad she is there.

On the fourth night, as they rest, Cador asks what will happen now.

Raimon shakes his head. 'There will be no more fighting,' he says. 'The king has broken the Occitan. He hasn't got the Flame, but he's won.'

'It's devilry,' Cador says.

'It's strategy,' Raimon tells him, because that is what Sir Parsifal would have said. It is the response of a knight.

He does not speak to Cador about the Inquisitors, though, for he is quite certain that they will not be suppressed. Indeed, buoyed up by their repulsive triumph at Montségur, they will doubtless redouble their efforts. Yet after this worst of all massacres, they need hardly bother, for the courage of the few Perfecti remaining in the Occitan will falter. Raimon does not waste his sympathy. Without the Cathars, the Occitan's story might have been very different. Yet as he feels

Galahad steady beneath him, the angry bitterness that has so often eaten him up eases. So much is lost but not everything. Yolanda has the Flame. At night, at least for some if it, he sleeps.

Only when Cador declares that they will reach Castelneuf the following evening does Metta, who has been almost entirely silent, rouse herself.

'I don't wish to go to Castelneuf,' she says in her quiet way. 'I want to go straight home.'

Raimon plucks at a passing branch and makes himself speak. 'Yes. I understand.' He shifts in the saddle. 'I'm sorry, Metta. You can't know how sorry I am. For everything.'

'I do know that.'

'I'm not proud of what I did.'

She presses with uncharacteristic fierceness against him. 'Never say that, Raimon. You *should* be proud of what you did, not to my heart perhaps, but of what you've really done. You saved my life and you saved the Flame.'

'But not the Occitan.'

She is gentle again. 'There are more ways of losing the Occitan than at the point of the French king's lance.'

Raimon feels for her hand round his waist and squeezes it. He has never loved her more genuinely than at this moment. She is the one truly good person he has met. More than either himself or Yolanda, she has something of the new Flame's hopefulness about her. He wants to believe that she is going to be happy. 'You're right about so many things,' he says.

'Not everything,' she replies and then falls silent again until, a mile or two further on, she says 'I should like to meet

Yolanda. Perhaps one day I will.'

'I wish you would come with me now.'

She shakes her head. 'Will you lend me Cador to see me home?'

Raimon is nervous for her. 'Will you still have a home? Your father gave up everything to go to Montségur.' He cannot bear anything else to go wrong for her.

He turns and she surprises him with a smile. 'Of course I'll still have a home,' she says with enough spirit to make it a declaration.

'How can you be sure?'

She lifts her face to the sun. 'Because despite everything, I still have faith.' And the look she gives him, in which there is neither self-pity nor recrimination, humbles him.

'I'll take you.'

'No,' she says firmly. 'Send Cador. That's what I want.'

'Metta –'

'I'll never forget you, Raimon.'

'Nor I you.'

They part soon after, and their embrace is long and tight. Once she is settled behind Cador on Bors, she looks back only once, to raise her arm. Raimon raises his in return and keeps it raised until she is out of sight.

Alone, he rides more quickly, not seeking out remembered places this time, only wanting to arrive. Galahad is driven hard until just before night falls, they gallop round the corner into the Castelneuf valley and Raimon looks up. He can see the château, its keep and towers stark in the purple dusk of spring. He also sees that there is no light. Nothing. Not the slightest twinkle of a torch, not the ragged shadow of a hearth-fire. Above all, there is no Blue Flame. The place is deserted.

He blinks, searching and searching. No, there is nothing at all, and his heart leaps into his mouth because better than he has allowed himself to understand, Yolanda has understood that there is no future for them in this place of their childhood. In this château, once so very dear to them both, they would simply be clinging to the past when all the clinging must be to the future. It is hard to leave the familiar old for the unfamiliar new, but Yolanda has taken the Flame and done it without even him beside her.

He hardly notices that Galahad is wandering apparently aimlessly away from the château's lumpy hillside, over the meadows, through woods and coppices, past shepherds' huts and up goat tracks. He is conscious only of stopping, hours later, and gazing between the horse's ears into a valley whose shadowy shape is unknown to him. It, too, has a river, unseen this evening, but which he can clearly hear spilling over stones. There is light here, small dots from fires and smaller dots from lanterns. Slipping from Galahad's back he walks downhill with the old horse at his side.

Yolanda is standing in the firelight holding Hugh's son aloft, the Flame beside her feet. Her face, always thin, is thinner, but no longer white with exhaustion. The baby begins to struggle and suddenly, from behind, in a flurry of corkscrew curls, Laila sallies forth, snatches the baby with the deftness of a conjurer and tosses him into the air. 'Oh, be careful, Laila!' calls Yolanda.

Laila laughs and tosses the baby back, making him laugh too. But Yolanda is not laughing, she is waiting. Galahad stands on a twig and Brees cocks an ear before his breathy, jangling welcome breaks forth. Yolanda starts, flushed with hope. Laila tries to take the baby again but Yolanda shakes her head. She must take the child with her. In slow motion, she picks up the Flame, bids Brees remain where he is and walks out of the circle of the camp.

They find each other near the water.

'There was no light at Castelneuf,' he says.

'Did you think there might be?' Her eyes are like ripe almonds, the blue of the Flame reflected in the brown. Here he is, living and breathing, when she has so often imagined him – she does not want to recall.

'I was afraid,' he says.

She smiles fleetingly. '*You* were afraid.'

'Hugh's dead,' he says and looks away for fear of her expression.

'Did you kill him?' she asks after a pause.

'No.'

'Do you wish you had?'

He strives for truth. 'I wanted to kill him. I went to kill him. But when he died –' he shakes his head. 'I didn't know any more.'

She nods. 'I wanted to kill him too, yet when the baby was born I didn't know either.'

'Yes. I saw.'

She brushes his sleeve. 'You shouldn't have gone without waking me.'

'I wanted to wake you.' He stops. 'No, that's not quite right. I didn't want to wake you because I had nothing nice to say. I could only leave you the Flame and hope you understood.'

The baby gurgles and Raimon stiffens.

Yolanda hands the Flame to Raimon and holds her son defensively. 'His name is Arthur Parsifal.' Her breath touches his cheek. 'Do you remember how we pretended to be Knights of the Round Table on the old pack pony?'

He nods, his breath mingling with hers. 'And we've already got Bors and Galahad –' she looks round. 'Where's Cador?'

'He's taken Metta to her father.'

'Ah, Metta.'

'Yolanda –'

She interrupts. She does not want to talk of Metta. 'How will our lives be now, Raimon, with so many people gone and so much over? Aimery, even.' She stops, her lips trembling.

'He was a traitor, Yolanda.'

'You think I don't know that?' She holds the baby so tightly that he squeaks. 'It's silly, I know, but there's nobody else who'll ever call me Yola.' Her voice rises. 'I didn't even like it! But somehow – somehow.' She steadies herself and releases the baby. 'I just don't know what's left. Gui and Guerau are here, and the huntsman and the dogboys but I didn't even know if you'd return.'

'But I have, Yolanda, and I'm never going again. I've behaved so stupidly.' He puts the Flame down and breaks away. 'Laila!' he calls. 'Laila!' The girl appears. Her hair is silver and sparkles against the starry waterfall of stones at her throat, the stones with the dragonfly clasp. 'Take the baby.' He cannot yet call it by its name.

'I'm not a nursemaid,' she complains, hands on hips. She has shaken off the past months as a cat shakes off bathwater, save a small tremor as she looks at Arthur.

'Take him anyway.' She flicks her shoulders but obeys.

When they are gone, he and Yolanda stand awkwardly again until, with one mind, leaving the Flame in its own hollow of light, they begin to walk along the riverbank. She trips, unable to feel her way, and at once he is there to catch her. In his arms, she gathers her courage. 'Raimon, Arthur and I come together now. I couldn't imagine life with him and now I can't imagine life without him.' He tries to interrupt but she won't let him. 'And I can't not tell him who his father was. I can't pretend. I know better than anybody that what Hugh did was awful, but he was not a bad man, not really. At least he was better than some and no worse than others. And what good will it do to make Arthur ashamed of being half a des Arcis?'

The water is a deep pool below. Raimon brushes her hair with the end of his nose and now he begins to speak. He tells her everything: of his seduction of Metta, of his incarceration by the White Wolf and of the siege's terrible end. When he speaks of Hugh he spares neither her nor himself anything. The details, the intricacies, the memory of how Hugh looked and exactly what he said somehow help to expunge the memory of Hugh as intruder in the night, of Hugh stealing from Yolanda what she did not freely give, of Hugh as the father of the child that Raimon is challenged to raise as his own.

Yolanda does not interrupt the flow and never takes her gaze from his face although she feels, rather than sees, the shifting contours of his every muscle. To stop herself from touching his eyelids and pressing her palms to his cheeks, she fiddles with the leather rings round her neck.

At last, as the moon vanishes into cloud, they sit in complete darkness. Even the Flame and the campfires are hidden. When the moon reappears, however, it illuminates an odd sight. Laila is standing on the riverbank and suddenly, where the river is strongest, with a flick of her wrist she hurls something in. For a moment, she teeters, as if she has made a mistake, and then spins and runs back to the baby. They hear her scolding him until he cries and then teasing him until he laughs again.

'What on earth's she doing?' Raimon is half on his feet. He remembers Laila's description of Aimery's last, terrible shriek. He has not told Yolanda of that.

'Who knows,' says Yolanda, silently rejoicing at Raimon's concern. 'She does odd things. She's just Laila.'

'And you trust her with the baby?'

'*Only* with the baby,' says Yolanda. 'I don't trust her with anything else. But for some reason she loves him, or at least likes to take care of him. One day she'll be off, though. Life here will be too dull for her so she'll return to Paris and probably end up back in the gutter with nothing but her wits and her box of tricks for company. Then, just when we least expect her, she'll reappear, still painted, still scolding, still Laila.' She smoothes her skirt. 'She helped me when I needed her and I'm glad to know her although I'm glad not to be her.' Her voice peters out.

Raimon hardly hears. The wonder of sitting beside Yolanda is like drinking in the sky but he still cannot relax. She feels a tremor shake him, and then, finally, a question bursts out. 'Did I fail, Yolanda? Did I fail you and Sir Parsifal and the Occitan and the Amouroix? Did I fail the Blue Flame?'

She takes both his hands in hers, makes him get up and leads him back to where the Flame is still sitting in its hollow. She bends down and holds it up, and it seems to Raimon that just as it did when he first saw it, before he ever met Sir Parsifal or Hugh or the White Wolf, the small blue curl begins to swells and spill out. This time, however, instead of making him dance as it did then, he finds himself motionless as the blue streams down the valley into a distance that has no end. 'I dreamed of this,' he says, wonderingly, to Yolanda, because he can say anything to her.

'Look,' she says. 'It hasn't finished.'

The distance seems empty to start with, but then Raimon realises it is not empty, not at all. People are making their way towards the blue, only this time not with swords drawn. All they carry, all they need, is that very particular type of untamed pride for which the Occitan was famous before division and ambition corroded its soul like a fungus.

Yolanda's gaze follows his. 'You see, Raimon? You did this. You rescued the Flame from the weary old world and brought it to the new one we're going to make, you and I —' she puts down the Flame and squeezes his hands hard together — 'and Arthur.'

Raimon wants to believe her, but not everything fits.

'Parsifal gave me Unbent and said I was to be a knight,' he says. 'Knights live in castles not valleys.'

'That's because you think being a knight is all about fighting, which is as silly as the White Wolf and the Inquisitors believing God is all about hating. Didn't –' she colours a little – 'didn't Metta teach you anything?' He stares at her. How did she become so wise? 'What did Sir Parsifal tell you was the most important thing?'

He feels his finger. Without any fuss, without him even noticing, she has replaced the leather ring he never wanted to give up. 'Love,' Raimon says. 'He said the most important thing was love.'

'And doesn't love flourish in valleys? It's where the crops grow, after all, and the Flame seems to like it.'

He can feel the nervous hope coursing through her as she leans against him just as she used to when, as children, they told each other stories of high romance. 'Doesn't it, Raimon?'

'Yes,' he says, 'love does flourish in valleys.'

'And for all a knight's prowess,' she continues, 'what's the Occitan without love?'

He twists the ring. That is not at all hard to answer. 'It's like the world without you,' he says.

She sinks her head deeply into his shoulder and now he can look without fear over her mess of hair first to the Flame and then to where he knows the campfires burn. He can hear Arthur chortling as he rolls amongst the dogboys and the huntsman's remonstrances when the play gets too rough. He can hear Laila laughing at some impossible joke of her own.

And he can hear something else. Gui and Guerau are quarrelling over a tune. He smiles. He has not heard them quarrelling since the old count was alive.

Yolanda raises her head. She, too, is listening. 'What are –'

'Ssssh,' Raimon does not want her to move.

When it eventually comes, the troubadours' song is filled with rich regret as troubadours' songs always are. They have to wait for the chorus to hear what they are looking for and the troubadours do not disappoint. Instead of ringing with the Song of the Flame handed down through past generations, the Song both Raimon and Yolanda have sung a thousand times, something different tentatively emerges. Yolanda raises her head again and this time Raimon does not try to restrain her. There are unfamiliar harmonies here, some of which clash in unexpected discord. There is another argument, but finally the two voices agree on a new melody that puzzles and disquiets all who hear it, as new melodies often do. Some listeners murmur with approbation, some with disapproval. Unabashed, the troubadours sing on until it is quite clear that they do not intend to stop.

Raimon takes up the lantern. 'Come,' he says, and with the Flame in front, Unbent at his back and Yolanda at his side, he strides forward. Surely, armed with such treasures, there is no challenge he cannot meet.

Galahad is grazing and Raimon does not bother to take his rein. The old horse will find his way. Raimon halts for a moment. When Cador returns, he will get him to polish Hugh's sword until it shines like Unbent. A good father should do no less. He turns to tell Yolanda but she is running to retrieve her son from the dogboy scrum. He opens his mouth to call, then smiles a smile broader than the valley itself and shakes his head. What is he thinking! There is no need to tell her because she already knows.

And so my tale is ended although my story is not finished. In a valley deep in my mountains, the Flame still burns. Indeed, it is still tended by Raimon and Yolanda, though not the Raimon and Yolanda you have met in these pages. They are long dead and free to haunt the ruins of Castelneuf when the fancy takes them. The Raimons and Yolandas who tend the Flame today are those with a secret in their eyes, those who will not tell you exactly where their valley lies, those who hold their lanterns carefully. Follow them with caution. Come like the White Wolf and you will find them difficult company. Come with a drawn sword and they will draw theirs in return. But if you come quietly, seeking only to warm your hand on the Flame, whilst they may at first be suspicious, I do not think they will turn you away.